DREAM LIFE

of

ASTRONAUTS

STORIES

PATRICK RYAN

THE DIAL PRESS · NEW YORK

Copyright © 2016 by Patrick Ryan

Published in the United States by The Dial Press,
an imprint of Random House, a division of
Penguin Random House LLC, New York.

THE DIAL PRESS and the HOUSE colophon are
registered trademarks of Penguin Random House LLC.

Some of the stories in this work were previously published
in different form in *Crazyhorse, Faultline, Catapult, Denver
Quarterly, The Chattahoochee Review,* and *Feedback.* "The Dream
Life of Astronauts" was originally published in *Between Men*
(New York: Running Press, 2007).

LIBRARY OF CONGRESS CATALOGING-IN-PUBLICATION DATA

Ryan, Patrick
[Short stories. Selections]
The dream life of astronauts : stories / Patrick Ryan. — First edition.
pages ; cm
ISBN 978-0-385-34138-7—ISBN 978-0-8129-8972-4 (eBook)
I. Title.
PS3618.Y336A6 2016
813'.6—dc23   2015025991

Printed in the United States of America on acid-free paper

randomhousebooks.com

2 4 6 8 9 7 5 3 1

First Edition

Book design by Diane Hobbing

To David McConnell

CONTENTS

The Way She Handles   3

The Dream Life of Astronauts   33

Summer of '69   63

The Fall Guy   86

Miss America   113

Fountain of Youth   156

Go Fever   175

Earth, Mostly   197

You Need Not Be Present to Win   233

THE DREAM LIFE OF ASTRONAUTS

THE WAY SHE HANDLES

L ate one night during the summer of Watergate, I was in
bed reading a Hardy Boys novel by flashlight when a car
pulled into our cul-de-sac, its headlights sweeping the
walls of my room. If I'd been reading something else I might
not have been so in tune to things, but a mystery by flashlight turns everything into a clue. A few paragraphs later, it
occurred to me I hadn't heard a car door slam. Which meant
someone either was lingering in the car or had closed the
door so quietly that it didn't make a sound, and why would a
person do either of those things if he weren't trying to get
away with something? I got up on my knees, inched back the
curtain, and spied a dark-blue Lincoln Town Car parked in
front of our house.

The headlights were off and, sure enough, someone was
sitting behind the wheel. Someone else was in there, too,
and their murky shapes were moving around suspiciously.

Donning black gloves, maybe. Pulling ski masks over their faces.

Then our porch light came on and I could see my father step out into the front yard. He was barefoot, dressed in his robe and pajamas, and he was holding a croquet mallet.

He was halfway across the yard when my uncle came running out of the house to catch up with him. My uncle was also barefoot, and he was wearing a pair of cutoff shorts. He patted my father on the back and said something to him I couldn't make out, and my father sat down on the grass so fast it was like he'd dropped into a hole. He let go of the mallet and clutched his head with both hands.

All of which did nothing to address the two people in the Lincoln and led me to have what my last year's English teacher, Mrs. LaPeach, would have called a *mature thought*. "I know you're just children," she would say to us, "but it wouldn't kill you to have a mature thought every now and then." Mine was, *This is why I watch so much goddamn television and read so many goddamn books. Because nothing interesting ever happens in real life.*

But then my father got to his feet again and walked the rest of the way across the lawn as calmly as if he were retrieving the morning paper—only he had the croquet mallet back in his hand. When he reached the front of the Lincoln, he pushed his glasses up the bridge of his nose, raised the mallet as high as he could, and brought it down onto the hood with a gargantuan *thunk* I felt in my chest. The head of the mallet broke off and went somersaulting behind him. And right on the heels of the *thunk,* one of the Lincoln's passenger doors opened and I heard a voice—my mother's, it turned out—screaming into the night, "JESUS CHRIST, PHIL, ARE YOU OUT OF YOUR FUCKING MIND?"

That was the end of my mother's foray into adult education. The next day, she withdrew from the one class she'd enrolled in and didn't even bother to sell back the textbook she'd been clutching when she'd scrambled out of the car. I glimpsed the book's title in the trashcan—*Economics for Daily Consumption*—and understood why she wouldn't want to stay in that kind of class, but I didn't know what had made my father so angry. When I asked him about it, he told me it was a grown-up matter and that I should have been asleep, anyway. When I asked my mother (after my father left for work), she said, "Wasn't that bizarre? The man was my teacher, after all. He was just giving me a ride home." And when I asked my uncle, while the two of us stood side by side in the bathroom brushing our teeth, he shrugged and said into the mirror, "Love, little guy, is a many splendored thing."

He was my mother's little brother, her only sibling, and he'd hitchhiked all the way from California to start a new life in Florida. Out west, he'd been a bread baker, a gardener, a songwriter, and a meditation instructor— occupations he'd listed in a letter to my mother before saying he was ready for a change and asking if he could come stay with us while he checked out "the east coast scene."

"I don't understand," my father had said midway through my mother's reading of the letter aloud over dinner. "What scene?"

"New people, I guess. New opportunities." She squinted against the smoke from her cigarette. "How the hell should I know?"

"Well, does he have any sort of plan?"

"Actually, he does. He says here he wants to pursue a career in music therapy." She took a sip of her drink. Her lipstick decorated the rim of the glass.

My father, still in his yellow Century 21 blazer, swirled what was left of his drink around until the ice collapsed. *"What?"*

A couple of Saturdays later, I was in the garage with my father, sweeping while he struggled with the fishing line on the weed-whacker, when a Volkswagen van rounded the cul-de-sac. The van stopped at the foot of our driveway, its side door slid open, and a man all but stumbled out, his blond hair sweeping his shoulders as he righted himself. A duffel bag was tossed after him, a tiny guitar case (which he managed to catch), and what I thought at first was a wicker basket, but turned out to be a crimped cowboy hat. "Thanks!" he hollered as the side door slammed shut and the van sped away. "You're beautiful people!"

My mother ran out of the laundry room and straight through the garage, squealing as if the house were on fire. At the end of the driveway, she jumped up and down and hugged the man at the same time. He put the cowboy hat on her head.

"This was a mistake," my father said, still clutching the weed-whacker.

We all moved inside to the air-conditioning, where my father shook my uncle's hand as if the two of them were entering a shady business deal. When I held out my own hand, Robbie grinned down at me and said, "Only squares shake hands, man." He slid his palm flat against mine in slow motion.

"Can I fix you a drink, Robbie?" my mother asked. "We have vodka, bourbon, Scotch, and gin."

"Water's fine," Robbie said.

"You're sure? Nothing stronger?"

"Don't flip your lid, Judy, but I went on the wagon about a year ago."

"*Really,*" my mother said, as if this were of particular interest to her. Still wearing the cowboy hat, she walked over to the sideboard in the dining room where the liquor lived.

Robbie dropped down onto the couch. "When you forget three whole days of your life and wake up on a beach in Monterey with no wallet or shoes, it's probably time for a change, right?"

"Probably is," she said, dropping ice into a pair of highball glasses.

I tugged my big red hand chair out of the corner and sank into it.

My father took his recliner. "And you're with us squares for how long?" he asked.

"Just till I figure out the lay of the land," Robbie said. "See what's what and, you know, get something started."

"Your cake baking and, what is it, music therapy?"

"It was bread, not cake. But, yeah, a little music therapy never hurt anyone, did it?" He glanced at me, grinning as he said this.

"See, here's what I'm a little cloudy about," my father said. "What exactly is music therapy?"

"Songs for the heart," Robbie said. "Songs for the soul. Get it out, make it sweet, soothe the world."

"Uh-huh," my father said. "And what does that mean?"

My mother came back into the room carrying a tray of drinks—a vodka and tonic for her, one for my father, a can of Pepsi for me, and a plastic tumbler of water for my uncle. As she distributed the drinks, she said, "Phil's our Welcome Wagon, can you tell? He's loaded with charm."

"Ha ha!" my father said.

She sat down on the couch next to my uncle. "I think music therapy sounds like just what we need right about now. We're living in crazy times."

"That we are," Robbie said.

"But what *is* it?" my father asked.

"You ever get into a bad mood, and then you hear a song, and for whatever reason it's just the right song to pull you out of that mood and set you down on an oasis?"

"No," my father said. "Not an oasis, no."

"Well, that's called music therapy. That's part of it, anyway."

"It's called turning on the radio," my father said. "It's not a career; it's a dial."

"Oh, for godsake, Phil, give it a rest," my mother said.

"Hey, I'm just making conversation. Just entertaining guests in the comfort of my own home."

"Yes, you wear the pants. We know." She pushed the cowboy hat back an inch on her head, took a sip of her drink, said, "Mm!" and pointed to the statue on top of the television. "Do you like my latest acquirement, Robbie?"

"Acquisition," my father said.

"Do you like it? I bought it at an art show in Cocoa. It's called 'The Lovers.'"

"It's great," my uncle said. "You've really got the place decorated nicely."

I'd never thought of our house as being "decorated" before. There was a vase of plastic flowers on the dining room table that we pushed to one side when we ate. A painting over the couch of a ship drifting through a sunset. Another painting by the front door of baby chicks in a box and a dog peering down at them. The statue on the television was nearly a foot tall, carved out of wood, and was supposed to be a man and a woman kissing, but for some reason they were shaped like Q-tips.

"I helped a couple of guys just back from Vietnam work through their night terrors," Robbie said. "And a woman with chronic insomnia who sleeps like a baby now."

"By turning on the radio?" my father asked.

"By helping them write their own song. Sometimes the inner demon's got the sweetest voice. The Chinese believe in something called Ghost Possession. Ever heard of it?"

"*I* have," my mother said.

My father rolled his eyes.

"Some people've got the ghost," Robbie said. "Charles Manson. Roger Mudd. Tricky Dick."

"The President of the United States," my father said.

"Phil voted for him," my mother told Robbie. "Twice."

"So did a lot of other people. You can tell by his eyes that there's something dead in there. It's like looking at a mannequin's eyes."

"You're really out there now," my father said.

"You should do some sightseeing," my mother said. "There are all kinds of things to do around here. The Space Center. The wildlife refuge. The beach! And Disney World's only an hour away. I'm sure Sam would be happy to give you a grand tour of the Magic Kingdom."

"Is that right, little guy?" Robbie asked me.

"Sure," I said.

"We should all go out and do something fun *right now*," my mother said.

But we didn't go anywhere. We stayed in the living room, and they kept talking. Finally, I got up and went to my room to read.

When I came out an hour or so later and peered into the living room, my father was still in the recliner, and my mother and Robbie were still on the couch. She was leaning sideways a little and had her feet up on the coffee table. "Is that your biggest complaint?" she was saying. "That I *flirt*? Honestly, Phil, I don't know whether to laugh or to feel sorry for you. I live in the world, okay? I *exist*. And if that means I smile at somebody at a party or the grocery store or the 7-Eleven, then so be it. I mean, really, boo fucking hoo. Right, Robbie?"

"I don't have a dog in this race," Robbie said.

My father muttered something under his breath.

"What was that?" my mother said. "You have to speak up, Phil. No one can hear you if you mumble."

"I said, would you please take off that goddamn hat?"

Still later, I was bored, hungry, and wondering what was for dinner. The door to the guest room across the hall was standing partway open and I could see Robbie lying on top of the bed, sound asleep, with his feet crossed and his hands folded over his stomach. His duffel bag had been emptied, and a pile of rumpled clothes sat on the floor next to the tiny guitar case.

I heard music coming from the front of the house: violins and an earnest-sounding woman singing that song from *The Poseidon Adventure*. I felt a momentary surge of excitement, thinking the movie was on TV, but the music was coming from the stereo—the *Love Songs of the Cinema* album my father had given my mother last Christmas. Their highball glasses were on the coffee table (along with the cowboy hat and one of the bottles from the sideboard) and they were standing in the middle of the room, facing each other. His arm was around her waist. Her head was resting on his shoulder. And though they seemed not to be moving at all, they were—just barely—dancing.

R obbie had come at a good time. There were a couple of other kids my age who lived in the neighborhood, but they were both on long summer vacations with their families. We got four channels on the television, but one of them was PBS and the other three were eaten up every day by Watergate. It was the only reason I'd been reading so much: daytime TV was either educational shows or men in suits talking into microphones. I'd spend all of a minute flipping the dial and watching their suits—and sometimes their complexions—change color just slightly from one station to the next; then I was done with Watergate. But Watergate didn't seem to be wrapping up anytime soon, and the summer was only half over.

With Robbie there, my mother seemed rejuvenated—at least, while my father was at work. She made quiches and frittatas for breakfast. She kept us at the table as long as possible, asking Robbie to tell stories about their childhood back in Ohio and then barreling over him to tell them herself. The time they stole a For Sale sign from a neighbor's house and planted it in the yard of their high school principal. The time they made rum and cokes from one of the booze bottles their father kept hidden in the garage and then rode their bicycles through the flowerbeds in front of the courthouse. "And you—*you!*"—lighter in one hand, cigarette in the other, rocking damp-eyed with laughter—"you mooned the mayor!"

"It wasn't the mayor," Robbie said. "It was one of the town councilmen."

My mother turned to me. "He did it on his bicycle and nearly crashed into a mailbox."

"Well, that part's true," he said.

"And we snuck in to so many movies. Back in the good old days, before all the doors had fire alarms, we put duct tape on the back door of the theater so it wouldn't latch. I think I saw *Singin' in the Rain* a dozen times. And what was that Western I couldn't stand, but you kept going back to?"

"*High Noon.*"

"With Gregory Peck—handsome, but boring as hell."

"It was Gary Cooper."

"Right," she said. "Also handsome and boring."

"Judy-paloodie," he said, shaking his head.

"Robbie-palobby." With the hand that held the cigarette, she reached over and jostled my shoulder, trailing smoke between us. "Sam-palamb!"

I felt like the three of us were siblings, only I hadn't been born for any of their shared memories. It was fun to see her so animated, so cheerful. We played board games. We went to lunch at the Piccadilly and Red Lobster and the restaurant at Mathers Bridge. In the afternoons, my mother would leave to run errands, and for long stretches it would just be me and Robbie. I asked him if it was easier to play a tiny guitar than a regular-sized one, and he told me it wasn't a guitar; it was a ukulele. He played me a few songs, then said, "If you could write a song about your favorite thing in the whole world, what would it be?"

I gave that some thought and told him my song would be about *The Six Million Dollar Man*.

"Shoot," he said, grinning. "How old are you?"

"Almost ten."

"Tell you what—in a couple of years you're going to be singing a different tune, but that's okay. The *Six Million Dollar Man* will do for now."

He played a succession of chords and helped me write the words. They went like this:

I'm a man with unusual power
I could prob'ly knock over a tower
If you fight me, good luck
I cost six million bucks
I hope I don't rust in the shower

He tried to teach me to meditate. We sat in the backyard, side by side and cross-legged on the grass, and he told me to close my eyes, touch my thumbs to my middle fingertips, and say "Om."

"Um," I said. I didn't understand what meditation was any more than my father understood music therapy.

"Each one of your thoughts is a cloud," Robbie said. "So when a thought comes into your mind, you just watch it float from one side to the other, and let it go. It's not you; it's just a thought. Got it?"

"Sure," I said.

"So here comes a thought. See it coming?"

"Yeah."

"What is it?"

"That I have to pee."

"Sam has to pee," he said. "Sam has to pee. And there it goes, drifting by. See how that works?"

"I still have to pee." He laughed, told me I had "monkey mind," and I asked him if we could play Barrel of Monkeys instead. We did, and eventually we invented our own game that combined the monkeys, Pick-Up Sticks, and dominoes.

Then my father would come home, and my mother would get back from her errand running. They would fix drinks and sit around and talk and laugh and eventually argue—about what we should have for dinner, about whether or not we should get an aboveground pool (since we couldn't afford a cement one), about anything that came up, really. Robbie wouldn't say much while they were going at each other. He'd watch the news and make a comment now and then, express an opinion on the president that would get a rise out of my father. And I think my father enjoyed that. He'd warmed up to Robbie a little since that first day. When he got tired of arguing with my mother—her appetite for it was always larger than his—he'd turn his attention to Robbie, start questioning him about what his life had been like back in California and grilling him about whether or not he was making any progress with his business ventures. His questions started sounding like setups for jokes, and he had a smile crimping his mouth more often than not. "Did you live in a commune, out there? Like a Moonie kind of thing?"

"I shared an apartment with a couple of people. But I did live in a commune for a while. Pagans, most of them. We had a garden about half the size of a football field."

"Pagans. What's that, devil worship?"

"No deities," Robbie said. "No creeds. More like universal pantheism. One nature, one mind."

"One something. And how's the magic-song business coming along?"

"Man, go easy on me. I've only been here a week," Robbie said. "Drip, drip makes a river."

"You tell him," my mother called from the pass-through to the kitchen. "Drip, drip mayzuh-river."

"Ah," my father said, lifting his glass, "first slur of the evening. We should have a bell."

Not long after that, my father came home from work one night looking different. I thought at first he'd gotten a haircut, but it was the look on his face. Utterly flat, like his circuit breakers had been popped. He fixed himself a drink and sat down in the recliner with the newspaper, but he didn't read it; he just kept his gaze low, focused on some spot on the floor beyond the footrest.

I was on the couch finishing another Hardy Boys book.

Robbie was at the dining room table flipping through the pages of a used-car circular. When my mother walked in, a little later than usual, she closed the door behind her and stood just inside the threshold, staring at the three of us. "What a lively bunch," she said. "Thanks for the greeting."

"Hi, Mom," I said.

"Sis," Robbie said.

She looked at my father. "How about you, Prince Charming? Don't I get a hello?"

"We need to talk," my father said.

"Well, I just walked in the door. Let me discombobulate."

"Alone," my father said as she was crossing the room.

The word put a jolt in her step, as if one of her shoes had caught on the carpet. "Well, *that* sounds ominous," she said, setting her purse on the dining room table. She took a bottle from the sideboard and carried it into the kitchen, and I heard the rattle of an ice tray being cracked. I knew how long it took her to make a drink, and this one seemed to take twice as long as normal. When she came back into the living room, she stepped around the recliner, sat down next to me on the couch, and kicked off her shoes. "It is *so* humid out there," she said, pinching her blouse and snapping it away from her chest. "And the mall parking lot smelled like rotting fish today. I had to pinch my nose just to get through it."

"Let's go to the bedroom," my father said.

"I just sat down. Can't we talk here? We're all family."

My father folded the newspaper into thirds. He held it in one hand and tapped it against his thigh. "You were at the mall?"

"Don't worry, I was just window-shopping. The end-of-summer sales haven't started yet."

"Where else did you go?"

"The Green Thumb, to look at some ferns."

"Play any ping-pong?"

"You're coming in fuzzy," my mother said. "What was that?"

He kept tapping the newspaper against his thigh. "I'm asking you a very simple question, *wife*. Did you. Play any. Ping-pong?"

In the books I'd been reading that summer, people seldom laughed. They *chortled* or *guffawed*. I would read those words with little idea of what they meant, but the sound that next came out of my mother seemed to fit the bill. "I think the heat's getting to you," she said. "Who wants chicken pot pie?" She pushed up from the couch and carried her drink back into the kitchen.

The meal that evening was painfully quiet. My mother tried to keep up the conversation, and Robbie did his best to participate. My father silently nursed a single drink while my mother had four, and when, after a long stretch of quiet—just the ticking of our forks against the plates—she lit a cigarette and asked my father if the cat had his tongue, he said, "You still haven't answered my question."

"Do you really want to pursue this?"

"I can do things," my father said.

"So can I. So can everybody. It's a free country, last time I checked."

He shook his head—so subtly, he might have been shivering. "I can do things," he said again.

What things? I wondered. We watched a variety show after dinner, and while the studio audience chortled and guffawed its head off, none of us laughed. When the next show started, my father got up and made another drink. Instead of carrying it back to the recliner, he opened the sliding glass door, stepped out onto the patio, and closed the door behind him.

"Go talk to him," Robbie said to my mother.

"He gets crazy ideas in his head, Robbie. I can't stop the world every time he gets like this."

"I'm not saying you should stop the world. Just talk to him."

She folded her arms. "Not when he's like this. He's drunk."

"He's not drunk," I said.

She took her eyes off the television and looked at me as if I'd just been beamed into the room.

"He's only had two," I said. "Not even. He just got his second one."

"Since when did you start counting drinks?" she asked.

From when I was about seven, would have been my best guess, but I didn't think she wanted that answer. I shrugged.

"You know what?" she said. "It's probably time for you to go to bed. It's probably time for all of us to go to bed. It's been a long, hard day."

None of which made sense, because it was just after nine and I got to stay up till eleven in the summer, and because what had been hard about the day for any of us—except maybe my father, who'd gone to work?

"I want to watch *Ironside*," I said.

"No, you don't. You said last week that he was a fat grouch."

I'd been talking about *Cannon,* not *Ironside.* As I was heading out of the room, Robbie said, "I still think you should go out there and talk to him, Judy. He's obviously upset about something."

"Men," my mother said. "You know what men are? Bizarre. With their little suspicions and their little tantrums. 'I can do things. I can do things.'" She flapped her free hand like a startled bird. "What does it even mean? What *things*?"

Exactly what I was still wondering as I said good night and walked down the hall to brush my teeth: What things?

A week later, she started her adult-education class in economics. And two weeks after that, my father attacked her teacher's car with a croquet mallet.

The mallet incident was never mentioned again—not around me, anyway. My mother kept making her fancy breakfasts; she and Robbie and I kept playing board games and eating lunches out. We churned up a strip of backyard along the fence and planted a vegetable garden (nothing grew but the tomato plants, which were spindly, and bore tomatoes the size of peas), and we had a picnic out there one afternoon while Robbie played "Garth, the Magic Garden" on the ukulele. When my mother looked at him, there was a brightness in her eyes I rarely saw, almost as if she were wearing a lot of eye makeup—though she put that on only when she was getting ready for her afternoon errands.

Sitting on the blanket we'd spread next to the garden, Robbie got me to sing my *Six Million Dollar Man* song for her while he accompanied me on the ukulele. She laughed and said it was the silliest thing she'd ever heard.

"Then you write one," I said.

"Oh, don't be such a sourpuss. I was only kidding."

"You ought to try it," Robbie said. "It might free your mind up, you know? I'll start playing, and you jump in whenever the spirit moves you."

"The spirit's not going to move me. I don't have a creative bone in my body."

"The ukulele says different," Robbie said, strumming.

"Ukuleles can't talk."

"Just close your eyes and say one true thing about yourself. The first true thing that comes to your mind. That'll be the first line of the song."

She had her legs folded beneath her. With her hands resting flat on her knees, she closed her eyes.

Robbie kept strumming, slow and steady. "Deep breath," he said.

She breathed in; her shoulders lifted and fell. I thought for a second she was going to smile, but a tremor set into her lips, and when she opened her eyes again, they were glazed with dampness. "This is ridiculous," she said. "What do you want to hear? That I'd like to buy the world a goddamn Coke?"

"If that's what's in your head."

"What's in my head," she said, suddenly getting to her feet, "is that I have a million errands to run. Will you all bring in the dishes and the blanket? I really need to get going." Without waiting for us to answer, she tugged on her blouse, straightening it, and marched back into the house.

"So much for that," Robbie said. "Want to go a movie and then test-drive some cars? I need wheels, man."

We walked to the movie theater connected to the mall. He wanted to see something called *Dirty Mary, Crazy Larry,* but I begged him to see *Death Wish.* "Too violent," he said. "Your parents would kill me."

"They won't care," I said. "They won't even know."

"What if they ask us how we spent our afternoon? You don't want to have to lie, do you?"

They wouldn't ask, I told him. They *never* asked. But he wouldn't give in, so we compromised—a word that, as far as I could tell, meant not getting to do what you wanted to do—and saw *Chinatown* instead. I had a hard time following it. But I liked the part where the private detective had a glove compartment full of watches and put one under a tire so he could tell what time somebody's car was moved, and I liked how he had to wear a bandage on his nose after the rat-faced guy sliced him with the knife. I was still trying to piece the story together when we walked to the used-car lot across the street from the mall.

"Corvette," Robbie said. "Too rich for my blood, but that's a nice-looking ride."

"So the lady who got shot at the end was crazy?"

"She wasn't crazy; she was just upset all the time."

"And that old man was her father?"

"Yeah. A real creep, too."

"And the guy at the beginning who was crying a lot—he beat up his wife?"

"We probably should have seen something else," Robbie said. "A comedy or something."

"Hey, there!" A salesman had come out of the office and was waving hello as he walked toward us.

I followed the two of them around the lot, still thinking about the movie. The salesman showed Robbie one car after another. They talked prices and gas mileage and down payments. "You got something on the low, low end?" Robbie finally asked. "A clunker you want to get rid of?" The salesman pulled a folded handkerchief out of his back pocket, dragged it across his forehead, and walked us over to a '65 Mustang the color of a beet. There were dime-sized spots where the paint was missing. The front and back bumpers were speckled with rust. "This one's talking to me," Robbie said.

We took it for a test drive. The salesman got behind the wheel first, Robbie took the passenger seat, and I sat in the back. I was wearing shorts and my legs stuck to the vinyl.

"You folks local?" the salesman asked.

"He is," Robbie said. "I might just be passing through."

This was news to me; I'd thought Robbie was here to stay.

"It's a beautiful place," the salesman said. "Some folks are in a panic about the Apollo program shutting down, but I think the island's got plenty to offer. You can't beat the weather."

Also news to me—sort of like hearing Robbie say our house was nicely decorated. You wouldn't know you were on an island unless you looked at a map, and as for the weather, it was either hot, or less hot.

"Feel that?" the salesman asked, bringing us to a stop at a red light. "New brake pads on her. New dust caps and bleed valves too. Let me find a place to pull off and you can see how she handles."

He drove another block and turned in to the parking lot of a motel that was chalk white, but decorated with sherbet-colored panels along its second-floor railing. They both got out while I stayed in the back, and as Robbie was rounding the front of the car, he came to a dead stop for a moment. Then he resumed walking and climbed in behind the wheel.

"You'll like the way she handles, I think," the salesman said. "Decent pickup. You might want to drive around the parking lot a little, first, just to get a feel for her."

"Nah, I'm good," Robbie said. He rolled the car forward, tugged the wheel as far as it would go, and U-turned us out of the lot with enough speed to make the muffler bounce off the asphalt.

"Whoa," the salesman said. "Easy, there."

Something was eating at me as we drove back to the car lot. It was like I was half-remembering a thought without even knowing what that half was. Some part of the movie we'd just seen, I assumed, because I still didn't understand what it was about. There was the kid on the horse in the dry riverbed. The guy who looked like a math teacher who drowned.

"Not today," Robbie told the salesman as we stood next to the car. "Soon, though. I've got a girl back in California who's holding some money for me. If I can get her to wire it over, we can do business."

"I've got tell you," the salesman said, "somebody was giving this baby serious consideration just yesterday. They might be back this afternoon."

"Yeah, yeah," Robbie said. "Do what you have to do."

During the walk home, he explained to me how car salesmen worked, how there was always somebody about to buy the car you were interested in, and how the previous owner was always a little old lady who only drove to church on Sundays. My thoughts were ricocheting around inside my head, and I felt an antsiness in my stomach that bordered on panic, all because I couldn't decide what I wanted to ask. The salesman hadn't said anything about a little old lady. What did water rights have to do with the woman getting shot through the eye at the end? And what the hell were water rights? Up ahead, something small and furry waddled from one side of the road to the other.

"Jeez!" Robbie said. "Did you see the size of that rat?"

"It wasn't a rat," I said. "It was a possum." And then it came to me: the colored panels on the second-floor railing, the name of the motel. "Was that the ping-pong Dad was talking about, that time?"

Robbie cleared his throat. "Say what?"

"The place where we turned around. The Ping Pong Motel." I could see the name spelled out across the sign. It was a building I'd ridden past so many times that it usually vanished into the background.

"Aw—no," Robbie said. "Heck, no. I think your dad was talking about *real* ping-pong. Like, with an actual ball and paddles? I think he was just jealous that your mom might have been out, you know, having fun while he was stuck at the office. I wouldn't even mention it, okay?"

I nodded.

"Okay?" he asked again.

"Yeah," I said, "I got it." But I was smarter than that. I could spot a clue for what it was, follow the evidence, and figure things out. Where there was smoke, there was fire, and where there was an argument between your parents about ping-pong, and a place called the Ping Pong Motel nearby, well, that mystery was at least partially solved. My mother had gone to that motel, and my father had spotted her there. She'd gone to meet friends, maybe have drinks. Whatever the reason, she'd gone there without my father, and it had made him angry. It didn't explain what had happened with her teacher and the croquet mallet, but in all likelihood there was a line connecting one thing to the other. You didn't have to be Columbo to figure that much out.

R obbie had been with us for almost a month when he went out alone one morning and came back with the Mustang. The sticker was still in the window as he drove me and my mother down to Mathers Bridge for fried shrimp and ice cream. We were sitting at one of the picnic tables and I was done eating and was staring at the river, wanting a ship to come by so I could see the swing bridge turn, when I spotted a dark shape on the surface of the water, close to the shore. A dead body, I thought. Or a shark. I asked if I could go look and my mother waved me away with her cigarette, telling me to be careful.

Not a dead body, I saw as I got closer to the water, and not a shark, either. Manatees—three of them. Then four. Then five. Moving around so quietly, they didn't make a sound except for an occasional whoosh from their air holes. The two big ones gnawed on the low shrubs growing along the bank. The smaller ones—probably no bigger than me—swam around them, nudged them, barrel-rolled against their sides. They were a family, I thought. Out for lunch, just like us. I watched them until they swam around a bend and out of sight; then I walked back to the picnic table.

My mother was crying over her ice cream. "Do you know what it's like?" she was saying. "I can't breathe. Literally, Robbie, when I'm around him sometimes, I feel the air being sucked out of me."

"You two need to work this out," Robbie said. "And not when you're liquored up. That's no good for anybody."

"Please," she said. "If I couldn't have a drink in the evenings, I'd go out of my head." As she touched a finger to the corner of one eye, she caught sight of me. "Hi, honey! Did you have fun?"

A few days later, there was another uproar. My father came home from work early, answered the phone in the kitchen when it rang, and said in a loud voice, "No, she's out. Can I take a message?" A few seconds later, he was all but shouting. "No message, huh? You don't even have the guts to tell me your name? Don't ever call here again, you son of a bitch!" He slammed the phone back into its wall cradle. Then he picked it up again and slammed it down three more times.

Robbie looked at me from across the living room and said, "Let's get out of here for a while."

We drove to the mall and saw the *Dirty Mary, Crazy Larry* movie. When it was over, he asked me if I was up for another one, and I said sure, but only if it was *Death Wish*. He relented.

It was dark by the time we got home, and long past dinnertime. I didn't care about missing dinner, because I was stuffed with popcorn and Twizzlers, but I wondered if we were going to be in trouble because we'd just disappeared—no note, nothing said to my parents. When we came in through the front door, the lights were off and there was only the television illuminating the living room. My mother was sitting at the dining room table, staring down into her lap. A glass was in front of her. "Hey, sis," Robbie said, but she didn't respond, didn't even look up. "Sis?" He walked over to the table and tapped her shoulder, then said, "Aw, Judy. Aw, jeez." He told me to get a towel from the bathroom.

She'd peed, right there in the chair. The lower half of her skirt and pantyhose were soaked, and the chair cushion was wet underneath her. When we tried to shift her over so we could wipe up around her, she made a couple of sounds, but they weren't really words. My father came out of the back of the house, saw what was going on, and said, "For chrissake." He told me to go to my room, but I wanted to help and kept pushing the towel under her as Robbie tilted her to one side.

"Maybe we should call somebody," he said.

"Like who?" my father asked.

"An ambulance?"

"No. She needs to sleep, is all. If she wakes up in the hospital, I'll never hear the end of it. Help me get her to the tub."

"I don't think she should take a bath right now, Phil. She's barely conscious."

"I don't want her to take a bath; I want her to sleep in the fucking tub until she's done pissing herself." He glanced at me, realizing I was still there, and winced. "Please, Sam, go to your room."

The house was dead quiet for the rest of the night, like

Paul Kersey's apartment after his wife had been murdered. I tried to read, but couldn't concentrate. I thought one of them might come check on me, but no one did. More than anything, I wanted to go back out to the living room so I could watch television, but I knew it was probably best to stay out of sight for a while. Eventually, I drifted off.

When I woke up, sometime in the middle of the night, I was lying on my side facing the wall, and an arm was draped over my neck. I started and wiggled myself around, half-expecting to see my mother, or even Robbie, for whatever reason. But it was my father—lying on top of the covers, still dressed in the shirt and trousers he'd worn to work. Sound asleep, gently snoring. It took a few moments to get my mind around the strangeness of his being there. I wanted to nudge him, get him to shift over a few inches so I could have a little more room. But I didn't want him to wake up.

The next Thursday, just as *The Streets of San Francisco* was about to start, the programming was interrupted so that the president could come on and talk about Watergate. My father was in the recliner. I'd given Robbie the big red hand chair and was on the couch next to my mother. She hadn't left the house since the night she'd messed herself. She hadn't put on outside clothes, either, but had stayed in her housecoat and matching slippers. The president's speech dragged on, and the camera kept moving in closer and closer, until the knot of his necktie was cut off by the bottom of the screen. He'd never been a quitter, he said, and then, a few minutes later, he told us he was quitting.

But he continued to talk, and talk. Finally, he said he would
leave each and every American with a prayer, and I felt like
groaning, but the prayer was mercifully short. "May God's
grace be with you," he said, "in all the days ahead." The
screen went black. Please, I thought, let it be over. Not just
the speech, but the entire whatever it had been that had
eaten up so many shows.

Robbie draped his head back and let out a low whistle.

My mother laid her hand on top of mine and squeezed it—
as if the two of us had suffered more than anyone else.

I was waiting for the show to come back on, but my father
lowered the footrest of his recliner, got up, and turned off
the set.

And even that wasn't the end of it, for the next morning
the programming was interrupted again so that we could all
watch the president say goodbye to his staff and then walk
out to his helicopter with his wife. She climbed the steps
ahead of him, and just before he ducked inside he turned and
waved, smiling, and then threw his arms open wide and
made the victory sign with both hands.

Robbie and I were sitting cross-legged on the living room
floor, playing domino-monkey-sticks. "Little guy," he said, "you
just witnessed history."

My mother was still asleep. My father was standing at the
front window, gazing out at the street. He'd taken the day off
and was dressed in his weekend outfit—canvas deck shoes,
khakis, a polo shirt—and he was holding a coffee mug.
"Whose car is that?" he asked without turning around.

"You mean the Mustang?" Robbie said. "That's mine. I
bought it a week ago. You're just now noticing it?"

My father said nothing for several moments. Then, still with his back to us, he said, "You know, things haven't been so good since you've been here."

Robbie had a plastic monkey in each hand. He looked at me and chuckled. "You can't exactly blame Watergate on me, can you?"

"I don't mean that," my father said. His voice was calm, level. "You move in, you eat our food, you sit on your ass like it's some goddamn resort. Like everything's a big joke. And all this time, you've got the money to buy a car?" He turned around. "You could have offered to help out a little."

Robbie opened his mouth, but hesitated. "I can," he said finally.

"You could have bought some goddamn groceries," my father said.

"I can do that," Robbie said. "I've got a little left over. I've just been trying to get on my feet."

"I think you should leave."

He stuck around for another two days. He didn't argue with my father's decision—my mother did that for him, but even she fizzled out after a few fights. She moped instead, and started drinking at lunch.

I asked each of my parents, in private, why Robbie had to go, why he couldn't just stay and pay for his own food. The sad truth of it, my father told me, was that people will take advantage of you, if you let them. People will railroad you, take the best part of you and twist it to fit their own needs. The only person who has your best interests at heart is you, he said, and the sooner I learned that, the better. My mother's answer was more succinct: "Your father's an ass."

I helped Robbie stuff his things back into his duffel bag and asked him where he was going to go.

"Not sure," he said. "Key West, maybe. I hear it's closer to Cuba than mainland Florida."

I didn't know anything about Cuba other than that it was a whole different country and sounded impossibly far away. Still, the antsiness crept back into my stomach until I figured out what it was I wanted to ask next. "Can I come?"

He grinned, and a shine surfaced on his eyes. "I guess not," he said, as if my coming along was an option and he was choosing not to take it.

For a long time—a year, maybe—I stayed mad at him for that. Then one day, out of the blue, it occurred to me that of course he couldn't have taken me with him. That would have been kidnapping. It would have enraged my father and upset my mother; it might even have been on the news—a manhunt involving the police, private detectives, witnesses who'd spotted us, and a team of FBI agents laying siege to the southernmost port in the country, just as my uncle and I were about to board a boat bound for Cuba. I had to stay; he had to go. Three years later, he sent a postcard from Prague, addressed to the family (*"Pozdravy!*—Robbie" was all it said). By then, my mother was gone, too: back to Ohio, where she got a job in a department store and called every couple of weeks—sometimes drunk, sometimes not—to talk to me, not to my father, and where she eventually married a fat man who had twin sons from another marriage, and where I had to start going for a month in the summers and hated every minute of it, and where she hugged and kissed me over and over again every time she had to put me on the plane back to Florida. I was in college when the fat man dropped dead. I didn't fly to Ohio for the funeral, even though both she and my father offered to buy my ticket, and I don't think she ever forgave me for that. But she came to my wedding, and she gave an impromptu speech at the rehearsal dinner that was kind-spirited, meandering, and, ultimately, incomprehensible. My father, at the far end of the table, had been about to speak, but he kept his eyes on his plate as she prattled on, and I saw him slip his notes back into the pocket of his suit coat. I wished, of all things, that Robbie could have been there. But Robbie and my mother had had a long-distance falling-out sometime during her second marriage, and she didn't want me trying to track him down. Anyway, it would have made him sad to see what she had become, which wasn't so different from what she'd always been. As for my father, he'd stopped drinking years ago. He'd switched over from real estate to life insurance. He hated Carter, voted for Reagan, voted for the first Bush but not the second one. He never remarried. We spoke once a week on the phone—about politics, the weather, his arthritis—until just after his seventy-third birthday, when he went to sleep one night, and that was it. I had to call my mother, of course. She surprised me by weeping.

THE DREAM LIFE OF ASTRONAUTS

Clark Evans finished his talk on his NASA experience with a description of the g-forces created in a Darmotech centrifuge. He held one of his large hands open in front of him, as if displaying a work of wonder, and then moved the hand in a circle that increased in speed as he described the sensation. Frankie, staring from the front row, felt nearly hypnotized.

The wheat-haired librarian who was moderating the event asked if anyone had a question for their guest. Frankie raised his hand. There were five people in the audience, scattered over a flock of twenty folding chairs. The librarian and Clark Evans sat on slightly nicer chairs at the front of the library's map room. She looked right past Frankie and pointed a wavering finger at an old man wearing a sun visor.

"Did you find being on the moon made you want to throw up?"

"Well, as I was saying—" Clark Evans began.

"The reason I ask is because Conrad, or maybe Bean—one of those guys from Apollo 12 or 14—said in an interview that the low gravity made him nauseous, and I was wondering what would happen if an astronaut threw up in his suit."

"I imagine that would be quite a mess," Evans replied.

"But it didn't happen to you?"

"Not to me, no. As I was saying a while back, I was lined up for three different missions, but they didn't come through. NASA politics and whatnot. But I can tell you from knowing a whole lot of guys who went up there that walking around on the moon is like nothing on this planet, that's for sure." He seemed to smile right at Frankie as he said this.

"Any other questions?" the librarian asked.

Evans's jaw looked smooth, but bore a five o'clock shadow. Only one of his cheeks had a dimple, which may just have been from the way he was holding his face. Frankie raised his hand, but the old man spoke up again:

"So you're saying there's no system in place for when an astronaut vomits?"

"Not that I'm aware of," Evans said, and the old man glanced at the other audience members, seemingly appalled.

The librarian cleared her throat and said in a trembling but authoritative voice, "Let's have another question."

She pointed to a woman who didn't ask anything but said, "God made the Earth for people to live on, not leave."

"How about this young man," Clark Evans said, nodding toward Frankie. "You've got a question, don't you, buddy?"

His face, Frankie thought, was a little like Buck Rogers's.

He had Han Solo's shaggy brown hair. Remington Steele's alluring gaze. It was the face Frankie saw every week on the back of the local TV guide in the ad Evans took out for his real estate business. Frankie straightened up in his chair and asked, "Can you comment on Gordon Cooper's UFO sighting and the photos he took during his Mercury orbit?"

"That's a great question," Evans said. "And, you know, I actually have an interesting story about that event—but it's a little long to tell right now." He turned to the librarian. "We're about out of time, aren't we?"

When she confirmed this, Evans stood and pulled his wallet out of his blazer, and from it he removed a small stack of business cards. He stepped forward and passed them out to each of the five members of the audience, encouraging them to call if they were ever buying or selling a home in the area. There was a small clatter of applause.

Frankie was unlocking his bicycle from the rack in front of the library when he heard a voice say, "I hope you didn't think I was dodging your question, buddy." He looked up and saw Evans standing several feet away, holding his car keys. The man had on a pair of aviator sunglasses and he was smiling. He had very white teeth.

"That's okay," Frankie said.

"I'd love to tell you that story sometime. These public talks are a circus. It's refreshing to run into someone who has a genuine interest in the space program."

The "circus" had only involved an audience of five, but Frankie was grateful for the chance to talk to the astronaut one-on-one. "I think there was a cover-up and maybe Cooper was in on it—only because he was scared. I think maybe he was afraid NASA would get mad if he talked too much about what he saw."

Evans held out his hand. "I'm Clark," he said.

Frankie's skinny arm snapped like a rubber hose in the man's grip.

"You live on the island?"

"Yes, sir."

"Good for you. No need to *sir* me, by the way. Do you want to be an astronaut?"

"Not for the government."

"Well, there aren't too many independent companies out there, though if there were, I'm sure they'd be better run than NASA."

"Do you think we're descended from aliens?"

"I haven't given it much thought. How old are you, buddy?"

"Sixteen. Almost seventeen."

"How about that. Well, listen, you still have the card I gave you?"

Frankie nodded and pulled it out of the back pocket of his jeans.

"That number on the front is my office," Evans said, taking the card from Frankie's hand. He turned it over, clicked a ballpoint pen, and began to write. "But this is my home number. Why don't you give me a call sometime, and maybe we can get together and talk—about space." He handed the card back to Frankie. "Ever been inside the Vehicle Assembly Building?"

"Not inside it, no."

"We could tour the facility. Would you like that?"

Beneath his Admiral Ackbar T-shirt, Frankie's heart was pounding. "Sure," he said.

"Give me a call and we'll see what we can work out."

"Thanks, Mr. Evans."

"Not 'Mr. Evans.' It's Clark." The man pulled his sunglasses down and gazed at Frankie for a moment. Then, spinning his key ring around his index finger, he walked across the parking lot to a midnight-blue Trans Am. He glanced back once before getting in, pulled out of the parking lot, and was gone.

Still standing next to his bike, Frankie looked down at the business card. He read the handwritten phone number, then turned the card over. The motto of the business, bolded and italicized, read, *I'll travel the galaxy to meet your needs!*

He had begun to think of his house as a network of pods where they all lived separately. His sister Karen's pod was off-limits and silent when she wasn't there, off-limits and noisy with heavy metal music when she was. His brother Joe's pod was a dark hovel Frankie rarely glimpsed; it smelled of sneakers, and the only sound that ever came out of it was the faint but frequent squeaking of bedsprings. Frankie's pod was lined entirely with tinfoil and had a cockpit at one end, fashioned out of his desk, a mounted pair of handlebars, and three dead television sets. And at the opposite end of the house was his mother's pod, where she sometimes spent whole days off from work with the door closed.

They'd taken to foraging for their dinners, crossing paths in the kitchen like competing scavengers. Joe, his chin speckled with a fresh outcrop of zits, was leaning against the counter, eating pickles from a jar, when Frankie walked in. "Do we have any Triscuits?"

"No idea," Joe said.

Frankie found a box of Triscuits behind the cereal and took it down from the cabinet. Before he could eat any, Karen walked in wearing her steak house uniform and grabbed the box out of his hand.

"Evening, losers."

"What, are you supposed to look like a winner in that outfit?" Joe asked.

"Bite it." Karen ate a cracker as she peered into the refrigerator.

"I met an astronaut today," Frankie told them. He was used to his family's not understanding him and normally he kept the events of his day to himself, but meeting Clark felt too big, too exciting to contain.

"On this planet?" Karen asked.

"At the library. He gave a talk on NASA."

"So he's been to the moon?"

"No. He never really went on a mission—NASA politics and whatnot. He gave me his phone number, though. He wants to take me on a tour of the Space Center."

"Lucky you." Karen finished what was left of the crackers, took the pickle jar from Joe's hand, ate the last pickle, then took a swallow of the juice.

"That's disgusting," Joe told her.

She wiped her mouth with her hand and gave him back the jar. "So when are you and the fake astronaut going on your date?"

"He's not a fake. And it wouldn't be a *date,*" Frankie said.

"Why else would an old guy want to hang out with you? He'll probably try to butt-fuck you in a Mercury capsule."

After Karen left for work and Joe had retreated to the back of the house, Frankie sat down on the couch and looked at Clark's picture in the quarter-page ad on the back of the TV guide. The picture was a head shot no bigger than a postage stamp. Clark was displaying the same smile he'd given Frankie that afternoon, and his slogan was printed below his face. Frankie was staring at the picture when his mother's door opened and she stepped into the living room. "Where is everyone?"

"Karen's at work. Joe's in his pod," Frankie said.

"In his what?"

He held up the TV guide. "I met this man today. He used to be an astronaut and he wants to take me on a tour of NASA."

"Is he sane?"

"He seems like it."

She walked into the kitchen. "Well, make sure he gives you a hard hat if he takes you anywhere with scaffolding." He heard her clacking dishes around. When she reappeared, she was holding a bowl of cereal. "And if you get into his car, don't let him drive unsafely." She carried the bowl back to her room.

In his own pod, liquid purple from the black lights reflecting off the tinfoil, Frankie sat at his desk and extracted Clark Evans's head from the TV guide with an X-Acto knife. He used his glue stick to anchor the head to a blank sheet of drawing paper, then sketched a body beneath it: naked, hands on hips, dick pointing up to the sky.

*

At school the following Monday, he met Melissa in the commons during lunch. She was eating an egg salad sandwich and had a cookie and a lemonade next to her on the concrete bench. "Don't even look at me," she told him. "I'm Godzilla."

"No you're not," Frankie said, sitting down next to her and unwrapping his own sandwich. "You look skinny."

"I'm a monster of grotesque proportions. How's life?"

"I met an astronaut this weekend at the public library. He wants to show me the Space Center."

"Haven't you seen it already? I thought your dad used to work there."

"My dad worked in a supply room. Clark said he wants to show me behind-the-scenes stuff. My sister says he's a phony and is just trying to get into my pants."

Melissa stared down at her half-eaten sandwich as if she didn't have the energy to lift it. Then she lifted it and took a bite. "He probably is. It's probably going to turn into some steamy affair. He's not gross, is he?"

"No. He's really handsome."

On his way past the bench, Curt Alberg stopped short and looked at Frankie. "Are you talking about me?"

Frankie shook his head no.

"Definitely not," Melissa said.

"Faggot," Curt said, and walked on.

Frankie turned back to Melissa. "Do you really think he might be interested in me—like that?"

"Lust rules the world," she said. "It doesn't rule *my* world, but it rules everyone else's. And you're an okay-looking guy, though you're kind of an oddball. You're not going to show him your bedroom, are you?"

"Why?"

"He'll feel like he's at work."

"He's not an astronaut anymore; he sells real estate."

"And he's handsome?"

"Really handsome."

Melissa sipped from her lemonade and let out a long sigh. "I guess I really am going to be the last living virgin on Merritt Island."

That afternoon, at the pay phone in C-wing, Frankie got up his nerve and dialed the number on the back of Clark's business card.

A woman answered. "Hello?"

He hung up.

A few minutes later, he dialed the business number.

"Evans Realty."

"Hi. Is this—is this Clark?"

"Speaking."

"It's Frankie. The guy you met at the library last week?"

"Hey, buddy! I thought maybe you'd be too shy to call. I'm glad you did."

Frankie swallowed. He realized he was nodding yes instead of speaking. "Me, too."

"You still interested in that tour?"

"Yeah. And I'd like to hear your story about the Gordon Cooper photo."

This coming Saturday at the library, they decided. Clark would drive.

*

They sailed up Courtenay Parkway in the Trans Am, bound for the Space Center. After a while, the buildings thinned out and the land on either side of the road turned green and feral. Clark told Frankie the story of how Apollo 12 was struck by lightning not long after takeoff. "The rocket generated its own electrical field on the way up. Those boys weren't even sure what had happened at first; they just knew some of the circuitry had gone haywire. Lucky they weren't blown out of the sky."

"Which missions were you supposed to go on?"

"That depends on who you ask. Supposedly, there was a rotation system in place, but it seemed like something was always mucking that up. Made me wonder if the system meant anything, since they could change it around whenever they wanted to. I had a chance on Apollo 18 and again on 19, but both of those got canceled. Then I got wind of a rumor that I was lined up for 20, but that was canceled, too, because they needed the Saturn for Skylab. Did you know when Skylab came down, pieces of it took out a bunch of cows in Australia?"

Frankie pictured this, hoping the cows' deaths had been instantaneous, then blinked and asked, "Why didn't they just transfer you to the Skylab team?"

"I wish I knew. Hey, look at those bad boys." Clark slowed the car down and pointed out Frankie's window. Just off the side of the road, a pair of alligators sat, half-submerged in shallow water. "They're all over the place up here. I saw one get run over by a little sports car one day, and it just kept walking." He mashed the gas pedal. Frankie felt his back press into the bucket seat.

They passed the turnoff for the Visitors Information Center, slowed down for a guard post that turned out to be unmanned, then rolled past it. Nothing much changed about the immediate surroundings; the marshland was the same as what they'd been driving through on the last stretch of parkway. But in the distance loomed the Vehicle Assembly Building: a massive structure slotted with a pair of narrow garage doors tall enough to allow a standing Saturn rocket to exit, once completed. "See that American flag painted on the side?" Clark said. "You could drive a bus up one of those stripes, they're so wide."

Frankie already knew this from having taken the bus tour. He asked if they were going to be able to get onto the roof of the building.

"With any luck," Clark said. "You know, that thing is so tall, I was standing up there one day and looked *down* at a helicopter flying by."

Long before they reached the V.A.B., the road was blocked by a guardrail and a man sitting in a booth. Clark brought the Trans Am to a stop and rolled down his window. "How's it going, chief?" he asked the guard.

"Can I help you?"

"Is Jasper around?"

"I don't know any Jasper."

"Well, I'm Clark Evans. If you'd be decent enough to raise that rail, I'd like to show my friend here the inside of the V.A.B."

"Do you have some identification?"

"Absolutely." Clark dug his wallet out of his back pocket.

"I meant your NASA ID."

"Oh. That's at home—framed and hanging with the other memorabilia. I used to be one of the Apollo boys, but I've moved on to other pastures."

"You don't work for NASA?"

"Not anymore," Clark said.

"Then I can't let you past this point."

"Sure you can."

"It's not going to happen," the guard said.

"Be a nice guy and raise the rail, would you? We're not Russian spies. I told you, I'm Clark Evans."

"Sir, turn your vehicle around and head south. The Visitors Information Center is on the right, at the overpass."

"I know that." Clark peered though the windshield at the V.A.B. "Thanks for your time," he said finally, and put the car in reverse.

"It's okay," Frankie told him.

"Jackass is on a power trip."

"But for me it's, you know, more exciting to get to talk to you than to see the inside of the V.A.B." He meant this in earnest and hoped it didn't sound weird, or too flirty.

Clark smiled. "Exciting, huh? You like excitement, I'll bet. Got a bit of a wild streak in you?"

Frankie nodded.

"Then let's get wild."

He took an abrupt right before they reached the overpass, putting them on a service road that connected to the space shuttle runway. "What would be *really* wild is if we could get out on the runway and open this puppy up," he said, gunning the engine. "We'll probably just have to settle for a look-see, though."

But before long they encountered another guard post. Clark's exchange with the guard was much the same as the one he'd just had. Again, he thanked the guard for his time. Again, he told Frankie the jackass was on a power trip.

He made a third attempt to get them off the beaten track by steering them onto a road clearly marked with large white signs that read *NO ADMITTANCE* and *NO VEHICLES BE-YOND THIS POINT WITHOUT ADVANCE CLEARANCE.* This time there was no guard post, but a rack of metal teeth lay across the road. Clark spotted them just in time and the Trans Am screeched to a halt.

They wound up at the Visitors Information Center.

Not for the first time, Frankie stood on scales that told him what his weight would be on Mars, Venus, and Saturn. He peered into a Mercury capsule (his sister's predicted setting for the butt-fuck). He wandered around the Redstones and Atlases and Titans in the Rocket Garden, while Clark trailed glumly alongside him, his eyes hidden behind his sunglasses and his hands tucked into his pockets.

"It's a literal changing of the guard," Clark said as Frankie tore open a package of astronaut ice cream. "The old boys knew me on sight. I had the run of the place."

"Want some?" Frankie asked, holding out what looked like a pink block of Styrofoam.

"Sorry we didn't get in there deep. I feel like I should make it up to you somehow."

"It's okay," Frankie said again.

"Seriously. You have any interest in getting a bite to eat tomorrow night?"

Frankie felt warmth climbing up his neck. The freeze-dried ice cream softened on his tongue. "Yeah."

"You could come out to the house, and we could go from there to this great restaurant I know called Pounders. It's a fun place."

"Your—your house?"

"In Cocoa. You drive, don't you?"

Frankie nodded. "I got my license this year. I called your house before I called your office. A woman answered."

Clark took off his aviators. "That was Pepper."

"Who's Pepper?"

"You'll *love* Pepper. She's top-of-the-line."

Karen's hair was soaked in mayonnaise and wrapped in cellophane and Scotch tape. She leaned sideways across the backseat of her Datsun and filled a trash bag with beer cans, Burger King wrappers, and empty cigarette packs, then tied the bag shut and tossed it onto the driveway. "Garbage."

Frankie carried the bag to one of the trash cans alongside the house. When he got back to the car, she was sitting behind the wheel with a spray bottle of Armor All and a roll of paper towels. "Why'd you offer to help me, anyway?" she asked.

"No reason," Frankie lied.

"Uh-huh. So how'd your top secret, underground NASA date go?"

"We couldn't really get in anywhere because he doesn't work there anymore."

"I *knew* it," she said. "He's fake. Which is creepy."

"Clark's not fake," Frankie said, though he was starting to wonder if Karen might be right. "He's taking me to dinner tonight."

"To a real restaurant, or a fake restaurant?"

"A place called Pounders."

"Ha! I've heard about that place. Billy Myers goes there and times it so that he takes a big dump right in the middle of the meal. He really sticks it to them, that way."

Frankie didn't know what she was talking about and tried to erase the image from his mind. He picked up the paper-towel roll from the seat and tore one off for her. She spritzed the dash. "Does Mom know there's an old guy after you?"

"He's not old. He's probably around thirty-five."

"And you're sixteen."

"Almost seventeen. And he's not after me. If anything, I'm after him."

"Oh my god, that's even creepier. Have you had anything up your butt yet? You better stick a cucumber up there or something. He's going to be kicking at the back door, mark my words."

"Clark's not like that."

"If it walks like a duck and talks like a duck, it butt-fucks like a duck."

Frankie tore off another paper towel and handed it to her. "It's fun, helping you," he said.

"For you, maybe."

"Can I borrow your car tonight?"

Karen sat back on the seat and looked at him. Thin rivers of mayonnaise ran down her temples. "I knew you wanted something. Do you have any idea what a hassle it is to keep up a car? I break my back in that steak house five nights a week to keep this piece of junk going. I'm an adult now, you know. I've got responsibilities and a livelihood to consider."

"Okay," Frankie said. "But I have to get to Clark's house in Cocoa. Can I borrow it—just this once?"

She narrowed her eyes, still glaring. "Hold out your arms." He did and she spritzed them both, elbow to wrist, with Armor All. "No," she said, turning back to the dash.

He examined the shellac-like coating on his skin as it glistened and dried in the sun, and decided he didn't mind it. He still needed a car, though.

His mother was in her pod, but the door was open, so he stuck his head in. She was on her knees in front of her closet, surrounded by shoes.

"Are you going anywhere tonight?" he asked.

She started, then returned her attention to the shoes. "I hope not."

"Can I borrow your car?"

"What for?"

"Clark's taking me to dinner, but I have to get to his house first."

"Do I know Clark?"

"He's the astronaut I told you about. The one who I was with yesterday at the Space Center."

"It seems like you're spending an awful lot of time with Clark. Is this a—dating thing?"

"Nah," Frankie said. Not long after he'd reached puberty, he'd told his family, Melissa, and anyone else who would listen that he was gay, and while Karen liked to tease him about it, his mother had asked them all not to bring it up—though she brought it up herself from time to time.

"And he doesn't seem like a felon?"

Frankie shook his head.

"Well." She picked up two brown shoes and studied them, discovered they didn't match and dropped them onto the carpet. "Be back by eleven, and replace the gas you use."

Later that afternoon, he sat on the kitchen counter and called Melissa.

"There's this Pepper person who answered the phone when I called his house," he said. "I asked Clark about her, and he told me she was 'top-of-the-line.' You think it could be his daughter?"

"Did she sound like a grown-up?"

"Kind of."

"Could be his wife."

"My sister still thinks he's trying to have sex with me. Maybe he's gay and it's some big secret?"

"Maybe he's AC/DC," Melissa speculated. "There *are* people like that, you know—bisexuals. I should be bi, now that I think about it. It would double my chances. Did I tell you I ate an entire package of Fig Newtons for lunch?"

"I think he at least likes me," Frankie said.

"There are even people who are into *fat* people. They only want to get naked with fat human beings. I should find out if they have a club and join it."

"You're not fat. You just have a bad self-image."

"Well, if I *am* fat, I hate myself, and if I'm not, it means not even the people in those clubs will want me."

He changed T-shirts three times, settling on a purple one with David Bowie on the front. Dusk was just under way when he backed his mother's Oldsmobile out of the driveway and drove over the bridge into Cocoa.

Clark's house was on River Road, across from the island. The yard needed mowing and the paint on the shutters was flaking off, but it was a nice, two-story house with a front porch and windows that looked out over the Indian River. Frankie parked next to the Trans Am, checked his hair in the rearview mirror, then walked up the steps and rang the bell.

The door opened a few moments later and a woman stood next to it, eyeing him. She wore jeans and a sleeveless white shirt that buttoned up the front. Her blond hair was pulled back in a ponytail. She was pretty and young-looking—though not young enough to be Clark's daughter.

"You must be Frankie," she said.

He nodded.

"I'm Pepper. Come in." He stepped past her as she turned and hollered up the staircase, "Clark! Frankie's here!"

Clark's voice called from above, "Can you come up here for a second, Pep?"

"Make yourself at home," she told Frankie, then bounded up the stairs.

Frankie stood in the foyer, listening to the muffled sound of their voices. Then he wandered into the living room. There was a long, lipstick-red sofa with round, white pillows at either end. A black, lacquered coffee table on which sat a Sears catalogue, a copy of *House & Garden,* and a glass ashtray. A treadmill in one corner. Nothing about the room indicated that an ex-astronaut lived there—until Frankie reached the bookcase. There were no books, but every shelf was crammed full of framed photos, nearly all of them pictures of Clark in his NASA days: smiling alongside a trio of crew-cutted men in the launch room; dressed in an orange jumpsuit and waving on a tarmac; sitting inside some sort of simulator and staring at a panel of gauges with a stern look of concentration on his face. In one photo, he was shaking John Glenn's hand. "For Clark," the inscription read, "—with high hopes!" and underneath it, Glenn's signature.

Relieved, almost giddy, Frankie moved on to the kitchen. There were dirty dishes in the sink, Evans Realty magnets on the refrigerator. Over the toaster, a large picture frame holding patches from each of the Apollo missions, and over the coffeemaker, Clark's framed NASA ID badge.

In the dining room, Frankie found Clark's official astronaut portrait. Standing before a backdrop of the moon, Clark wore a spacesuit and was looking not at the camera but slightly above and past it, his helmet under one arm, his eyes filled with glitter and promise. He looked godlike to Frankie, who had an erection.

Adjusting himself in his jeans, he turned away from the portrait and spotted a bell jar nearly a foot high on the middle of a sideboard. Inside the jar was a pedestal, and on top of the pedestal was a jagged gray rock no bigger than a golf ball.

"Buddy!"

Frankie jumped and spun around. Clark and Pepper were standing at the entrance to the dining room, smiling at him. "Hi," he said, folding his hands in front of his crotch.

"You and I are becoming a habit. And good news: Pepper approves."

Pepper squeezed Clark's elbow and ruffled a hand through his hair.

Clark pointed toward the bell jar. "You know what that is?"

"A moon rock?"

Clark seemed disappointed that Frankie already knew. "A *bona fide* moon rock. Buzz Aldrin gave that to me."

"He won't even let me touch it," Pepper said.

"I let you hold it once," Clark reminded her. "How about you, buddy? Want to hold it?"

"Yeah," Frankie said. "I'd like to."

Clark stepped around the table, lifted the bell jar, and set it aside. Delicately, he picked up the rock and placed it on Frankie's palm. Frankie imagined it humming against his skin, charged with some sort of space energy that would give him special powers here on Earth. His palm twitched and the rock rolled to the side.

"Careful!" Clark said. His reflexes were quick; in the same instant that it moved, he grabbed it back.

"Thanks for letting me hold it."

"I'd say 'any time,' but it probably won't happen again," Clark said, returning the rock to its pedestal and covering it.

"He loves that rock more than he loves me," Pepper said.

"Not true. I love *food* more than I love you." Clark rubbed his palms together. "Who's hungry?"

Pounders was one town over, in Rockledge. Just inside the door, a hostess stood next to a large scale that had a digital readout. Her T-shirt had a cartoon pig on it, its mouth smeared with barbeque sauce. She welcomed them and invited Pepper to weigh in first. Pepper stepped onto the scale.

"One-eighteen and twenty-four ounces," the hostess said. She asked Pepper's name, then wrote it and her weight on a card with a red Sharpie.

"One-seventy-one and six ounces," she announced when Clark stood on the scale, and "One-oh-nine on the dot," when it was Frankie's turn.

"Lighter than me." Pepper feigned jealousy.

"Nobody's hiding lead in their pockets, I hope," the hostess said.

"Not us," Clark told her. "We're tried and true."

She smiled, opened her hand to the dining room, and said, "Pig out!"

They chose a table, sat down and ordered drinks (iced tea for Pepper and Frankie, bourbon and Coke for Clark), and then got up again and stood in a buffet line. There was barbeque, fried chicken, fish squares, meat loaf, mashed potatoes, and four different kinds of dessert, including an enormous pan of banana pudding, which was half gone and sliding forward like lava. "Want to compete?" Clark asked Frankie as they filled their plates.

Frankie still didn't get it. "How?"

"We weigh in again at the end of the meal. They charge by the ounce. Whoever gains the most wins."

"I don't eat much," Frankie said.

"Doesn't matter," Pepper said, reaching for the banana pudding spoon. "I'm going to win."

Clark drank three bourbons. Both he and Pepper went back for seconds before Frankie was halfway through his plate of food. He'd taken too much because he'd wanted to try everything on the buffet, but he realized it didn't matter because if he didn't eat it, it was free. "This restaurant makes the most sense of any around," Clark said, chewing. "Eating out should be like buying a shirt. You go into a store and try on a few shirts, but you only pay for the one you actually walk out with."

Frankie sipped his tea from a cup so wide he had to use two hands to lift it. He was beginning to doubt Clark was gay. Pepper smiled whenever he caught her eye. He smiled back, but felt uncomfortable. "Are you two married?" he asked.

She waved her left hand and showed Frankie her wedding band. "Seven years."

He spotted a matching band on Clark's finger and was surprised he hadn't noticed it before. "Do you have kids?"

This, for some reason, made Clark laugh, and Pepper reached over and lightly slapped his arm. "No," she said.

Clark wiped his mouth with his napkin. Then he downed the last of his bourbon, pushed back from the table, and lit a cigarette. "Frankie's interested in space travel, but he doesn't want to do it through NASA."

"You want to be a cosmonaut?" Pepper asked.

"I'd like to have my own space ship," Frankie said. He

looked at Clark. "Can we talk about Gordon Cooper now? The sighting?"

Clark winced. "You're not going to bring up that did-we-descend-from-aliens business again, are you?"

"No. I'd just like to hear about what he saw."

"Look, call it what you want, but my theory is that being out in all that space does something to people's heads. Certain big-ego types, that is."

"What do you mean?"

"It can make certain kinds of people a little—" Clark see-sawed the hand holding the cigarette, zigzagging the smoke.

"But what's the story?"

"The story is, there is no story. Cooper saw ice, or something like ice, coming off the back of his ship. From what I heard, the boys in Ground Control groaned big-time over that one. Same thing happened with Carpenter."

"Scott Carpenter photographed a saucer," Frankie said. "I read about it in a book, and saw the picture."

"He photographed a tracking balloon. He *said* it was a saucer."

"He believed it."

"Yeah, well, that's my point. Certain kinds of people—with an inflated sense of their own importance—get blasted up there and then get a little, I don't know, light-headed. They start seeing things. It's loony tunes."

"Clark's a little bitter," Pepper said around her last spoonful of pudding.

"I'm not bitter. I'm realistic."

Frankie said, "I read that NASA officials told reporters not to ask questions about that stuff."

"Exactly. Because it was embarrassing. Glenn started it on his Mercury orbit with voodoo fairy lights zipping around his head, and a bunch of the other boys jumped on the bandwagon. Most of them couldn't go up there without thinking they saw some alien whatever. It's nonsense."

Frankie thought of the photograph of Clark shaking John Glenn's hand, and Glenn's inscription.

"Lovell and Aldrin?" Clark continued. "You know what they were looking at when they cried UFO? Their own jettisoned trash bags. If that had been me, and reporters had been allowed to question me about it, I'd be ashamed to show my face. 'I saw a UFO! I saw a UFO!' Please."

"Buzz Aldrin gave you the moon rock," Frankie said.

"Yeah. Well." Clark snubbed out his cigarette in a plastic ashtray. "Even a loony can give a nice present."

They weighed themselves again before leaving. Clark paid the bill. On the drive back to Cocoa, in the backseat of the Trans Am, Frankie decided he was still attracted to Clark, but no longer liked him. There was something mean about him. As for his opinions on the UFO sightings, he was just—wrong. In their driveway, Frankie thanked them both for dinner and started to say good night, but instead of shaking the hand he held out, Clark said, "Whoa, buddy, what's the hurry? Don't you want to come inside?"

"What for?"

Pepper looked out over the river and adjusted the purse hanging from her shoulder.

Clark shrugged. "Wild times. A little excitement."

Frankie looked at Clark in the moonlight. His solid shoulders, his treadmill-tended waist. The shaggy brown hair falling over his forehead.

"Come on in," the astronaut said, nodding toward the house.

He sat in the living room on the sofa and accepted the beer Pepper offered him. He'd never drunk alcohol before, but stepping over the threshold into the house for the second time felt like crossing a border into another country, where a whole new set of rules and customs existed. The beer tasted awful, but he drank it, while Pepper sat next to him and talked about the kindergarteners she taught and Clark drank another bourbon and smoked, standing next to the picture window. Clark's mood had changed. A redness had come over his face, and he stared at Frankie as if he might not even want him there. But when he'd taken the last swallow of his drink, he nodded toward him and said, "Why don't you chug that thing and the three of us go upstairs?"

Frankie followed them up the staircase. Expect nothing, he told himself, even as he became aroused. This is a tour of the house. Clark's a realtor, after all. Maybe they're selling the place. But Pepper led them into the master bedroom, where she turned around and smiled and said to him, "If you're not comfortable with this, that's okay. You just tell us. But I thought I'd take my clothes off now."

Frankie felt Clark's hand rest on his shoulder.

"You don't mind, do you?" Pepper asked.

"No," Frankie said.

"Do you want to take yours off?" She asked this in a polite way that really did seem to leave the matter open.

"Okay," Frankie said.

"How about you, Clark?"

"Why not," Clark said, releasing Frankie's shoulder. He began to unbutton his shirt.

Pepper moved slowly but efficiently; she was naked in what seemed like no time. Frankie liked her body as a scientific wonder: the movement of her breasts as she bent to pull back the bedspread; the patch of hair between her legs. He matched Clark item for item, pacing himself against the astronaut's progress, and by the time he was naked, his dick was sticking straight up against his belly. Clark's was soft and hanging like a third ball.

"You look sexy," Pepper told Frankie. "Do you want to lie down here with me?"

"What about Clark?" Frankie asked.

"I'll be in this chair," Clark said and dropped down into a floral-patterned, wingback chair in the corner.

Frankie hesitated, watching him.

"Come lie down with me," Pepper said.

"But—" Frankie began.

"Go on, buddy," Clark said. He put his hand on his dick and started squeezing it as if it were the bulb of a blood-pressure cuff.

Pepper had pulled down the top sheet along with the bedspread and was stretched out flat on her back now. "It's okay," she said. "This is what we do. Clark likes to watch."

"Pretend I'm not here," Clark said.

Frankie felt a little dizzy—from the beer, maybe. "I can't— touch you?"

"Not if I'm not here," Clark said.

"But you *are* here."

"No, I'm not. You're doing this, just you and her. I'm not even in the room, buddy."

"It's going to feel so horny to have you lying here with me," Pepper said.

Frankie's bare feet felt weighted to the floor. His toes gripped the carpet. But he made himself walk the several steps it took to get to the foot of the bed and climbed onto it. Pepper turned onto her hip, patted the mattress, and he scooted up alongside her.

"Really nice," she said.

Was it? Frankie supposed so. At least, it wasn't gross, lying naked in the air-conditioning, in the company of people who had invited him, who wanted him to be there. And for as disappointed as he was that he wouldn't get to touch Clark, it actually helped him relax to imagine Clark was there, watching, and that Pepper was enthusiastic. Pepper, whose voice had dropped to a whisper as she'd said *Really nice* and who was petting the top of Frankie's head, the way his mother used to when she put him down for his afternoon nap.

But then her other hand moved to his dick, and his dick, he realized, had gone soft.

When she began to pet it—much the same way she was petting his head—he flinched.

"What's wrong?" she asked sweetly.

"Nothing," he lied.

She touched him down there again, and he flinched again, and moved a hand to cover himself, both embarrassed by his limpness and wanting to be left alone.

"Do you not want to do this?" Pepper asked.

"It's just—I thought maybe with all three of us. But—maybe not?"

She exhaled through her nose. "I think I get it," she said.

"What's going on over there?" Clark asked from the corner.

Pepper rolled over. She moved backward until she was sitting against the headboard and drew her knees toward her chest. "Nothing," she said.

Frankie heard the wingback chair creak. "Nothing?"

"He doesn't swing my way, Clark."

"Sure he does."

"I swing," Frankie said, suddenly conscious of wanting to be a good guest. "But toward guys, mostly. Mostly only, I mean."

"Are you kidding me?" Clark asked.

Pepper pushed a strand of hair behind her ear. For a while she just sat there, glancing around the dimly lit room. Then she got out of bed and reached for her panties and bra. "Jesus, Clark, can't you do anything right?"

"How was I supposed to know?" Clark asked.

"You're such a screw-up," she said. "I don't know why I expect anything different." She was as smooth at dressing as she was at undressing. She was already buttoning up her shirt. "Sweetheart," she said to Frankie, "you swing any way you want. That's just fine. I'm really sorry about the misunderstanding." She cut her eyes over to Clark again and said, "Jesus."

"So I'm supposed to be a mind reader that he's a closet case?" Clark asked.

"I'm not in the closet," Frankie said.

"Well, you might have told me that, buddy."

"He shouldn't *have* to tell you," Pepper said. "You could intuit, you know? You could learn for once in your life how to read people. Then maybe you'd get somewhere." She turned to Frankie again. "Get dressed, honey. And please don't tell anyone about this."

"Hey, *you* didn't do such a great job, either," Clark said. "And what's that supposed to mean, 'get somewhere'?"

"In your life," Pepper said. "In your marriage."

"I'm somewhere."

"No, you're not. You're not even here, remember?"

Clark shifted his gaze from Pepper to Frankie, and for a moment he just stared at Frankie as if trying to make sense of him. Finally, he said, "Guess it's time for you to leave, buddy."

Frankie gathered his clothes and clutched them in front of him as he made his way down the stairs.

"There's no end to the sickness and depravity of the human spirit," Melissa said upon hearing the story before lunch the following Monday, on a bench in the commons. "I guess that's the good news."

"Maybe," Frankie said.

"I wonder if people like that would go for a chubby girl like me."

"He's not nice. She is, but not him. You think he'll come after me?"

"Did you give him your phone number?"

"No."

"Does he even know where you live?"

"No." Frankie had his backpack open on the ground between his sneakers and was holding the moon fragment, turning it in his hands.

"You're a minor and they tried to have sex with you," Melissa said. "*And* they gave you alcohol. If they came after you, you could go public and expose them as extreme molesters."

Frankie brought the fragment up to his face and peered at its knobby surface. It smelled like gunpowder. "I don't feel molested."

"I know. But it means you get to keep the rock."

SUMMER OF '69

We never would have laid eyes on Ike if his dad hadn't gone to sleep on a pair of railroad tracks somewhere in Jacksonville. The man was either drunk or simpleminded—either way, he was gone and it must have been gruesome. I was untangling the garden hose when Mr. Beal told me Ike was coming to stay with us and help out.

"We've got more than enough day workers for the grove," I said, "and there's not that much to do around here. How old is he?"

"Young, I guess. Maybe ten."

"Why can't he stay where he is?"

Mr. Beal spat a dark rope of tobacco juice onto the dirt, wiped a finger across his lip, and said, "Hannah, you're about as friendly as a possum." Then he told me the boy's father used to work for Mr. Merrick, and I knew the matter was settled. Mr. Merrick owned the orange grove and a handful of other groves in Brevard County. He owned a trucking company and half a dozen packinghouses. He was letting the Beals live on the farm because Mr. Beal had driven one of his delivery trucks for most of his life and Mr. Merrick wanted to show his gratitude. Whatever Mr. Merrick wanted was pretty much how things went.

I asked Mr. Beal for a pinch of his Skoal. Skoal wasn't for girls, he reminded me, but he dug the can out of his pocket and handed it over. My spit was too soon, hardly even brown. "We might have cabbage loopers," I said, jawing toward the garden. "Something's eating holes in the lettuce."

"You heard what I said, though."

"Ten years old," I said, giving the hose a snap. "What good's he going to be around here?"

"I want you to be nice to that boy," Mr. Beal said.

"I've got no use for him."

"Nobody's asking anybody to have a use," he said. "If it's going to kill you to be nice, then you might as well get on with dying."

Such was life at Cassandra Grove.

Up till then, it'd just been the Beals, their adopted son Gary, and me. I didn't live in the house with the rest of them. I'd moved out to the barn two years earlier when I was fifteen, not long after Gary arrived—partly because I was tired of hearing Mrs. Beal's record player coming up through the floor of my room, and partly because I didn't much care for Gary, who was two years younger than me, nosy, and a boy. I dragged my mattress up to the barn loft, along with an orange crate to use as a nightstand. From up there, out the south side, I had a view of the field, the road, and the Indian River. Out the north side, I could see the orange trees, the swamp beyond them, and, way off in the distance like a mountain, the enormous building where they were putting together the next rocket, the one they said was going to the moon. If nothing else, the view reminded me there was more to the world than just the farm and the grove.

The Beals were old, at least seventy when they adopted Gary. They were calm, quiet people. The only time I ever heard Mrs. Beal raise her voice was when she caught Gary playing with himself on the tire swing behind the house. Mr. Beal and I were up on the roof fixing the shingles when she started hollering, and we edged over and looked down in time to see her walking in a circle and waving at the air while Gary swung around trying to get his pants buttoned.

That night at dinner, when the four of us were sitting around the table, Mrs. Beal said maybe we should have a family discussion about what was okay to do in private and what wasn't okay to do in public—say, in the backyard. In the tire swing, she added, just in case we didn't know what she was getting at. Gary flushed. I rolled my eyes, and Mr. Beal said, "That's okay, Mother." It *was* okay, she said, but not in the tire swing, and Mr. Beal said her point was understood.

Gary and I had to wash the dishes together every night—it was the last thing I did before heading out to the barn—and I was staring at his hands and trying not to smirk, wondering which one he used to play with himself, when he dropped a pot into the sink and splashed water onto my shirt.

"Klutz," I said.

"You're the k-klutz."

"So what were you thinking about? Girls? Naked girls?"

"N-not you, that's for sure," he said.

I hadn't been wondering that at all. I didn't want him or anybody thinking about me when they touched their penis. But I knew he was trying to be mean, so I asked, "Have you ever noticed your head is crooked?"

He told me to shut up.

"It is," I said. "Your entire head is crooked. They probably squeezed the forceps too hard when you were born."

"They p-probably squeezed your *five*-ceps too hard," he said.

Not the sharpest nail in the toolbox, Gary. But even if he'd been sharp, I wouldn't have liked him much.

The truth was that, thankfully, not a lot happened at Cassandra Grove that involved other people. The day workers who picked the oranges had almost nothing to do with us and were gone by sundown. (I'd nod to a few of them now and then, but even the women eyed me with suspicion and wanted nothing to do with me.) The farm bordering the grove was hardly a farm at all. It sat far back off the road, tucked into the northern swell of the island, just below the Space Center. There was a gravel drive that ran from the road to the front porch and curved off to the barn and the rusted silo. Behind the silo was the shed where Mr. Beal kept the tools for Mrs. Beal's garden. Mrs. Beal hadn't worked in the garden for years, said she couldn't bend over anymore, but I kept it up. Lettuce and radishes, mostly. Kale, when I could get it to grow.

Mr. Merrick kept about forty head of cattle in the field past the barn, fenced and gated off from the house and the orange grove. We never had much to do with them besides giving them water and replacing the salt licks. Every so often, Mr. Merrick would send a truck over to take a few of them away. The cows would walk onto the truck like they were walking across the field, then they'd be gone. And the ones who were left behind seemed unbothered. They collected themselves around the gate near the house, until they got tired of Mr. Beal honking his horn every time he wanted to get his Nova through. Then they'd move out near the road and just stand there, all of them facing the same direction. Every once in a while we'd hear a gator growling out in the swamp, or a fruit bat banging against the inside of the silo, and one time something bit one of the cows and made its leg swell up to the size of a grapefruit for a few days. But for the most part, it was a stagnant place. Nothing moved unless it had to.

The cows were all out by the far gate the morning Mr. Beal drove to the bus station to pick up Ike. I watched him leave while I was sweeping the front porch of the house. Mr. Beal had had to drive on a schedule for most of his life, and now that he was retired, he was a slow driver. His Nova crept to a stop when he had to open and close the gate, and then crawled off toward the highway.

Behind me, I heard the screen door open. Mrs. Beal stepped out and stood on the porch, watching her husband drive away.

"It'll be nice to have a new member of the family," she said.

"I thought he was just coming for a little while."

"As long as he needs to stay. You want me to braid your hair so you look nice when he gets here?"

I didn't even answer that. Why in the world would I care how I looked? "Doesn't he have other family besides his dad? Doesn't he have a mom?"

"He does, but not that he can go to," she said. "His mother's in the state hospital, tried to hurt herself. Don't you go talking about it, though. It's none of our business."

"But he's got somebody."

I felt her hand pat my arm, then rub up and down a little. It was the same rub she'd given me when I first got there. The same rub she'd given me when she tried to school me, with the help of some textbooks Mr. Merrick had sent over. She'd struggled, trying to keep me focused for two hours a day, but I felt like I'd already learned all I needed to in school before I'd come to the farm, and I had no interest in math or science. Or history. Or English. The books Mr. Merrick had sent over had illustrations in them. They were meant for kids.

But Mrs. Beal would rub my arm and tell me I deserved an education. She'd tell me not to forget how blessed we were to have one another, to be a family, and it always sounded strange when she said that, because the Beals hadn't asked for me to be there, and I hadn't asked to come. My dad was already out of the picture when I was still little. My mom had taken work as a cook at one of Mr. Merrick's camps and had done that till her cough got worse, when I was around twelve. Then she coughed for a whole year, lost weight, and died. Next thing I knew, one of the foremen from the camp dropped me off at the farmhouse. The Beals had had no choice in the matter.

For whatever reason, they'd decided they wanted a family in their ripe old age. After nobody else laid claim to me or took an interest, they asked me how I felt about being adopted by them. I told them I didn't feel right about that since I still had a dad out there somewhere, so they said I could stay on anyway. Mrs. Beal sewed me a dress, which I felt silly in and wore only once. They said I could call them Mom and Dad, or Mama and Papa, or Mother and Father, but that didn't feel any more right than letting myself get adopted. I was thankful for how welcoming they were, and I appreciated Mr. Merrick's generosity, especially given that I'd never even met the man. But I wasn't an orphan.

There were deliveries now and then. Things Mr. Merrick wanted us to store in the barn. Farm equipment, fertilizer, sometimes furniture—like whole houses somewhere had been tipped to one side and emptied out. We stored whatever we were sent until someone came to take it away, sort of like what happened with the cows. Earlier that morning, Mr. Beal had told me there would be some feed sacks coming in on a truck in a few days, so when I was done sweeping the porch, I walked out to the barn to clear one of the stalls.

I was dragging the tooth end of a chisel plow across the floor when Gary walked in.

He nodded at me, and I nodded back. He took off the work gloves he often wore—not that he ever did anything you'd call work—and laid them on a bench, then wiped his hands on his hips. His fly was open, but I didn't feel like saying anything about it.

"Dad's gone to get that boy," he said.

I told him I knew that already and walked back into the stall.

Gary sat down on the bench. He was the bona fide orphan around here. He'd come from an actual orphanage, had been brought here by the Beals' choice, and he'd started calling them Mom and Dad almost from the get-go. He followed them around, those first few days, looking at me over his shoulder like he was trying to figure out who I was. Eventually, he started following me around, too. I would glare at him until he'd pick up a mud clot or an orange and throw it—not at me, but nearby, sometimes at the side of the barn—and then run back into the house.

In the evenings, after he'd gone to bed, I'd sit in the den and read to the Beals from *National Geographic*. Or we'd watch the news on the black-and-white television Mr. Merrick had sent over. The world's longest suspension bridge being built somewhere. The war on poverty starting up somewhere else. The stories we saw had nothing to do with us and felt just as exotic as *American Bandstand*, which I watched almost without blinking, I was so taken by the dancing and the way that entire room full of kids seemed to know one another. "Go up and ask Gary if he wants to watch the news with you," Mrs. Beal had said one night, and I'd told her no way, I didn't like Gary almost as much as he didn't like me. "Nonsense," Mr. Beal had said from his chair. "He's just sore because you got a head start on him." What head start was that? I'd asked, and he'd said that, in Gary's eyes, I'd gotten the jump on his new life and he was coming to terms with that in his own way. I kept it to myself, but I thought that was one of the stupidest things I'd ever heard.

"Boy's dad got hit by a train," Gary said from the bench.

I told him I already knew that, too. I told him I was busy.

"Busy doing what?"

"Whatever it is you're not doing," I said, picking up a stack of empty crates. "Why don't you go play with your pecker?"

He got up from the bench, but then he just stood there. "Why don't you go p-play with your cooter?"

Cooter, for godsake. He scooped up his gloves and walked out of the barn.

It was July and it was hot. I still felt like a kid around the Beals every now and then, which was okay, but I wanted to feel like a grown-up around Gary and sometimes that was a challenge. I finished clearing the stall and then walked out and stood on the gravel between the barn and the house. Every window I could see was wide open, even the rooms the Beals didn't use. Mrs. Beal was playing one of her records, some ancient swing music. It filtered out through the windows, sounded further away than it was. I walked over to the oak tree, put my boot against the base, grabbed the lowest branch, and hoisted myself up. The tree was taller than the house. I heard Mrs. Beal's record fade out and then come back again when I climbed past the second-story windows. I climbed as high as I could, until the branches got thin enough to scare me.

From that height I could still make out the flattened tracks in the grass from where Mr. Beal and I had driven out to the pond two weeks earlier. There'd been a storm in the middle of the night and a tree had been struck by lightning, the snap-bang of it waking us all up. Mr. Beal had come out of the house and I'd come out of the barn and we'd both squinted into the dark, against the rain, but we couldn't see anything. So the next day we'd driven out to the pond and had found the tree lying on its side, the trunk going right down into the water. There wasn't much we could do about it.

I saw the Nova turn onto the gravel drive from the road. Mr. Beal stopped at the gate, got out to open it, rolled through, and then stopped again to close the gate behind him. Then he stopped in front of one of the cows and honked until it moseyed out of the way. I heard Mrs. Beal's music cut off as the car reached the house, and I hung on to the branch and leaned out so I could see better. The top of her gray head appeared as she came down the steps. Her arms were stretched out in front of her. Mr. Beal stepped from the car and walked around to the passenger door, but it opened before he got to it. "This must be Ike," said Mrs. Beal.

He was small, from what I could tell, and he had a small, brown suitcase in his hand. He was a towhead.

Gary came out of the house and stood near Mrs. Beal. Mrs. Beal reached down and hugged Ike like she'd known him her whole life. Then the four of them went into the house. After a few minutes, I heard Mr. Beal laughing and the record started again.

Ike wasn't ten, it turned out. He was eight. They introduced me to him that night—"Ike, this is our Hannah"—and the five of us ate dinner together. Mrs. Beal had baked what she called a no-surprise orange pie, all the browned orange slices showing on the top of it, and I didn't even like oranges, so I didn't have any of it. After the meal, we moved into the den, where Mr. Beal sipped coffee and Gary showed Ike his comic books. I sat at Mr. Beal's rolltop desk and watched the two of them. Mr. Beal had little use for a rolltop desk, but it had come in with one of the deliveries from Mr. Merrick and had never been moved on to someplace else, so eventually we'd carried it into the house. Gary and Ike looked at comic book after comic book—all of them found in a box of old magazines that had been part of one of the deliveries, though Gary acted like he'd been collecting comic books for years. Mrs. Beal watched the two of them with a glint in her eyes. Bored, I started going through the desk drawers and found a box of matches. I took one out, turned it in my hand, scratched the sulfur end against one of the brass drawer handles. It flared up and I shook it, hoping none of them had noticed, but when I glanced at Mr. Beal, he was eyeing me over his coffee.

Mrs. Beal asked Ike if he liked it here and Ike said he did. Then Mr. Beal coughed up what sounded like a dumpling and started to tell Ike all about Mr. Merrick, how Mr. Merrick lived in a big house near the south end of Merritt Island, how he provided everything we needed, and how he wanted what was best for us and that was why we were all here together. I listened for a while, then got up and said good night.

"Stay a little longer, Hannah," Mrs. Beal said.

But I shook my head and walked out of the house. Outside, the dirt and the barn looked the same shade of dark, and the gravel was glowing with moonlight. I dragged my feet over the gravel, listening to it move under my boots as I made for the barn.

*

The next morning I was in the garden on my hands and knees, pulling up weeds, when I heard a voice ask what kind of animals I took care of. I looked around and saw Ike standing there, holding a milk carton.

"Where'd you get that?" I asked.

"The old lady gave it to me."

"She gave you the whole thing?"

"There's only a little left in it. She said I could have it." He asked me again what kind of animals I took care of.

"I'm not a zookeeper. There's cows, but I try not to have anything to do with them. And if you walk out that way far enough, there are gators who'd probably love to eat you."

He upended the carton and finished off the milk. "In Jacksonville, there was a man who had a monkey he kept chained to a tree in his front yard."

"That's great," I said. "I'm busy."

"The old lady said you'd show me the lake."

"It's not a lake. It's barely even a pond."

"She said you'd show it to me."

I ignored that for a little bit. Then I stood up, smacked my hands against my knees, pulled my handkerchief out of my back pocket and dragged it over my face.

The carton was standing on the ground now next to his feet, and he was staring at me, the milk drying on his lip. I figured it was probably a safe bet Mrs. Beal was watching us from the house.

"Come on," I said, and started walking.

We crossed the yard. I hopped the fence and watched Ike

climb up one side of it and down the other. Then we made our way out into the field. He walked with his hands in his pockets, taking extra steps to keep up with me. What would it be like, I wondered, to have friends who weren't half-pints, or half-wits, or old people? What would it be like, at seventeen, to know other girls—just *one* other girl—who would want to spend time together without having to talk about every stupid thing under the sun? I had to remind myself sometimes that I'd once lived in a town a whole county away, in an apartment down the street from a school my mom would send me off to and tell me to behave at, and I had friends in that town, and we made dollhouses out of Saltine boxes and stole Cokes from the drugstore and changed the secret password every week for the club we'd formed that we didn't want anyone else to join (not that anyone else even knew about it, since the club was secret). I had to remind myself sometimes that I'd had that life. That I'd had almost seven years of schooling, in a real school. That if my dad hadn't taken off and my mom hadn't gotten sick, I wouldn't be here at all.

When we got to the pond, Ike climbed right up on the lightning-struck tree that was sunk down into the water. He said, "You catch fish in here?"

I leaned against the trunk. "There aren't any fish. Mosquitoes, but no fish."

He was peering down at the water like he was trying to spot fish, never mind what I'd told him, and he had his fingers on some kind of pendant hanging from his neck. I asked what it was.

"My mom gave it to me."

I asked if I could see it.

Without hesitating, he pulled the chain over his head and reached down to hand it to me.

The pendant had one round edge and one jagged edge and was stamped with words. *The Lord between thee we are one another.* "It doesn't make any sense," I said.

"Her half's got the other words," he said. "It's a prayer."

I let the necklace pool in my hand and bounced it up and down a little. I knew that with a toss I could have it out in the middle of the pond. With a toss, I could ruin his day.

I handed it back to him and started walking. "That's the pond," I said.

He followed me, and by the time I reached the garden he was already starting up the porch steps, calling for Gary.

Mr. Merrick took his time sending the feed sacks over. I carried buckets of water out to the troughs for the cows, and worked in the garden, and watched Gary and Ike playing in the yard. They'd hide from each other and find each other. They'd sit in Mr. Beal's Nova and steer and make noises. I pulled every weed I could find, but the garden still looked ragged.

At dinner, Mrs. Beal would ask us how our day had been, and Gary would tell her everything he and Ike had done together. Then she'd ask what I'd done and I'd say I'd worked and waited for the feed. On the fourth night, while Mrs. Beal was in the kitchen cutting up dessert, Mr. Beal mentioned how he'd met Ike's father once and how he was a respectable man. "He had an eye for chickens," he said. "He could always pick the winners at a 4-H fair."

I half-suspected he was making this up and had, in fact, never met Ike's dad. "That's not so hard," I said. "A fat chicken looks like a fat chicken."

For a moment, the only sound was what was coming through the windows: field crickets and frogs.

Ike looked at me with half his face scrunched up. "Where's *your* dad?"

"Somewhere else. Like your mom."

"Hannah." Mr. Beal shifted in his chair. "Why don't you go see if Mother needs any help?"

In the kitchen, Mrs. Beal was sinking a big knife into a pound cake, making slices for the plates she'd laid out. I leaned against the wall by the back door. The kitchen was painted yellow and it made the one lightbulb seem brighter than it really was. I watched her wipe the knife on a dish towel between slices. With her back to me, she said, "You know he's just getting used to everything."

"What's to get used to?" I asked.

Instead of answering, she said, "It seems like you two would get along fine. Just seems like you naturally would."

I heard the blade connecting with the plate. "We're not family."

"But you could be. You've both lost people, and you're both here now." She set the knife down in the sink.

"Doesn't matter to me."

"Well, it should." She gathered up two plates in each hand and motioned for me to get the remaining one.

Pound cake was a far shot better than no-surprise orange pie, but I was done being around all of them for the night. I told her I'd have mine tomorrow.

Then I was down the hall and outside, crossing the gravel, crawling up the ladder to my loft in the barn. I'd never talked to the Beals about my dad, and they'd never really asked—at least, not a question as direct as Ike's. I always assumed Mr. Merrick had given the Beals the story on both my parents, which meant that at some point my mom must have given Mr. Merrick the story on my dad. That was enough for anyone to know, wasn't it? It should have been, if it wasn't.

When I walked out of the barn the next afternoon, there were at least a dozen cows milling around the house. A few of them were sitting in the shade of the oak tree. One of them had its face up to the dining room window.

I ran toward the gate that separated the driveway from the field and before I got there I could see it was wide open. A cow on the other side tried her footing on the cattle guard, jumped over it, and walked toward the house like she had a bone to pick with someone inside. Ike was sitting cross-legged in the grass next to the fence.

"Did you open this gate?" I asked.

"No," he said. "The old man left it open when he drove his car into town."

"Then why the hell didn't you close it?"

He pointed at the metal grill set into the trench across the driveway. "Gary told me those things are supposed to keep them from getting across."

I grabbed the gate and shoved it closed. "Any moron can see they don't work. You could have closed the gate and saved us a lot of trouble. It's going to take hours to get these cows back out to the field."

I was angrier than I needed to be, but I couldn't help it. He stood up and looked toward the house, then started running.

"Get back here, you jackass!" I hollered.

The screen door slammed behind him.

When you have a dozen cows in one open area and you need to get them to another open area, it's not exactly a breeze. Not without a dog, or another person. You clap at two cows, and one of them walks in the opposite direction you want it to. You get three lined up to move and two of them drift away, like canoes. It didn't take all afternoon to get them back out to the field, but it took a chunk of it. By the time I went in for lunch there wasn't any, just the stale slice of pound cake from the night before. I waved a fly off of it and carried it out to the barn.

The stall I'd cleared for Mr. Merrick's feed was empty, but looked like the dirtiest thing I'd ever seen. I swept it, then swept it again. There was always more dirt. By the time I had it in somewhat better shape, my nose and eyes felt clogged with grit. I was heading out to wash up at the hose when Gary walked in. I started past him, but he stepped in front of me.

"Don't call him any more names," he said.

I told him to get out of the way, but he took hold of my forearm.

"Leave him alone."

"I'm in a bad mood, so you ought to just watch it."

"Sh-*shit*," he said—the first time I'd ever heard him swear. "You've been in a b-bad mood since the day I met you."

I stared hard into his eyes, put my hand on top of his and squeezed it, then lifted it off my arm. "Go to hell," I said. "Both of you."

I pushed past him and walked outside.

The rest of the day I spent walking along the edge of the grove, as far away from the house and the barn as I could get and still be on the property. The workers were up and down their ladders, picking oranges as fast as their hands could move. Some had burlap sacks hanging from their shoulders, some had baskets with leather straps. They filled whatever they had, climbed down, found the truck they were assigned to, and dumped their oranges into it while a foreman on a folding chair kept track. There were all kinds of day workers—white ones, black ones, in-between ones (Cubans, I guess), some who looked almost as young as Ike and some who looked even older than the Beals. The ones I was watching on my walk around the perimeter didn't talk to one another much and didn't stop moving. I thought it might not be so bad, picking oranges for Mr. Merrick. You'd get shade when you were up in the trees, have plenty to do, wouldn't have to talk to other people too much. I was standing next to the furthest fence from the house, with the grove on one side and the swamp on the other, when one of the day workers noticed me looking at him. He was tanned red from the sun, had deep creases in his face, and looked like he could have been somebody's grandfather. He was halfway up a ladder, his fedora pushed back on his head. I was about to say hi when he said, "Keep walking, you green-moneyed bitch."

I kept walking, and walked faster once I was out of his sight. I followed the chain-link fence because I didn't want to cut through the grove, and I was all but running when I got to the end of it. My heart was pounding in my ears. I started toward the field, and just as I cleared the grove, I spotted Ike in the distance. He was back at the pond, sitting up on the fallen tree.

I would have walked in another direction, but he had already seen me, had maybe even seen how fast I was going, so I made myself slow down. Pushed my hands into my pockets. Wandered toward him.

"Hey," I said when I got to the edge of the pond.

"Who's chasing you?"

I glanced behind me. I kicked at a chunk of mud and sent it into the water. "Does it look like someone's chasing me?"

He shrugged.

"Sorry I called you names, but you could always just call me names back, you know?" It wasn't much of an apology, but still it tasted bad, saying it.

He was straddling the log the way you'd sit on a horse. "How come Mrs. Beal's not your mom now, if your mom's dead?" he asked.

And that made me angry all over again. Loose-cow angry. Life angry. "Because I had a mom, and now I don't. Why'd you go crying to Gary?"

He looked down at the water, staring into it like he had when he was waiting for a fish to jump. "Gary's my best friend. And he's my brother now."

"He's not your brother. You just met him. You don't even know him."

He kept his head down. "He can be my brother."

I took a step toward him, but then stopped and kicked at the mud again.

He was holding on to the log with both hands. "Why can't he be *your* brother?"

"Why isn't Mr. Beal your dad?" I asked, caught up in what felt like a question loop, my voice starting to tremble. "Because someone else is your dad, only he's dead, that's why. He was hit by a train."

His face darkened. I saw two of him, above the water and reflected down in it, the trunks pulling away like a giant, open beak.

"Hit by a train," I said. "Gone."

"But my mom's coming back, once she gets better."

"Ha!" I said. "Not in a thousand years. Trust me, that won't happen."

Part of me felt awful, telling him that, but part of me wanted to tell him everything again—that the Beals weren't his parents, that Gary wasn't his brother, that his mom was crazy in a hospital and the sooner he swallowed that, the better.

He wouldn't look at me. Only down, at the water.

*

U p early the next morning, I sat by the south window paging through one of the magazines that had come in the box of comic books. *Today's Teens,* it was called. There were picture spreads of The Beatles, Freddie and the Dreamers, Herman's Hermits. Articles with names like "What Fellows Say About Girls," and "Too Shy to Be His Steady." There was something called a "Self Quiz" for rating your personality— ten multiple-choice questions designed to tell you what kind of person you were. The heat swarmed under the metal roof and I could feel the sweat running down my back, inside my shirt. I circled my answers. Added up my score. A horn sounded in the distance, and through the window I saw a few of the cows moving and dust clouding up from the gravel road. I was "tempestuous," according to the quiz, but I didn't know what "tempestuous" meant.

There were eighteen sacks of feed. The driver helped me unload them onto the ground near the front of the barn, but said he didn't have time to help move them inside. He was in a hurry. People were waiting. I thought this was how Mr. Beal must have spent his years as one of Mr. Merrick's drivers: always in a hurry, always with people waiting.

The sacks were fifty pounds apiece. To lift them, I had to bend down and work my arms under them, leverage them up and shift my footing around. When the first one landed in the stall, all the dirt I thought I'd swept out came clouding up. After that, they just got heavier. The gravel sounded like it was powdering under my boots.

I was lifting the last sack, and I was trembling with the weight of it, thinking about Ike and his mother and what I'd said. I was thinking about my dad, and wondering for the first time if Mr. Merrick knew where he was—dead or alive—and wasn't telling. Because Mr. Merrick seemed to know everything about us, but when it came down to the spit and chaw of it, he didn't do a whole lot to help, did he? I imagined I could stay in Cassandra Grove for the rest of my life, quiz myself once a year and be "tempestuous" every time, and never see an improvement in my situation or anybody else's. Just more orphans trickling in.

I turned around.

Ike was standing just a couple of feet away, staring, like maybe he wanted to help, but maybe he only had something he wanted to say. And that's when my arms gave out and the sack went down.

Gary called his name from inside the house. The rocket was on television, he hollered. It was about to lift off across the swamp. Come see.

Ike took a step backward. He spat onto the feed that had landed between us. Then he turned and ran.

I wiped my sleeve across my eyes, stepped out of the barn, and blew dirt into my handkerchief. When I reached the garden, I looked north.

The flame was about as big as my fist and was just lifting over the furthest line of palm trees when the screen door smacked open. Ike and Gary ran down the porch steps, the Beals coming after them. Ike seemed to have already forgotten what had happened in the barn, which made me wonder if it had happened at all. He was jumping up and down, saying he'd never been this close to a rocket before. Gary picked him up and hoisted him onto his shoulders.

The flame rose on a column of gray smoke. The ground shook under my boots, and I heard a frantic twitter and a flap of wings—doves roused from the hole in the silo roof. Then the rumble, which sounded far away but grew louder until it matched the shaking in the ground. The flame climbed higher and higher, and the trail of smoke behind it began to coil.

"For Pete's sake, Hannah, what are you looking at?" Mrs. Beal asked.

I was down on one knee, squinting at the lettuce. "Cabbage loopers," I said, lifting one of the bright-green worms with my thumbnail.

THE FALL GUY

Ever since his stroke, Leo Burke felt a constant flutter in his left eye. His neurologist—perky, effeminate, bearing a brotherly resemblance to Tony Randall—had told him several times that it wasn't the eye itself he was feeling; it was the ligaments, specifically the lateral palpebral ligament. "You've been traumatized," Dr. Loudon had said. "You can't shake the house without upsetting the china." Some doctors believed patients drew solace from having their medical conditions expressed in everyday terms, but Leo wasn't one of those patients. Dr. Loudon would sit on the edge of his desk with his hands folded in his lap and listen to whatever Leo had to tell him—smiling all the while, as if he were hearing a child describe a day at the zoo—then ask if Leo liked to play Yahtzee. "Think of yourself as a cup filled with Yahtzee cubes. You got shaken up and tossed out. Things aren't going to be exactly like they were before the stroke." Then he'd reach into his blazer pocket, pull out that goddamn stick with the little red ball on it, and ask Leo to follow it with his eyes.

There was a palsy, too. Dr. Loudon had said that would probably go away with time, but it had been two months since the stroke and the left side of Leo's face still sagged. When he braved the mirror each morning, he saw a man who looked like he was trying not to laugh at something he found only half-funny. Combine that with the flutter in his eye and the pulsing of his lower lid, and he looked like a candidate for the nuthouse.

"Think of yourself as a car," Dr. Loudon had said. "Something got knocked loose and kept the gas from reaching the engine for a little while. It might never happen again."

Cold comfort. Dr. Loudon had encouraged Leo to get back to his normal routine as soon as possible, so Leo had pushed through the doors of Technicolor just a week later. He'd also resumed his part-time job at the hardware store, his deaconing at the church, his Scout meetings. But it wasn't the same as before. He tried to hold the left side of his mouth just slightly higher than the right, and to squint his eyelid just enough to suppress the flutter, but he wasn't successful. When people talked to him now, they talked to his left eye. And when they listened to him, which no one really did anymore, they focused on the downward sag of his mouth.

"If the pulse and the palsy are bothering you that much," Dr. Loudon had said, "just think of yourself as a trusty old appliance. A Westinghouse. You might have a few new rattles, but you're still running."

Leo wouldn't have minded punching Dr. Loudon in the stomach.

He also wouldn't have minded screaming into the faces of the people in his life who used to respect him and who now only saw him as weak. His coworkers at Technicolor. The customers at the hardware store. The congregation at First Baptist.

His wife.

His two boys.

Just a couple of blasts from his whistle used to bring Mitch and Howie home for dinner; now Leo had to stand at the foot of his driveway and blow his lungs out: three blasts, then three more, then three more after that. The boys weren't afraid of him anymore; they tuned out the whistle just as they tuned out his voice. And they looked at him differently. If they weren't focused on his eye or his drooping mouth, they were looking at his hair, which had turned half-white over the past eight weeks. They were obstinate, but they weren't idiots: they worked it to their advantage. They pissed and moaned now about having to do their chores. They complained about having to go to church, having to wear Toughskins instead of Levi's, having crew cuts. They'd begged for puppies last year—one for each of them—and Leo had brought home a pair of six-week-old springer spaniels on the condition that they take care of them, walk them, train them. But the dogs went largely ignored and slabbered around the backyard like wolves.

For godsake, he wanted to tell his boys, life is *short*. Shut the hell up and appreciate what you have. But they were too busy griping. They were too busy punching stop signs and running over snakes with their bicycles. A week ago, they'd taken one of the younger boys from the neighborhood—a fellow Scout in Leo's troop, no less, and a boy who they knew full well was the son of one of Leo's underlings at Technicolor—and tied him to a palm tree, then pulled down his pants and stuffed a dead myna bird into his underwear. It had been irksome for Leo to have to hear about it from Marie, who'd heard about it from Skip Ferris's wife. It had been embarrassing to have to apologize to Skip Ferris at work the next day. And it hadn't been nearly as satisfying as it should have been to take Mitch and Howie, one at a time, over his knee and smack their backsides. In fact, Leo had felt a little silly doing it, wondering if their cries were genuine or fake, all the while feeling his eye flutter like a telegraph key.

J ulian Ferris heard the first, faint blows of the whistle and felt something close to relief. The Burke brothers had dragged him into the side yard of an empty house at the end of their street, where they'd dug a hole to bury him in, and he was kneeling in it now while they fought over who got to use the shovel.

"Keep reaching for it," Mitch, the older of the two, told Howie as he held the shovel away from him, "and I'll flatten your head into a birdbath."

Howie snorted, said, "Fat chance," and reached for it again.

"Keep reaching for it," Mitch said, "and I'll shove it so far up your ass, the handle will come out your mouth."

"Hug a nut," Howie said.

It went on like this for a while. Julian's knees started to ache, and he counted to ten over and over again, waiting for the next set of whistle blasts. Climbing out of the hole and making a run for it wasn't an option, since the blond, crew-cutted Burke brothers were faster and stronger than him; the last time he'd tried to escape, they had nabbed him easily and had taken turns slapping the back of his head.

Whole days could go by wherein they seemed to forget he existed. Then they'd descend upon him, drag him off somewhere, and explain what they had in store for him. One day they'd tell him they were going to make him eat a lizard, and if he threw up, eat the throw-up, and if he pooped, eat the poop. Another day, they were going to stuff him into a garbage can and throw in a live hornet's nest. They were going to make him eat an ant pile with a spoon. They were going to cover his dick with peanut butter and tie a squirrel to his ankle. Poor planning usually saved him—they weren't able to find a lizard, had no way to handle a hornet's nest, couldn't locate an ant pile or catch a squirrel. But the day they'd threatened to tie him to a tree and stuff a dead bird into his pants, they'd surprised him by actually having a dead bird on hand, and today they'd already dug the hole before capturing him on his way back from 7-Eleven. Fortunately, they were lazy and had dug down only about a foot and a half.

The second set of whistle blasts rose up through the warm air.

"If you were any stupider," Mitch told Howie, "you'd forget to breathe."

"If you were any uglier," Howie told Mitch, "you'd make the whole island drown in its own puke."

The only thing they disliked more than each other, it seemed, was Julian. And there was no avoiding them because their lives were so miserably wound up with his. They lived in his neighborhood. They went to his school and were in his Boy Scout troop. Their father, Mr. Burke, was not only his dad's boss and the scoutmaster, but he also drove the three boys to the weekly Scout meeting.

Mitch and Howie couldn't stand Julian's name, which they only ever pronounced "Julie-Ann." They couldn't stand his face, either, which they said looked like a steaming plate of balls. And they *hated* his hair. It was girl's hair, they'd said. Long and brown and stringy, like Mackenzie Phillips's, if Mackenzie Phillips never took a bath. Julian's hair wasn't that long; it barely reached his shoulders, but they'd grab it when they caught him, and twist it, and once they had him pinned to the ground, wipe their hands on his shirt and say he could end the oil crisis if he'd only turn himself in to the government.

The third set of whistle blasts finally arrived—clipped and mean sounding, louder than it was before. The Burke brothers both turned in the direction of their house.

"You're lucky," Mitch said after a moment, looking down at Julian. "You were almost dead."

"So almost dead," Howie said.

As they started out of the yard, the shovel resting on Mitch's shoulder and Howie, for some reason, still reaching for it, Mitch called back, "Till next time, Julie-Ann."

Julian was eleven years old and was convinced he'd suffer for the rest of his life at the hands of the Burke brothers. He'd certainly never grow big enough to fend off Mitch and Howie, who were not only older than him, but just a little bit fat in the middle. Still, he thought as he stepped out of the hole and brushed the dirt off his legs, wouldn't it be wonderful to get exposed to radiation and wake up so enormous that he couldn't be caught by anyone? Wouldn't it be the best thing in the world for his new mega-self to walk over to the Burke house and tap a finger on their roof, and when the Burkes came running out and looked up in terror at the giant looming over them, say hi to Mrs. Burke (who seemed nice), and hi to Mr. Burke (who had a scary-looking twitch in one eye but had never been mean to him), and then raise his foot into the air and say *"Ha-yaa!"* as he brought it down on Mitch and Howie? He'd take one step to the east and wash his foot off in the river. And then Mr. and Mrs. Burke, all the residents of Merritt Island, and even President Ford would say, *Thank you, Julian Ferris. Now and forever, thank you.*

S cout nights were the only times Leo ever laid eyes on Julian. The boy was small, only a year behind Leo's youngest, but about half the size. He was quiet and skittish, looked rattled much of the time. It wasn't any great surprise that Mitch and Howie picked on him, even though they'd been told not to and had been punished for doing so. How could they resist? They were boys, after all, and Leo had once been a boy—and a small one, at that. He'd never told his sons, but he'd taken his own share of knocks back in Mississippi until he'd gotten wise and learned how to throw a punch, learned how to make sure there was at least one kid in his neighborhood who crossed the street when he saw Leo coming. It was a natural part of childhood to either wallop or get walloped now and then. But, for the love of God, let there be no more dead animals shoved into people's underwear.

Leo blamed himself a little. He'd tried to teach the boys boxing once, but he'd lost his patience too soon. He'd bought them gloves and headgear and a stand-up punching bag and had tried to teach them the rules he'd learned in basic training at Camp Shelby. But he made the mistake of calling them "queens rules" instead of just "rules," and the little idiots couldn't get past the phrase, thought it was the funniest thing they'd ever heard. They lisped and pranced around with their gloved hands dangling from their wrists until finally Leo said forget it, snatched back the gloves and everything else, and donated the whole kit and caboodle to Goodwill.

In theory, Scouting should have instilled the kind of confidence that brought focus, and the kind of focus that undermined dumb behavior. Having a uniform to wear, a troop number to be proud of, badges to work for—what could be better for both men and boys alike? But, as with anything lately, there were hassles to deal with. For one thing, enrollment was down. There were only five other Scouts besides Mitch and Howie, and two of them were Jewish. Leo had nothing against the Jewish, but every time you turned around they were having some sort of holiday that kept them from attending meetings. And of the three boys who weren't Jewish, one of them had a doctor-certified heart condition, poor kid, and couldn't do much more than sit on a folding chair and highlight his Scouting manual. That left the Stelzel boy, who was promising, and Julian Ferris, who wasn't.

Julian had poor initiative, didn't even seem interested in earning his Tenderfoot. He also had a nervous habit Leo found irritating: he scrunched his shoulders up and rolled his head around like he was rubbing the back of his skull against his neck. It wasn't exactly a shrug, but it looked like one, and he did it whenever he was tongue-tied or restless. Mention the Tenderfoot badge, and there went Julian, scrunch and rub.

Another hassle for Leo was dealing with Dan Messer. Dan—shaky and spindly—was the only person Leo had been able to find on Merritt Island who was interested in being assistant scoutmaster, and he was nice enough, but he was a bit of a wet-brain. As in, he came to the weekly meetings drunk. He hiccupped during the Pledge of Allegiance. "Bring your own personality and excitement to instructing the sessions," the training manual said, but Dan didn't bring any of those things. At the close of the meeting one night, right in the middle of the Stelzel boy's clunky but earnest rendition of "Taps," a flask bottle of Old Crow had fallen out of Dan's windbreaker. When he'd dropped by to see how Leo was doing in the days following the stroke, and had been trying to buck up Leo's spirits by saying they were robust for men their age, both of them just fifty, Leo had been astonished. He would have put Dan at sixty-five.

Mitch and Howie, as far as Leo knew, were still committed to the idea of Scouting and of one day becoming Eagle Scouts. But they took the pageantry of it all far less seriously than they had before his stroke. They used to sit like ironing boards in the backseat of the station wagon on Scout night. All the way to the meetings, they would barely say a word, but would check, over and over again, the hang of their sashes, the stitching of their badges. Now they rode like monkeys. They yanked on each other's neckerchiefs. They tried to throw each other's hats out the window. They tormented

the Ferris boy, who did nothing to defend himself, just covered his face with his arms. When all this became intolerable,
Leo would slam his foot down on the brake and throw gravel
as he steered the station wagon to the side of the road. He
would turn around in his seat and holler that they, Mitch and
Howie, were going to get it; they were already going to get it,
but if they didn't settle down and leave Julian alone, they
were going to *really get it.* But next week, it would be the
same thing all over again.

They were suspiciously quiet at the moment. Leo turned
off their street and into the newer section of the neighborhood and peered at them in the rearview mirror. Both of
them in uniform, hats on, neckerchiefs tied. Both of them
tight-lipped and red-faced and wearing false mustaches.
Where the mustaches came from, Leo had no idea. And, really,
for obnoxious behavior, this was small-time. One on a scale of
ten. But in another way this tiny infraction—false mustaches
on the way to Scout night—was worse than if they were
smart-mouthing and was exactly the kind of thing he felt certain he wouldn't have had to deal with if he hadn't had the
stroke. There was no rationality to it, but since his brush
with death, the smallest of annoyances had become intolerable. Already this evening he'd had to deal with Marie's berating him for having skipped both his last neurologist
appointment and his physical therapy. Then had come the
excusatory phone call from Dan Messer, saying he had some
sort of flu and didn't feel well enough to make it to the meeting (Leo had recognized the familiar booze-scrape in his
voice, like someone had shoved a shoehorn down his throat).

The windows were down. The air smelled of gardenias

and cut grass. Another person might have felt glad to be alive, given the circumstances, but those false mustaches were eating at Leo. The boys wouldn't speak until he told them to knock it off, clean up their act, get those goddamn things off their upper lips, and it felt like his whole life was in their sticky little hands, his entire existence funneled into the moment when he finally gave in and started yelling.

And now here came the Ferris boy: out of uniform, bounding down his driveway as Leo made the turn.

Julian ran right up to the driver's door as Leo was coming to a stop and announced that he wasn't going to the meeting tonight.

What forces, Leo wondered, had aligned to take such a colossal crap on his day? But he had no one to pose such a question to—no one wanted to hear it. "Are you Jewish?"

"No," Julian said, "I'm Catholic. But it's my birthday."

One of the mustached devils snorted from the backseat.

"What's that got to do with anything?" Leo asked.

"I guess there might be a cake and presents," Julian said, scrunching the back of his skull against his neck. "My aunt and uncle are coming over. My parents want me to stay home."

"We're voting tonight," Leo said. "Halloween's in two weeks, and it's on Scout night. We're voting on whether or not we'll meet."

Julian glanced into the backseat at Mitch and Howie. He didn't wave at them, didn't say hi, didn't even seem to notice their mustaches. "I guess I'd vote not to meet, if it's going to be Halloween."

"No proxies," Leo said and put the station wagon into reverse.

Julian's birthday haul included a new pair of roller skates (from his parents), a Daredevil T-shirt and a baseball cap with the Apollo-Soyuz logo (from his aunt and uncle), and a nickel-clad bicentennial dollar (from the old man who lived next door and who'd spent so much time talking about the coin as he showed it to Julian that Julian had wondered if he was ever going to give it up).

For several days following his birthday, it rained in the late afternoon—flat and heavy, knocking against the driveway and the sidewalk. On the third day, when he got home from school, he asked his mother if she would move her car out of the carport. She did and then dashed back into the house under the cover of an umbrella. For an hour or so, Julian skated in a circle around the empty carport, avoiding the oil stain in the middle and the curtain of water that fell on all three sides, listening to the rain batter the roof. But it wasn't much fun. There was barely enough room, and he wasn't that good of a skater yet.

Finally, almost a week after his birthday, the rain let up. He got home from school and changed out of his Divine Mercy uniform, pulling on a pair of shorts and his new T-shirt. He put the bicentennial coin into one of his pockets, adjusted the strap of his new baseball cap, and tugged it down onto his head. Then he carried his skates outside and laced them around his feet.

He stuck to the sidewalk. He watched for cracks and avoided palm kernels. It was sort of like swimming, in that he got a little braver each time, ventured further away from his house before turning around and wobbling back to the driveway. He fell twice, but his only damage was a bruised elbow and a bloodied knee. He imagined himself as an explorer on the banks of a river no one had ever traveled. Around the bend, where Letty Drive met Compton Street, were winged beasts with fangs secreting poison. He'd capture one, he decided, wrap it in a titanium net and keep it hidden from society until he'd trained it to recite the entire *Encyclopedia Britannica.* At which point he'd call together all the scientists of the world and make their jaws drop.

Then, suddenly, there *were* beasts coming toward him. He should have expected as much, though he'd never seen them on Compton Street before; their house was on the other side of the neighborhood. Like him, they had wheels—skateboards, in their case. They also had propulsion: the springer spaniels on leashes, galloping like a pair of Shetland ponies. The Burke brothers didn't even have their feet on the ground; they stood on their boards, arms stretched out in front of them, serpentining like water-skiers—until one of the dogs crossed in front of the other, Mitch yelled, "Go left! Go *left!"* and in a glorious moment of impact so slam-bang you could actually hear their bodies collide, the boys went down.

Let there be peace on Earth, Julian thought, feeling giddy, *and let it begin with Howie's shattered limbs, and let it end with Mitch's head bursting open like a melon someone took a knife to and carved out just enough space for a stick of dynamite.*

But the brothers were intact. Their boards had sailed off in different directions and yet they'd both managed to hang on to their leashes, and the dogs were already jumping around them spastically as the boys got to their feet and started fighting.

"That was the most boneheaded thing I've ever seen someone do!" Mitch said, shoving Howie away from him.

Howie fell back to the ground. "Snot-faced ball-licker," he said, jumping up again and lurching toward Mitch.

"You don't know your left from your right," Mitch said, shoving him back.

"Tits," Howie said, stumbling but managing not to fall this time. "Tits."

"Well, look who it is."

Being on roller skates in the presence of the Burke brothers and not being a very good skater was poor planning, Julian realized. When he got himself turned around and started down the sidewalk, he felt like he was trudging through quicksand. He made it across three, four, five squares of cement before a hand grabbed the back of his shirt and the iron-on Daredevil logo pulled tight across his chest.

"Cross-your-heart bra thinks he's going somewhere," Howie said.

Mitch stepped in front of Julian and peered at him, taking stock of him—as if it were the Burke brothers, and not Julian, who'd discovered a new species. "Maybe he is," Mitch said, his face glistening with sweat. A stench was coming off him that reminded Julian of cabbage. "Get the dogs."

"We *got* the dogs," Mitch said.

"Then get the boards, and make sure he doesn't escape."

"Where are we going?"

"Painville," Mitch said, his gaze fixed on Julian's.

"Where?" Howie asked.

"*Home,* asswipe. We're taking him home."

The dogs pulled Mitch at a pace more trot than gallop. Julian pulled Howie, who hung on to the back of his shorts and rolled alongside him.

When they got to the house, Julian's heart sank at the sight of the empty carport, because it meant that no grown-ups were home. Carrying their skateboards under their arms, the brothers led him across the lawn, through the side gate, and into their backyard, where they turned the dogs loose and told Julian to stand against the toolshed.

They seemed undecided on the manner of execution. Howie suggested they pour Windex into Julian's ears, but Mitch wasn't interested in the idea. Then Howie said they could just "throw stuff at him until he dies," and when Mitch asked what stuff, Howie said cumquats, grapefruits, potted geraniums. Julian knew they could throw fruit at him for about a month and it probably wouldn't kill him, but the potted geranium plants lining the patio looked heavy.

He reached into his pocket, pulled out the bicentennial coin and showed it to them.

"What the hell's that?" Mitch asked.

"It's a souvenir coin, but it's real money too. It's an actual dollar. I could buy my freedom."

Mitch squinted at the coin, said, "Cool," and took it from him. He tucked it into his own pocket and looked back at his brother. "We'd get into huge trouble if we broke all those geranium pots. I've got a better idea."

By order of the good state of Florida, Mitch declared, the prisoner would be drawn and quartered. Specifically, by dogs.

This prompted some follow-up questions, since Howie didn't know what it meant to draw and quarter someone, and then, after it was explained to him, wanted to know how they'd quarter Julian with only two dogs.

"Don't worry about it," Mitch said. "We'll catch him on the rebound."

They dragged Julian away from the shed and told him to lie flat on his back on the ground. They tied one leash to his right ankle and the other to his left wrist. Then they hooked up the dogs. But the dogs wouldn't sit still, so they had to hold them, aim their heads away from Julian, tell them to *Sit!* over and over again and then, finally, *Go!* The dogs walked over to Julian and began to lick his face. One of them nudged the baseball cap off his head.

The brothers tried throwing tennis balls for the dogs to fetch. They tried holding the dogs' attention with pig ears and walking backward away from them. This worked in that each dog leaned as far as the leash would allow, stretching Julian crossways, but it was hardly a dismemberment. In fact, the execution was such a failure that Julian started to giggle— and immediately regretted it, for Mitch declared the dogs brain-damaged and told Howie to untie them, then squatted down and planted his knee on Julian's chest.

"Open your mouth," he said.

Julian mashed his lips together.

"Open your mouth and eat this, or eat something worse."

Julian couldn't see what Mitch had in his hand but knew

the threat to make it worse was real. When he opened his mouth, Mitch shoved in one of the soggy pig ears. Julian clutched it with his teeth to keep it from touching the back of his throat while Mitch took hold of his arms and Howie his legs. His body lifted off the ground as the brothers strained in opposite directions.

And that was when Mrs. Burke, having finally come home from wherever she'd been, stepped out onto the porch, purse in hand, and gasped.

For a while after the stroke, Leo had tried an eye patch. He'd ordered it from an address he'd found in the back of a fishing magazine while waiting to get a haircut, and it had taken almost three weeks to arrive. Marie didn't like the patch. She said there was nothing wrong with his eye other than the tic (she called it "the tic"), and there was no reason to cover it up. Not that she knew what it was like, having a traumatized palpebral ligament. Not that she'd ever tried to carry on a conversation with herself, or the boys, or the Technicolor staff, and seen how even the most well-meaning person was drawn to the fluttering eye.

Leo had worn the patch to work and had told his coworkers that a sensitivity to light had set in. Nothing major, just a temporary adjustment. But the patch, it seemed, made everyone even more distracted than they'd been before. They stared at the black oval as if trying to discern the problem it was hiding. They asked him if the patch was elastic or if it tied around back. They asked him if it itched.

"You sure it's not leaching toxins into your eye?" one of

ouch! "No one has their hair like this anymore, Dad," Mitch said.

Leo might have reminded them that he'd worn a crew cut since his army days, that their grandfather had worn a crew cut his entire life, that the astronauts had always worn crew cuts. But it was nothing he hadn't said before. "Do you realize how humidifying this is for me?"

He hadn't meant to say that, but it's what his brain had served up. The same thing had happened, only more severely, in the moments leading up to his stroke. It had been a Sunday afternoon, the boys had been watching football on TV, Marie had been walking into the kitchen and saying she might make pepper steak for dinner, and Leo, sitting at the kitchen table with the newspaper open in front of him, had opened his mouth to say, "I'd rather not have pepper steak, if it's all the same to you," but what had come out was akin to Dr. Loudon's Yahtzee analogy.

"'Mother flap steak on a blue-skinned cruller?'" Marie repeated back to him word for word, tacking a question mark to the end of it, looking bewildered and a little put out. "What am I supposed to say to that?"

Leo remembered pushing his chair back and standing. He remembered feeling like his balance was somewhere outside his body, and resting a hand on the table, and then thinking it was a good idea to lie down flat on the linoleum floor.

"Leo!" Marie said. "What in the world are you doing?"

"Something's happening," he said—or tried to say; he wasn't sure what actually came out of his mouth.

She knelt down and leaned over him. "Oh god, oh god, oh god," she said.

"Get away from me," he said. "Let me breathe. Call an ambulance?"

"Oh god," she said, "I can't understand a word you're saying!"

You might still call, he thought. She was doing just that. He could hear her talking to the operator, and then waiting while the operator connected her to the hospital. As she was frantically repeating their address into the phone, Leo stared up at the swirls in the ceiling, trying to swallow, trying to stay calm. And then the boys came in from either side, their two yellow heads blinking down at him, eclipsing his view.

"Not 'humidifying,'" he said now, feeling even more agitated than he'd been a few moments ago. "Humilifying. *Humiliating.* Skip Ferris works for me. He works *under* me, you know that. It's humiliating to have to keep apologizing for the two of you."

Their eyes were like spiders crawling over his face.

"I need you to promise me something," he said, "both of you. I need you to promise you'll stop acting like little assholes all the time. Because kids who act like little assholes grow up to be big assholes. And nobody wants to be around a big asshole." He tried to think of something he could add to this. "Nobody who's an asshole becomes an Eagle Scout. That's a known fact." He tried to think of something else. "And you shouldn't be picking on this Ferris boy, anyway. He's half your size."

Slipping, he thought. He was slipping by inches, losing his grip.

"If it takes smacking you both across the face each and every time I hear that you've picked on this boy, then that's what's going to happen. And the dogs, the TV privileges, the basketball hoop you want for the driveway—you can kiss all that goodbye."

His lateral palpebral ligament was throbbing.

"Look, it's my job to make sure the two of you learn common sense," he said. "And one day I won't be around to try, and you're going to wish I was. You both know that, don't you?"

Mitch didn't respond, was looking at either Leo's fluttering eye or at the sag in his mouth, hard to say which. Howie sank his hands into his pockets.

"Don't you?"

S everal days before Halloween, Julian asked his mother if he could use his First Holy Communion blazer as part of his costume. She said yes. A day later he asked his father what was the strongest tape they had, and his father said duct tape. "Duck tape?" Julian asked, and his father told him no, *duct* tape, for ducts, but when he pulled a roll out of the utility closet to show Julian, the brand was, indeed, called Duck Tape.

"How about that?" his father said.

Julian asked if he could borrow the tape, and his father said, "Go for it, champ." Then Julian asked if they had any black spray paint, knowing they did because his father had used some to paint their house number on their garbage cans not long ago.

"What for?"

"My Halloween costume."

His father stepped onto his toolbox to get the can down from the shelf. "Outside only," he said, handing the can to Julian. "And aim it away from your face."

Alone in the backyard, Julian folded up the bottom flaps of the Communion blazer and used the duct tape to hold them against the lining, shortening the blazer at the waist. Then he lay the blazer on the grass and spray-painted it black: front and back, sleeves, collar, armpits.

Halloween night, he put on jeans and a white T-shirt, his school shoes, the jacket. He took a bottle of Wesson Oil down from the kitchen cabinet, carried it to the bathroom, and combed a handful of oil into his hair, catching the drips with a towel. The oil flattened and lengthened his hair—not what he'd been going for. He did his best to swoop it up in the front.

He was carrying the bottle back into the kitchen when his mother looked over from the couch, where she was watching a game show.

"What are you doing with the Wesson Oil?" she asked.

"I needed it for my costume."

"Well, I hope you didn't make a—is that your Communion blazer?"

He set the bottle down, cocked his head to the side, and gave her two thumbs up. *"Heeeyyyyyy."*

His mother brought a hand to her mouth.

After dinner, with his parents trailing him, he traveled up and down their street and the next street over, rang the bell at every house, did his double-thumb maneuver, and by dark he'd made a decent haul, nearly filling his plastic pumpkin.

Back at home, still in costume, he ate Zotz and waited for the doorbell to ring, answering it every time with *"Heeeyyyyy."*

He recognized the Burke brothers right away. Mitch was dressed as Spock, in black dress pants and a blue pajama top, with masking tape crowning his ears. Howie was in the store-bought Dr. Zaius costume Mitch had worn the previous year. They were about to laugh at his getup, Julian thought. They were about to muss his hair, congratulate him on finding a way to make it even greasier than it normally was. But, no: they just stood side by side, holding their pillowcases open.

He dropped a single piece of candy into each case.

Howie lifted his mask and peered down at the candy, a smirk set into his face, but Mitch knocked his little brother with his elbow and said, "Let's go." Even more surprising, he added "Thanks" over his shoulder as they were walking away.

Julian was about to close the door when he spotted Mr. Burke moving into the porch light.

Mr. Burke was dressed in his scoutmaster's uniform and was holding a plastic tumbler. Of course, he was the one who was responsible for the change in Mitch and Howie's behavior. Just looking at him, Julian knew this was true, and he felt a rush of gratitude.

Mr. Burke adjusted his stance on the cement slab of the porch, then adjusted it again. "Trick or drink," he said.

"What?"

Leo cleared his throat. "You heard me. I'm doing drinks, not treats."

"Dad," the boy called into the house.

Leo swallowed what was left in his cup. He batted a moth away from his face.

When Skip Ferris appeared in the doorway, he was smiling and rubbing his hands together as if he'd been making something. "Mr. Burke," he said. "How are you?"

"Trick or drink," Leo said.

"Ha ha. What's the trick?"

"You're fired," Leo said.

Skip Ferris laughed again, but it sounded forced. "All right. One sec, I think we have a beer."

He left them there—Leo clutching his empty cup, Julian holding the tray of candy. Mitch and Howie's voices bubbled up in the warm night, already several houses away. Listening to them, Leo tried to decipher who Julian was dressed as. A punk was his best guess. A hippie. Julian wondered if Mr. Burke had put on the uniform because he'd forgotten they weren't going to meet that night. Then another thought came to Julian, a question, and because he was still feeling grateful he asked it as nicely as he could.

"Is that your costume?"

"You need a haircut," Leo said.

The boy looked distracted, didn't seem to have heard him. Leo tightened his hold on his fluttering eye, hitched up the drooping side of his mouth, and leaned down so that he could speak in a near whisper. "You look like a goddamn girl."

MISS AMERICA

On the Wednesday that I'm supposed to go with Emerald to meet the talent scout, I get home from school and find a box that comes up to my knee sitting out by the curb where we put the trash. Wednesday is not trash day. The box isn't taped up or even closed, and when I dig through it I see a stack of Tom Clancy paperbacks, our crockpot, and a framed eight-by-ten photograph of my mother and stepfather, dressed up and smiling in front of the Polynesian Hotel at Disney World. Their wedding portrait. As I walk into the house, I hear what sounds like chains being rattled. My mother is in the kitchen rifling through the silverware drawer.

"This is absurd," she says when she notices me standing there looking at her. She's dumping forks and knives and spoons by the handful onto the counter. "Some of it has to go, don't you think? There must be four different patterns here."

There are six patterns—some plain, some with curlicues, some with plastic handles—but I don't correct her. And I don't mention the box out by the curb. She's home early from work, which is inconvenient because I wanted to have Emerald come in when she got here so she could help me choose an outfit to wear, and my mother doesn't like Emerald and doesn't want her in the house anymore. (Emerald flipped her the bird once from the foot of our driveway when my mother told her she needed to wash her car.) I drop my book bag onto the dining room table, go to my room and change into one of my newer blouses and a striped skirt I hope are flattering, check my hair in the bathroom, then head back outside to wait for Emerald on the front porch.

I'm not sure that meeting a talent scout is the ideal thing for me right now. I'm on-and-off panicky, on-and-off queasy, on-and-off unhappy with who and where I am. But Emerald has been talking about Derek for what seems like weeks. He's one of the people she's met since she dropped out of school and got a fake ID, and she thinks he's going to like me as much as he likes her. She thinks he's a dream ticket—and who, according to Emerald, deserves a dream ticket more than us?

Emerald has always been good at making me feel better about myself. According to her—and I'd like to believe it's true—I am an almost fully realized human being. I'm five feet, ten inches tall, have good cheekbones, and freckleless skin. I have what's called perfect pitch: I can hear a song on the radio once and sing it back to you without getting any of it wrong; I can even play it on the guitar, so long as I already know how to make the chords. And I have excellent brain-

power. I can read a whole paragraph in a magazine and re-
peat it word for word, no problem. At rapid speed, I can tell
you the names of every Miss America winner since 1921,
from Margaret Gorman to Kellye Cash. I can list all their talents and all their causes and all their home states, including
six each from Ohio and California, five from Pennsylvania,
two from Washington, D.C. (which isn't even a state), and
not one from Florida.

According to Emerald, I could change that.

My mother, on the other hand, likes to temper her encour-
agement with cynicism. She doesn't mind dishing out a compliment, but she usually shatters it with what she calls a
"medicine bomb." I'm beautiful, she'll admit; I've got all of
her looks, and then some. But looks aren't everything, she
says, and my attitude needs some serious adjustment. "Just
remember, when you're staring into that mirror you're so
fond of," she once told me, "for every beauty, there's a beast."

To which I said thank you, thank you *very* much, and
could I quote her on that some day?

I'm sweating up a storm by the time I see Emerald's pale
yellow Chevette coming down the street toward our house.
She taps the horn as she drives up onto the strip of grass between the curb and the sidewalk, and for a second I'm worried she's going to smash right into the box with the
paperbacks and the crockpot and the wedding portrait. Then
I realize: what difference would it make? And there's something sad about that, but I don't have the space in my head
to make room for it.

"All aboard, bitches!" Emerald says, leaning toward the
window on the passenger's side.

I open the door and climb into the car without looking back at the house.

Three months ago, my stepfather made the big announcement at dinner that he was ready for some major changes in his life. Specifically, he was ready to quit his job and relocate. My mother, who likes to read magazines while she eats, asked him without looking up what in the world he was talking about.

"Wyoming," Roger said.

"The state?"

"I've been mentioning this to you for a while now. Leaving my practice? Buying a buffalo farm? I'm ready to pursue that."

"Please," she said. "Dream on, buddy boy."

"I haven't come to this decision lightly. Not lightly at all. But I'll be flying out next week to look at a ranch that's gone into foreclosure."

"So you can do what?" my mother asked, turning another page. "Uproot us all? Pull your daughter out of school at the beginning of her junior year? That doesn't sound very considerate."

"Gail," Roger said. Then he did what he always does when he needs a moment to collect a thought: he took off his glasses, squinted at them as if they might have belonged to someone else, and put them back on. "I don't expect you to come with me."

"And we wouldn't," my mother said. "I don't know if I've ever heard such a half-baked idea."

"Dani can come, if she wants," Roger said. "I know she

needs to finish out the school year, but she's welcome to visit, once I get settled."

And right about the time I was thinking that if they divorced, they wouldn't be able to sit in a room together and talk about me as if I wasn't there, it seemed to dawn on my mother that he was leaving. She looked up from her magazine, at least.

Here's what she's gotten good at, since he left:

Deciding she can no longer bear certain household objects—like the wedding portrait, the rattan coatrack, and the marble sculpture of a pelican he gave her a few Christmases ago—and hauling them out to the curb.

Collecting paint chips from the hardware store and taping them up on the walls of every room in the house, including mine. (When I told her I didn't want my room painted anything called "Fruit Punch," she told me there was nothing wrong with a little color in our lives, now that we were free of my stepfather's obsession with taupe.)

Putting away desserts in the evenings. She's always been good at that, but she's gotten better over the past year. She can put away a pound of cookies and a half-gallon of sherbet when she gets revved up. And if there's nothing she feels like watching on TV, she sits down with the phone and starts dialing. "Everything's just rotten," she tells my one aunt in Wilmington or my other aunt in Carson City—whichever sister will take her call. "My life stinks, and why should I have expected it to be any different? Stupid me for marrying a Gemini, right?"

What I don't mention to her is that she used to say she needed the sweets because of how emotionally absent my stepfather was. Now that he's *completely* absent, she's gnawing through them from the minute she walks in the door after work till around the time she falls asleep—usually on the sectional sofa with a blanket pulled up to her neck. Her eyes dart like frogs just under the surface of a pond when she's sleeping. Her lips smack together and her nose sounds like an exhaust pipe. If I've been out, I try to come in quietly so she'll stay under, but she usually wakes up and wants to hear all about my day, or—worse—she wants to cuddle. "Come here, sugar," she sometimes says. "For godsake, just come here and hug me and let's weather this thing out together." *This thing* always has to do with her and never has to do with me.

Here's what I've gotten good at:

Whatever's going on, I pretty much tell her the opposite. I started doing this not long after my stepfather left, after she said it was high time she and I became friends. (All I could think was that she'd never seemed to care much before, so why all the sudden enthusiasm?) And, besides, she would have a meltdown if she knew what was really going on with me. Her life already stinks; the last thing she needs is more bad news. So how am I doing in school? I'm getting straight A's in everything, including Advanced Calculus, thank you very much. Have I given any thought to college? I have, and it's going to be law school for me, Ivy League all the way. Am I still seeing Brian Watley, the most respectful and handsome young man she's ever met? Yes, Brian and I are in love, but we're both saving ourselves for marriage one day because that will make it *so* much more special. And what about Emerald, that bad penny who needs to clean up her act before she gets into trouble with the law? I don't see much of Emerald these days, couldn't tell you where she is or what she's up to.

"I know you better than you think I do, little lady," my mother sometimes says.

I wonder.

"The thing about Derek is that he's pretty much brilliant," Emerald tells me as we sit in her car on Cullen Avenue, waiting for a funeral procession to pass. "He knows all about people, what makes them tick. He says the key to life is figuring out what you want and what kind of person you are. Some people shoot heroin, and some refuse to take an aspirin. Some eat raw steak, and some chew on tree bark. Some people cuss up a storm, and other people wouldn't say a bad word if they were looking the Grim Reaper in the face. They could be driving over a bridge and have the steering wheel come off in their hands, and it wouldn't even occur to them to say, 'Dammit.' And there are some people—like your mother, for instance—who let every stupid thing happen to them just because there it is, and there they are. And then there are people who see their lives *about* to be potentially fucked beyond belief and realize they can do something to change it. That's Derek, through and through. He says it's not astrophysics; it's common fucking sense."

That sounds reasonable, I guess. I want to be someone who doesn't live on Merritt Island, someone who lives in

New York or Los Angeles; I want to be someone millions of people love and admire for her beauty and her kindness and her talent; I want to be Miss Brevard County, and then Miss Florida, and then Miss America. But I don't know how to make any of that happen.

"Jesus, how many friends did this fucker have?" Emerald says, glaring at the line of funeral cars. She turns to me. "So are you one of those people who lets every stupid thing happen to them?"

"Maybe," I say. Her air conditioner's been broken for over a year. I feel like I could throw up from the heat.

"You're not. You just have to *know* you're not. You just have to say it out loud."

"I'm not one of those people," I say.

"Right on," she says. "To thine own self, cut the crap."

Emerald's name isn't really Emerald. It's Rowina, but she hates Rowina and has been saying since seventh grade that she'll punch in the throat anyone who calls her that. Before she dropped out, she even had some of her teachers calling her Emerald—which would be an amazing accomplishment if there weren't already two girls at school who'd gotten their math teacher to call them Peaches and Tinky. Emerald's hair was wispy and brown as a Hershey Bar all through school; now it's full-bodied and blond. Recently, she's started wearing lipstick and rouge and eye shadow. If somebody asks her where she works, she'll say she's an actress, like that's a place, when, in fact, she clears tables at Lobster Heaven in Cape Canaveral. All this is in keeping with her philosophy about not bullshitting thine own self because she's made every decision to change who she is on a calculated basis.

The funeral procession is just barely past the intersection when she takes her foot off the brake and guns the engine. She lays into the horn as the Chevette fishtails around the last car, and it feels like we're being dragged instead of just moving fast.

"Derek's going to put us on the right track," she says.

"I hope so."

"He gets people television and movie deals all the time. Modeling, too. Like I said, he's kind of brilliant."

I'm wondering how she got such a high opinion of this guy just from talking to him in a bar every now and then. Maybe he bragged about himself the way she bragged about me. I feel my forehead tighten. "You didn't tell him, did you?"

"About what?"

"The thing with me and Brian."

"What's to tell? Brian's out of the picture, isn't he?"

He is. And part of me wishes he wasn't, but I could never admit that to Emerald. She met him only once, and from those five minutes at Burger King she concluded that he was weasel-faced and spineless (he's not; he just has narrow features and bad posture). She didn't understand why I would want to date him, but that was right at the beginning of the summer when she was spending more and more time with her bar friends. What else did I have to do in the evenings? Sit at home with my mother? Brian and I started going out three or four times a week, went to the roller rink and the movies together, and ended up having a lot of sex in the backseat of his Pinto. "Here I go," he'd say every time, "oh, god, here I go," and it was cute, the way he sounded so much like a little boy. I'd give Emerald updates over the phone—

only because she asked for them. She thought the sex sounded boring, and she thought it was hilarious that I'd gotten Brian to take me to *Dirty Dancing* four times. ("What a pussy!") But then the stupid thing happened. The queasiness kicked in, and I started having to pee more than usual. My nipples started hurting just from rubbing against my shirt. And, of course, no period came. When I told Brian, in the parking lot of the movie theater, he took hold of both sides of his head and squeezed like he was trying to crush his own skull. Then he started sobbing. He said he was sorry. And he said he had a life. He kept saying this over and over. "I have a life, you know?" I thought at first he was talking about what we'd done, what was inside me, but he was talking about himself. He asked me to please, please, please get rid of it, and I told him of course I would. But as soon as I said it, I thought, maybe not. I was on the fence, which surprised me as much as finding out I was pregnant after we'd used condoms almost every time. I mean, I could see the advantage of having the whole situation just go away, but I could also see me with a baby. Being motherly with it, all-the-time sweet. Sitting right there in the parking lot, I started thinking up names. Trevor if it was a boy, because I've always liked the name Trevor. Rachel if it was a girl. Or Becca. Brian was taking deep breaths, like somebody who'd almost drowned. He asked me not to tell anyone, and I said I wouldn't. Then, as if the whole thing were a done deal, he thanked me. And kissed me. And thanked me again. He thanked me about a dozen times on the way home, his lower lip trembling and his hair mussed from when he'd squeezed his head. And he thanked me two days later, when he called to tell me he needed "some space."

Emerald came right over when I told her. She took me to Jetty Park and sat with me and let me cry as much as I wanted. When I was done crying, she told me she hated to admit it, but she agreed with Brian: I should get rid of the baby. Did I want my whole world taken over because I suddenly had to be a mom? Did I want to get fat and stay fat? No I didn't, she said. She bought us root beer floats at Carvel. She drove to the mall and paid for us to have Glamour Shots taken (it wasn't the best time because my face was puffy, but it was still nice of her). Afterwards, sitting by the fountain, she eyeballed the pictures and the little stamp-sized proofs they'd given us. That was when she told me about Derek the talent scout. Derek was going to like these pictures a lot, she said. She couldn't wait for me to meet him. As for Brian, she wanted to cut his dick off, put it in a hot dog bun, and make him choke on it.

We turn off Cullen Avenue onto a side road lined with one-story, cinder block houses. The windows are down because of the broken AC and my hair is blowing all over and sticking to my forehead. "Yeah, Brian's definitely out of the picture," I say. "But did you tell Derek about the thing with me?" My hand, I realize, is rubbing my still-flat stomach as I ask this; I pull it away and let it rest on the seat.

Emerald snorts. "You're kidding, right? That's about the last thing you'd want a talent scout to know."

*

My stepfather calls from Wyoming to talk to me every Sunday night at eight o'clock on the dot. Like my mother, he's taken an interest in me only since they split up, and now he asks all kinds of questions (about school, about my guitar playing, about my plans for the future). But Roger is easier to keep at bay because of the Florida-Wyoming thing, which means we don't have to see each other not looking at each other when we'd rather not be talking. And while I don't bother telling him the opposite of whatever is really going on, I can usually avoid any topic just by asking *Why?* and then going quiet.

"How are your friends?" he asked me last week. "Are they treating you okay?"

"Sure."

"And what about your grades? You're keeping those up, I hope."

"They're so-so," I said.

"And is your mother doing all right?"

"Oh, yeah," I said. "She couldn't be better."

He's not a dummy; he picked up on the sarcasm. "Listen, Dani, I'm very sorry about this whole—situation."

"Why?"

Silence.

"Because I don't want you to think it's any reflection on you. And I don't want you to feel like you need to side with either one of us."

"Why?"

Silence.

"Because you're the innocent party here. Not that anyone's

guilty. Your mother and I just stopped functioning on a—sufficiently cohesive level."

I wonder if he used this same sort of language with my mother. *Gail, I've been meaning to tell you: we're not functioning on a sufficiently cohesive level.* Anyway, one more *Why?* and I knew I'd be home free. He didn't want to go into the private details of their marriage with me, and I certainly didn't want to hear them. But before I could ask *Why?* again, he changed the subject.

"You really should think about coming out here for a visit. It's not all cowboys, you know; it's a lot of regular folk, too. A lot of teenagers. There's a community center right down the road from me, and they have a newsletter that lists all kinds of events for young people." He paused for a moment; I pictured him taking off his glasses, squinting at them, putting them back on. "And Wyoming has a lot of natural wonders. It has Yellowstone and Old Faithful. Some interesting history, too. It's where the very first J. C. Penney opened. And did you know it was the first state to grant women the right to vote?"

I don't care about natural wonders, I can't vote for another two years, and I wouldn't step foot in a community center if you paid me. "Okay," I said. *Okay* can also shut down the back-and-forth in a heartbeat. It's basically what everyone wants to hear.

He asked me to say hi to my mother for him and I told him, not for the first time, that I wasn't doing that for either of them; they could do that themselves.

He told me he missed me and loved me, and I told him I

missed him and loved him, too. We said goodbye and hung up for another week.

The thing is, I guess I do love Roger. My real dad died when I was a baby (he had a rare cancer, my mother told me, but she doesn't like to talk about it). My first concrete memory of my mother is of her pitching a fit—I mean, screaming her head off—in the checkout line of a grocery store because the cashier wouldn't take her coupons. She was always pitching fits when I was little. Then Roger came along when I was seven, and they got married, and she calmed down some. We moved into a new house, I got a bigger room, and we started buying real trees at Christmas. So I love him for that. But I don't miss him, not really. Maybe that makes me a cold person, or emotionally wounded, whatever a psychiatrist would call it. I don't *feel* wounded, or like I need to choose sides. Roger was never mean to me, never once yelled at me, never even scolded me that I can remember; he was always just there: calm and reserved and focused on some inner thought, like the most patient man in the world waiting for an elevator that would take him to some other floor—and then the elevator arrived, and he got on.

"So what did Wild Bill Hickok have to report?" my mother said when I came into the kitchen. She had various ways of asking about Roger's phone calls, but she always asked. She was sitting at the table, going through a week's worth of mail.

I opened the refrigerator and stared into it. "I've told you, if you want to know, you should call him yourself."

"Is he out there riding buffalo all day with his new girl-friend?"

There might have been something in the fridge that I felt like eating, but I couldn't see it, could only see things I didn't want to eat, and I had to close the door fast, because lately the sight of the food I don't want to eat is enough to make my stomach turn. I picked up an apple from a bowl on the counter and checked it for spots. Then I didn't want just the apple. I wanted the apple with peanut butter, but by the time I got the jar down from the cabinet, I only wanted the peanut butter. So I set the apple back in the bowl, took a spoon from the drawer, and started out of the kitchen.

"Wait just a minute," she said before I'd rounded the corner.

I stopped and looked at her.

A faint dusting of coffee cake crumbs was on her lips. She looked like an overgrown child, a puffed-up baby-woman about to throw a tantrum because snack time was over. "I swear to god," she said, "with you, it's like speaking two different languages. I just asked you if he's riding buffalo with his new girlfriend. Why didn't you answer me?"

I stuck a spoonful of peanut butter into my mouth and turned away again.

"Don't you dare," she said, putting a little more volume in her voice. "Don't you dare walk away without answering me."

I've got a bun in the oven, I imagined blurting out. *I am one hundred percent, baby-on-board pregnant, and I don't even have a boyfriend.*

"Are you enjoying yourself?" she asked. "You need a reality check, Dani. If you can't answer this one simple thing for me, if you can be that cruel, then you need a reality check. You think everything's a game? Life is cruel, little lady—

much crueler than anything you can wrap your head around. If you're not careful, the world will chew you up and spit you out onto the sidewalk."

"All right!" I said. I couldn't resist giving her a hard time when she was acting crazy. It's like how you can't resist kicking an empty milk carton someone's dropped on the cafeteria floor—not because you enjoy kicking things so much, but because the carton and your foot are in the same place. Still, I didn't need to hear her telling me I might end up as someone's cud on the sidewalk. "He sounds fine, and he didn't mention anything about a girlfriend, okay? And *people don't ride buffalos*!"

She folded her napkin and touched it to her mouth. "A direct answer," she said. "How refreshing. What did I do to deserve that?"

"Made me feel crummy," I said, and carried the peanut butter to my room.

know there are counselors for this sort of thing. Ours at school is named Mrs. Portofino. She smells like pine needles and has a sweet, Mrs. Claus–sounding voice. She wears earthy colors and has pamphlets on a rack outside her office with titles like *Avoid Tomorrow Today* and *Who Deserves to Know?* But I can't imagine talking to her about what's going on in my body. It's probably her job to follow up, not to let something drop after she finds out about it. She might even be legally bound to contact all interested parties, which would be aggravating since I'm really the only party that needs to be interested. Even if she counseled me and then never brought it up again, I can't imagine having to pass her in the halls for the next two years with *that* conversation under our belt.

I also know I'm not the first and am probably about the millionth teenager to be in this predicament, but there's no comfort in that, not one ounce. This girl Katie Hess transferred to Merritt Island High from Lake Wales near the end of freshman year. Because she was new, she was aching for friends and was always coming up to me and telling me things about herself I didn't really want to know. Just before summer break, she was sitting next to me at a pep rally and whispered into my ear that she was pregnant by a boy from Cocoa and was scared to death. "Wow," I said—because I barely knew her and what else was I supposed to say? But three months later, when the new school year started, she wasn't pregnant. So either she got rid of it, or she lost it without trying. I was tempted to ask and still am, but she's somehow landed herself a whole new set of friends and avoids me now, so I can only assume she wishes she hadn't told me to begin with.

Sometimes I think I don't have to talk to anyone about it. Talking is just thoughts that overflow out of a person's head, and thoughts aren't always rational. I can spend all of homeroom fantasizing about a time machine that will take me back to the moment right before Brian, on that fated night, said, "Oh, god, here I go," and pulling away.

For about the length of time it takes me to brush my teeth, I can picture not having this baby at all. I can picture going to the bathroom and having a little speck fall out of me, straight into the toilet (that happens, doesn't it?), and feeling relieved as I watch it swirl away.

For as long as it takes me to figure out a new song on the guitar, I can picture me having it, full-term, and then giving it to some nice, loving couple who can't have children of their own and who would raise it and let me visit it now and then.

But I can also see me keeping it.

I'd be a good mother, I think. I wouldn't want to cuddle up with it just because I was feeling sorry for myself. I wouldn't ask it crazy questions and get bent out of shape because I didn't like the answers.

Imagine you're you, and you have this little person growing inside you that you haven't met yet. You don't know what its voice is going to sound like, you don't know what its favorite color is going to be, you don't even know what sex it is. Wouldn't you be curious?

Imagine having a tiny little person that wants your boobs— just *one* of your boobs—more than a pot of gold.

Imagine holding your baby on a sunny day, and pointing at a palm tree and saying, "See that? That's an elephant. Just kidding, baby; that's a palm tree."

E merald stops along the curb in front of a squat, orange house with a gravel roof. A Yugo is parked in the driveway; two more Yugos are sitting on the strip of grass alongside it, one of them raised up on blocks. In the front yard is a Big Wheel, and a kiddie pool with a hose sunk into it. I tilt the mirror on the passenger's side and frown at my reflection. "I look awful and I feel like crap," I say. "I'm getting a zit on my chin."

"You look pretty," Emerald says. "You just have to *tell* yourself you look pretty."

"Okay, I look pretty. But I feel like crap."

Music is coming from inside the house. On the front porch, Emerald rings the bell, knocks on the door, rings the bell again. She turns to me and curls her lips back. "Do I have food on my teeth?"

I shake my head.

She bugs her eyes out. "Crusties?"

"No crusties."

She knocks and rings the bell again.

"What do you want?" a voice calls from inside.

"It's Emerald!" Emerald says. "And Dani. Emerald you met at the ABC Lounge that time, and Dani I was telling you about. You said to come by."

"Wait," I say, "you met this guy *once*?"

After a few moments, we hear a bolt unlock. Then a chain sliding out of its track. When the door opens, there's a man who's around my stepfather's age, maybe younger. He's barefoot and is wearing shorts and a white T-shirt with high sleeves that show off his muscled-up arms, and he's wiping his hands with a rag. He looks a little like the guy who works at 7-Eleven and a little like the guy who cuts keys at the hardware store, but maybe that's only because he's stocky and has reddish hair, like they do. There's a tattoo on the side of his neck, a kind of little, blue crescent, and there's this unfortunate thing with his eyes: the left one is focused on us and the right one is angled out, as if it's been fixed to his temple with a tiny rubber band. He's staring at us and that Big Wheel at the same time. "You're kidding me," he says.

"Nope," Emerald says.

The song is that awful "Love Touch" the radio stations have been playing to death for over a year now. "You're blowing my mind," the guy says. "I gave you my address?"

"You wrote it on a napkin, remember? You said to come by."

I'm about to take hold of Emerald's arm and pull us off the porch, because either we're at the wrong house or this guy's got a screw loose. But then his mouth curls into a smile and he points right at Emerald's chest and says, "Had you for a second there, didn't I?"

"Goddamn!" Emerald says in a voice so loud it startles me. "You did! You sure did!"

"Get in here," he says, backing into the house to make room for us.

Emerald steps inside, and even though I still have the urge to grab her arm and tug her back to the car, I follow.

The shag carpet is the color of avocado meat. Along one of the wood-paneled walls is a pair of bracketed shelves full of ceramics. People and animal figurines, vases and bowls, ashtrays and peace signs—all painted and glazed and shiny. The coffee table is draped with newspapers and has pencil-sized carving tools on it, little sheets of sandpaper, and another ceramic: this one an unpainted, chalk-white turtle. Over the couch is a framed poster of the St. Pauli girl with her bare boobs hanging out of her getup.

"Cool place," Emerald says.

"That it is," the guy says, still wiping his hands. "Not the Ritz, but I think a living space should be hands-on, you know? Utilitarian."

"Totally," Emerald says.

"People tell me coming in here is like climbing into my brain." He drops the rag onto the coffee table and holds his hand out toward me. "I'm Derek," he says. "You must be Dani."

"That's me." I don't want to shake his hand because it doesn't look too clean, despite all the wiping. But I do.

"You've got a face like an angel," he says. "Like a Charlie's Angel, if there'd been a fourth one."

"Thanks."

"Make yourself at home."

Emerald sits down on the couch. I move to sit next to her, but Derek touches my shoulder and nods toward a puffy leather recliner. "You should get on that," he says. "Most comfortable seat in the house."

I sit down in the recliner.

"It rocks," he says. "Try it."

I rock the chair back and forth a little.

"And don't forget about this." He bends over so close to me that I can smell his breath—gum and, just behind it, beer—and pulls a lever. The chair slides forward and flattens out a little, and the footrest swings up, elevating my legs.

"Who'd like a little libation?" he asks, straightening up.

"Me," Emerald says. "I'd like a little libation. A gin and tonic would hit the spot right about now."

I've had beer with Emerald before, and wine coolers, but I've never seen her drink anything as fancy as a gin and tonic.

"The problem with that," Derek says, "is there isn't any gin. I've got Heineken, vodka, and Sunny D."

"A screwdriver, then," Emerald says.

"How about you, angel?"

I feel a little silly, having just walked into a stranger's house and suddenly reclining with my feet up. I'm still queasy, but at least the air conditioner is on and I'm not sweating like I was in the car. "Sunny D," I say.

His left eye is watching me. "That button on the front of the arm?" he says before heading to the kitchen. "Magic fingers. Just so you know."

"How long are we going to stay here?" I ask Emerald.

"Relax," she says. "Go with the flow."

The radio must be in the kitchen, because I hear him turn the dial from "Love Touch" to Starship's "Nothing's Gonna Stop Us Now."

"He doesn't look like a talent scout," I whisper. "And he doesn't really seem all that brilliant, either."

"He wants to help us." Emerald picks up one of the finished ceramics from the end table. "Look—a monkey with a boner."

A few moments later, Derek comes out of the kitchen holding two plastic Slurpee cups and a bottle of beer. The Slurpee cups look like they've been through a dishwasher about a hundred times. He hands one to Emerald, saying, "For the painted girl," and hands the other one to me. "For the angel." Then he straightens up, takes a swig of his beer, and rolls his head around. "The thing is," he says, "I'm no more brilliant than any other guy who's plugged in to the energy around him." Apparently, I wasn't whispering softly enough. "There's good juice everywhere, right? You've just got to tap into the vibe."

I'm pretty sure the juice he's talking about isn't what he just handed me. And the "vibe" is probably something he thinks is spiritual. Or sexual. Not that it makes any difference to me.

"And while you're right, I don't look like a talent scout," he says, "I *do* have some experience in the field."

"Told you," Emerald says.

I ask him if he has a business card, and he says he'll get me one. But then he just sits down across from Emerald on the couch and takes another swig of his beer. Emerald is still holding the monkey with the boner. She wags it toward him, grinning, and he takes it from her and sets it on the coffee table.

"So who've you worked with?" I ask. "Anybody famous?"

"That depends," Derek says. "You know the girl on the Wynn-Wynn Windows commercials?"

I shake my head.

"I got her that gig. And another girl who was working at Mister Donut when I met her, she just finished starring in an industrial for Lockheed Martin."

"Industrial what?" I ask.

"Industrials are movies a big company makes for its employees. For training purposes."

Emerald says, "God, Dani, do you live under a rock?"

"But they don't get shown in theaters?"

"I hear you," Derek says. "You want exposure, right?"

I glance above his head at the topless St. Pauli girl. "I don't want to be boobs to the wind in a beer poster, if that's what you mean. But, yeah, I want people to know who I am. I want them to feel happy when they see me, and when they hear me talk."

"She wants to be Miss America," Emerald says. "Miss Florida first, but Miss America after that. I'm the one that wants to be in the movies. I want to be on TV, too."

Derek doesn't look at her. He leans forward and rests his elbows on his knees. "You want to be a role model," he says to me.

I don't know what I was imagining a talent scout would look like. Maybe the guy from *The Idolmaker,* but that's not Derek. He's got this slight smile set into his mouth now, and it's not a sarcastic smile. It's an interested smile, an impressed smile—like Reuben Kincaid when he listened to the band play at the end of every episode of *The Partridge Family.*

"Dani and I both want to be role models," Emerald says, reaching into her purse. "We want to be stars, but Dani's got no confidence. She thinks she's ugly—"

"No I don't!" I say.

"—and I tell her she's crazy. We're pretty, and we've got more talent in our pinkies than most famous people do in their whole bodies. Look at these proofs from our Glamour Shots."

Derek raises a hand toward Emerald and says, "Shh-shh-shh." He keeps his eye on me. "What talents do you have, Dani?"

"I can play guitar."

"She's really good, too," Emerald says.

"What else?"

"She can sing."

"I mean, I can carry a tune."

Emerald tells him I sound just like Cyndi Lauper and that she sounds like Sheena Easton.

Derek shushes her again. "What else?" he asks me.

"I have a good memory."

"For?"

"What I read, and just about anything I hear. Words and music."

"She's like a computer. One time, somebody asked her if she could recite all fifty states in reverse alphabetical order—"

"Emerald," Derek says. He frowns, squints his eyes shut, and grinds his thumb and forefinger into his eyelids. When he opens his eyes again, they're lined up just fine. It's like the rubber band came detached and let that right eye swing true. I don't even know if he knows it's happened. "Could you tone it down a little?"

Emerald looks confused. "Tone what down?"

"The jackrabbit routine." He turns back to me. "Any other talents?"

I'm all out of talents, but he looks more interested than ever now that his eyes are lined up. "I've got strong feet," I say. "I can stand on point—you know, like in ballet."

"So you can dance?"

"Sure."

"Want to show me?"

There isn't even any music on now. The radio is playing a commercial. I make myself laugh a little and say, "Not really."

"Well, I'm a good judge of people," Derek says. "And I think you're something special, Dani. You've got what I call high-octane promise."

"Thanks."

"Don't thank me. Just trust me. You see this?" He angles his head and shows me the tattoo on the side of his neck. "It's a comet."

"I can dance," Emerald says softly, and then takes a swallow from her cup.

Derek sits back and picks at the label on his beer bottle with his fingernail. "It's a comet, girls, because I can recognize rising stars when I see them."

Okay, a comet is about as opposite as you can get from a rising star, since comets are always falling, so that's pretty dumb. And I'm well aware that nothing going on in this room is going to lead to the Miss Florida contest, or even the Miss Brevard County contest. But look at me: I've got the best seat in the house and the air conditioner's aimed right at it. I'm a little nauseous, but I've got magic fingers if I want them. And Derek's paying a lot more attention to me than he is to Emerald—who didn't need to be called a jackrabbit, true, but who also didn't need to ask me if I lived under a rock. The fact is, I feel as close to being okay as I have in weeks. I almost feel special. How's that for a reality check, Mom?

As opposed to, say, falling asleep last Friday night with my Walkman on continuous play—Blondie's *The Hunter*— so that it keeps switching from one side of the tape to the other, all night long, until the batteries die. And in the morning waking up because my mother's leaning over me, holding one half of my headphones away from my ear, and saying, "How a person can get any rest with music pounding into their brain all night long is beyond me."

"What are you doing in my room?" I asked.

"Getting rid of dead weight."

I sat up, yawned, and glared at her. She was holding the pole of the floor lamp from the den in one hand and had the decoupaged *God Bless Our Home* sign from the kitchen tucked under her arm. "What can we get rid of in here? And don't say nothing because I'll bet you haven't touched half this stuff in years."

"It's *my* stuff," I said. "I don't want to get rid of anything."

"Baloney." She crossed the room and opened my closet. "I wish I was the FBI. I'd dust every single thing in this house for fingerprints. Anything without fresh prints—out it goes. Anything with just Roger's prints—out it goes."

"You can't keep putting stuff out by the curb," I said. "The neighbors are going to complain."

"It's been free bounty up till now. Whatever I put out there, someone takes away. But today we're having a yard sale, you and me. Out with the old, in with the moola. We're going to make some serious lemonade."

"God, I *hate* living here!" I said.

"I'm not so crazy about it, either," she said. With her free hand, she pulled out a raincoat I hadn't worn in years and laid it across my desk, then laid on top of that the coat hanger that had all my belts on it, and from the top shelf she took down the wicker basket full of hair bands and scrunchies. "Go through everything. Take no prisoners."

"People don't buy used hair bands."

"You'd be surprised." Her head roostered around, scrutinizing. "This goes, for sure," she said, reaching into the back of the closet to take hold of my beanbag chair.

The beanbag chair had been a present from Roger, not long after he and my mother had gotten married. "Let go of that!"

"If you can tell me the last time your butt touched it, I will. I'll bet you can't even remember."

You know how when you first wake up, it takes a few heartbeats for your life to come back to you, and how that's not always such a pleasant experience? Mine was coming back to me as she turned to walk out of the room, and the sight of her dragging that big tangerine blob across the floor made me feel both panicked and furious. I scrambled out of bed, and she saw me coming and quickstepped down the hall. I ran after her, smashing my big toe on the doorframe. "Fuck!"

"Language!" she said, but I was still coming and she was practically running now, the floor lamp scraping along the wall.

I threw myself onto the beanbag chair just as she reached the living room. She didn't let go of it, lost her balance instead, and went down. Her head connected with the wall and made this loud, awful thump.

"Are you all right?" I asked.

The lamp was lying next to us, its shade buckled in. She

rolled herself into a sitting position and cupped the back of her head with her hand, her face contorted and her eyes squinted shut. She was either nodding yes or just rocking with pain, I couldn't tell.

"Mom?" I reached over and touched her arm.

You don't have to pop a balloon to let the air out of it. All you have to do is stretch part of it really thin and bite a little hole so the air squeaks free. That was the sound that came from her while we were sitting there on the floor. At first, I didn't realize she was crying; I thought she was just gearing up to cuss me out. But then she stopped rubbing the back of her head and let her hands drop into her lap, and her whole body started jerking up and down with sobs. I sat there with my hand on her arm.

"Does it still hurt?" I finally asked.

She sucked in a wet shot of air through her nose. "Everything hurts!" she snapped. "Would it have killed him just to have stuck around for a little while longer? Just till you graduated? We could have gotten through that much, at least—like a family—and then you could have moved away to college and he could have gone off to ride buffalo, and I could have disappeared for a while, gone on one of those half-year cruises, instead of sitting here like everybody in the world's worst ex-wife."

Deep-end stuff. I didn't know where she came up with "the worst ex-wife" part, since it wasn't her fault my real dad had died of rare cancer and, technically, she and Roger were only separated.

"He's a jerk," I said.

"He is, isn't he?"

"A *boring* jerk, and that's the worst kind. How's your head?"

She took a couple of deep breaths, then wiped her nose with her hand. "Thick," she said. "I'll live. Do you really want to keep this hideous thing?"

I glanced at the beanbag. "I guess not."

"Let's get moving, then," she said, pulling herself up onto her feet. "It's already ten o'clock."

And this, I thought, was surely going to be one of the most miserable days of my life: co-manning an impromptu yard sale with my mother. Only, it wasn't. We spent the next hour dragging stuff out of the house: things we didn't care about anymore or had never used in the first place (like the pizza-maker, the fondue set, and the umbrella stand). We arranged it all on blankets and then sat down in lawn chairs and drank Cokes while the neighbors showed up one by one and mulled things over. "Get a load of that one," my mother whispered out the side of her mouth, motioning with her chin toward a woman wearing sunglasses and a headscarf. "Jackie Oh-Brother. Ugh," she muttered as an old man peered into a box marked *Misc.* "Tell Rip Van Winkle the alarm clock works." But whenever anyone expressed a hint of interest, she sprang up from her chair, polite as could be. I just sat back and watched, for the most part. When one of the neighbors asked how much we wanted for the fondue kit, she said, "Good afternoon!" then told him the set was made in Boston, had never been used, and was only twenty dollars. The man said he'd give her fifteen, and she beamed at him as if she'd just won a prize. She wanted twelve dollars for the Franklin

Mint plate set but sold it to a woman down the street for seven. We got rid of almost everything, including the *God Bless Our Home* sign—bought by old Mr. Burke, the cranky, white-haired scoutmaster who had a perpetual grimace and who hooked his cane over one arm while he counted out his money. By dusk, the only items left were the beanbag chair—maybe because I'd been using it as a footrest all afternoon—and the lamp with the dented shade. I dragged them both to the curb and left them there.

"Whew!" my mother said, once we were back inside. "That was something, wasn't it?"

I followed her into the kitchen, where she dropped the money onto the counter, opened the refrigerator, and took out a Sarah Lee pie. I got the peanut butter down from the cabinet. I heard the pie box being ripped open and the tin plate waffling as I brought the spoon to my mouth, and a moment later I heard her let out a sigh. When I turned around, she was leaning against the counter, fork in hand, smiling at me—the same smile she'd been giving people during the yard sale, but her eyes were filled with tears again. "There's just no knowing," she said with a shrug. "That was so much *harder* than I thought it would be!"

Derek is done with his beer. He's got a finger sunk into the bottle and is swinging it like a pendulum between his knees. "Who's ready for another?" he asks.

"Me," Emerald says. She gulps down what's left of her screwdriver, then shudders as she holds out the empty cup for him to take.

"Angel?"

I've barely had any of my Sunny D because my stomach is wobbly, so I tell him I'm fine. He smiles, stands, and walks into the kitchen.

Emerald crosses her arms over her chest and stares at me. I roll my eyes as if to say, *Isn't all this wild?,* then glance at the shelves of ceramics along the wall. Dolphins, cats, big-breasted mermaids. I slide my hand down the arm of the recliner and turn on the magic fingers, but they feel kind of like having your bowels rumble, so I turn them off. When I look back at Emerald, she's still staring.

"What?"

She swoops toward me, leading with her chin. "You think you're hot snot, don't you?"

I want to laugh because I haven't heard anyone say "hot snot" since maybe fourth grade, but I can tell she's angry. "No, I don't."

"You're not that good of a dancer, you know. I wouldn't go dancing around anybody if I were you. Not if you're trying to make a good impression."

"I was just answering his question."

"Right," she says. "Goody fucking Two-shoes. *I'm* the one who can dance." She sits back on the couch.

"Girls, girls," Derek says, coming into the room. "Are we getting along?"

"Sure." Emerald takes the cup from him. "How soon do you think you can start getting us auditions for stuff?"

"Depends on what you want to go for. Also depends on how bad you want it. The key to success is talent plus what?"

Luck, I think. *Timing.* I don't really care at the moment, because I'm still surprised by Emerald. She's always been quick to get mad, but never at me.

"Nice skin?" she says.

"Doesn't hurt," Derek says. "Speaking of which, you might want to go easy on the makeup, Emmie. You're looking a little like a color wheel." He squats down beside my chair and rests his arm next to my elbow. "The key to success is talent plus *hunger.*"

"Talent plus hunger," Emerald repeats, then tilts the Slurpee cup so high that it eclipses half her face.

"So which one of you is hungrier?" Derek is touching my arm now, and I can smell the beer and gum on his breath.

"Why does it have to be a competition?" I ask.

He shrugs. "Everything's a competition. You ought to know that if you want to be Miss America."

"Yeah," Emerald says. "That's kind of a no-brainer, Dani."

This, coming from the girl who once labeled Cuba "Hawaii" on a geography test. "You don't want to be Miss Anything," I tell her. I'm not trying to sound bitchy; I'm just trying to point out that I've never heard her mention wanting to be in a beauty pageant before. But as soon as I say it, I'm glad it came out bitchy. And as soon as I feel glad about that, I feel guilty. I can tell by Emerald's expression that she's even madder than she was a few minutes ago; around the blush and eye shadow, her face has turned red as a beet. Derek's right eye is creeping out of whack again. "Can I use your bathroom?" I ask, moving my arm away from his and reaching for the footrest lever.

"Sure thing," he says. "Second door on the left."

Walking down the hall, I decide it would probably be better if we weren't here. Whatever Derek can do for us, is it really worth fighting over with Emerald? A local TV commercial, a company training film? Actually, I'd take either one of those in a heartbeat and so would she, but I can see now that we'll both have to succeed at the same time—at the exact same *moment*—if we want to stay friends, and that's not going to happen if Derek is more enthusiastic about me than he is her.

I'm sitting on the toilet, finishing my pee, when I hear a sneeze that sounds like it's right next to my ear. I whip my head around, and after a moment I yank the shower curtain back and see a boy sitting in the dry tub. He's around five and is dressed in a T-shirt and underpants, and he's surrounded by little piles of Legos and is holding a knobby cluster of them in one hand. His hair is red, like Derek's, and he's got a booger bubble pulsing under one of his nostrils.

"What are you doing?" I ask.

"Taking a bath."

"There's no water."

"I'm not *really* taking a bath. I'm making my own Transformer."

"Were you spying on me?" I ask, reaching for the toilet paper.

He shakes his head. "Did you just poop?"

"No!" I say. "I only peed."

"Then why are you using toilet paper?"

I think about how I might answer this, then decide not to answer it at all. With one forearm covering my lap, and without lifting my butt much, I manage to get my underwear and skirt back up. Then I stand, flush the toilet, and wash my hands in the sink. "My name's Dani," I tell him. "What's yours?"

"Philip."

"Nice to meet you, Philip. How long have you been in here?"

"*I* don't know," he says.

He's an only child, I suppose—like me. Only children don't keep track of things the way other children do. I squat down in front of the tub and compliment him on his Transformer. Then I reach over, pull off some more toilet paper, and hold it to his nose. "Blow," I say.

He barely blows at all.

"Harder," I say, and he blows harder, flooding the toilet paper with so much junk I can feel it on my fingers. "Good job," I tell him, tossing the paper into the toilet. "Sounds like you've got a little cold."

"We're going camping next weekend," he says.

"You and your dad?"

He nods. "I get to make the points on the ends of the marshmallow sticks with my pocketknife."

I find it surprising—and a little worrisome—that a boy so young would have his own pocketknife. But I'm even more surprised that Derek is the kind of person who would take his son camping. "I bet you'll have fun," I say.

"Can I see your squeezebox again?"

"My what?"

"Your squeezebox." He motions with the cluster of Legos toward my crotch, which I guess I wasn't so good at hiding when I was pulling my skirt up.

"I have to go," I say.

When I come back into the living room, Emerald is leaning a little to one side, resting her body against the arm of the couch. I can't get much of a read on her expression, other than that she looks a little grouchy and a little sleepy. She's peering at me with her eyes half-squinted, like she's never seen me before.

"Emerald thinks we should take you for a test drive," Derek says.

He's back on the other end of the couch now, sitting forward, holding the ceramic turtle in one hand and a piece of sandpaper in the other. He's sanding the turtle's shell, then blowing on it. Sanding, then blowing.

"What does that mean, test drive?" I ask.

"Your memory," Emerald says. "Have you read something and tell it back to us. Show us what a goddamn computer you are."

Derek scans the coffee table and the surrounding carpet. He puts the turtle down, reaches under the couch, and produces a section of newspaper. "How about something from this?"

"No," I tell them both.

"Nervous?" Emerald says, then looks at Derek. "Maybe she's lost her touch."

Derek is grinning and holding the newspaper out for me. Feeling a flush rise into my neck, I snatch the paper out of his hand and ask, "What, like, a whole article?"

"Just part of one," he says. "For kicks."

I peer at the tiny print. There's a story about Black Monday and the stock market crash, but that looks so boring I'm worried I wouldn't be able to keep track of more than a few sentences. There's a story on how a porn star got elected to the Italian parliament, but I'm not touching that one. Baby Jessica is in stable condition, which is uplifting, but I don't feel like reciting her story in Derek's living room, so I skip that one too. Finally, I settle on a story about some German guy who landed his plane in the middle of Red Square, which apparently is a very big deal because of the whole Iron Curtain thing. I read the first three paragraphs silently, then hand Derek the newspaper, point at the article, and recite the paragraphs back.

It turns out Derek has an ability I've always wanted to have: he can lift just one eyebrow to show his reaction to something. Unfortunately, it's the brow over the eye that's out to lunch. "Almost perfect," he says. "That'll come in handy when you're giving acceptance speeches."

"Thanks." I look at Emerald. "You about ready to go?"

She's drinking from the Slurpee cup and squinting at me over its lip.

"Wait, now, don't rush off," Derek says, dropping the newspaper onto the floor. "I understand there's something I might be able to help you with. Something that's not necessarily career oriented, but kind of is. Seems like there's this—Brian person? Who ought to have his joystick cut off?"

I feel my stomach drop. I look at Emerald. "What the hell?"

"Wuh," Emerald says, her shoulders jumping like she's just felt a tiny electrical shock.

"So you're offering to do it?" I ask Derek. "Cut off Brian's 'joystick'?"

"No, no," Derek says, laughing through his words. "I'm not the mafia. I'm into ceramics, show business. Good times. What I'm talking about is something a little more—listen, do you want to step out to the back porch with me so we can talk in private?"

I don't, and I'm about to tell him so, but then Emerald says "Wuh" again. And leans forward. And vomits into her Slurpee cup. To her credit, not one drop gets on the floor.

"Oh, for the fucking love of god," Derek says.

He seems not only surprised, but truly irked, and I don't have a strong stomach these days and am worried Emerald's going to make *me* throw up, so I say, "Let's go outside."

The back porch is closed off, has a corrugated tin roof, and is windowed on three sides with horizontal planks of greenish glass that eat up most of the late afternoon sun. It's a little like *20,000 Leagues Under the Sea* in there, except for several boxes that say LYDIA'S SHIT stacked against one wall. I get about two feet in and turn around to see Derek standing right behind me.

He puts his hands in his pockets and leans against the doorframe.

"Sorry about Emerald," I say.

"Nothing I haven't seen before," he says. "So, listen, Dani. Your situation"—he bobbles his head around a little—"isn't exactly earth-shattering. The sky's not falling, is what I mean."

I wait for him to say more, but he doesn't. "Why?" I ask.

"Because it's not. I mean, what's going on with you right now doesn't necessarily have to get in the way of the life you want."

I wait a little more. "Why?"

"Because there are things you can do about it. One thing, in particular."

"I kind of know this already."

"I'm sure you do. But you might be wondering how to go about it. How to get it done without everybody and his uncle finding out. Bottom line is, it's not a big deal. Quick and easy. It's basically like a glorified checkup."

And how many glorified checkups have you had? I want to ask.

"Don't worry about what it costs," he says, as if either one of us has said anything about money. "I'll front you the funds, I mean. That's what friends do for each other."

A dragonfly pecks on the outside of one of the window slats. Derek is *almost* blocking my way back into the house. "Why?" I say again.

"Look, how many Miss Americas you think had bastard kids when they were crowned? I'd venture to say none, unless they were keeping it a secret."

"I met Philip."

"Did you? I hope he didn't talk your ear off."

"He's in the bathtub."

"Funny kid. Really funny. I call him my new and improved me. But I want to help you out," he says, setting the needle back down on his thought. "As your friend. Let me do this for you, and one day maybe there'll be something you can do for me, down the line. That's how people learn to trust each other, right?"

The dragonfly's fluttering shape through the glass is like a floater in my peripheral vision. I listen to it peck-peck-peck as Derek takes one of his hands out of his pockets, reaches up, and rubs a dusty thumb along the side of my jaw.

"Okay," I tell him, knowing this is what he wants to hear, hoping this will shut him down.

He looks a little surprised. "You'll let me help you?"

"Okay," I say again.

"Then you and I should get together and talk logistics. Sooner than later, of course. You could come back by tomorrow, if you want—on your own, just you."

I move fast but try to be graceful about it, fluid, like it doesn't make any difference to me where I am, only right now I happen to be just barely sliding past him, back into the kitchen. "I have to check on Emerald," I say over my shoulder.

I'm half-expecting Emerald to be passed out, but she's still sitting more or less upright, hunched forward, head tilted down. The cup is nearly full and is sitting on the coffee table next to the turtle.

"Come on," I say. "We're going."

When she looks at me, openmouthed, I see tears running down her cheeks. "I screwed this whole thing up," she says.

"No you didn't. Let's go."

She stands, and I take hold of her elbow to steady her. I pick up her purse from the couch, and the Glamour Shots, and guide her toward the front door.

"What time are you coming tomorrow?" Derek asks, coming in from the porch.

"Any time's good," I say. "Thanks for everything!"

The sky is just starting to turn periwinkle as I walk Emerald across the front yard, past the kiddie pool, to the Chevette.

"I guess I shouldn't drive," she says.

I fish her keys out, get her into the passenger seat, and climb in behind the wheel. Before I drive away, I see Derek standing in the doorway, watching us.

Emerald is quiet for most of the ride. She sits with her hands in her lap, staring out the side window. We're almost to her house when she tells me she doesn't understand what happened—meaning, I assume, the way Derek was more into me than her, the way he insulted her, his mention of something happening between us tomorrow that she's not in on.

"There's nothing to understand," I tell her. "I'm not going back there."

"No, I mean how did I get drunk so fast?"

When we get to her house, I help her out of the Chevette and walk her inside. Beyond the sliding glass door, I see her dad on the patio in the backyard, squatting down over a hibachi and holding a spatula. Her mom is setting out plates on the picnic table. It's like stepping into a TV show whenever I come over here, it's *that* nice. Emerald's mom waves at us. I wave back, and steer Emerald to her room, where she flops down onto her bed and hooks an arm over her eyes. I take off her shoes and put them beside the bed. Then I set her keys on the nightstand, close her bedroom door behind me, and walk the five blocks home.

*

Half of our silverware has been added to the box sitting out by the curb. It's scattered over top of the wedding portrait. My mother is sitting at the dining room table with a box of Pecan Sandies and an open, spiral-bound notebook. She's holding a pen with a heart-shaped piece of plastic attached to the eraser end. "I've decided to start keeping a diary," she says. "What do you think of that?"

I'm thinking it would have been better if I'd thrown up, because I'm feeling too full. Of everything. Of being somebody's friend, somebody's daughter, somebody's mother. I pull the chair out across from her and sink down onto it. "Can I talk to you about something important?"

She looks up from the notebook and blinks at me. She says, "I'm right here."

But how do I do it? And what's the use, really? I've gotten myself into this, and expecting anybody to understand, trusting anybody to hear me out and maybe talk a little but mostly just shut up and let me *be*—I'm about ready to give up on that.

"Well?" she says.

I look at the paint chips taped to the wall behind her. The picture hooks that used to hold the still lifes she and Roger bought at an art show in Orlando. "Don't worry, I'm not pregnant," I say.

She seems to get taller by a couple of inches, her back straightening against the chair. The little heart on the pen is also the cap, it turns out; she pulls it off, fixes it to the other end, and sets the pen down.

"So I'm not looking for anybody to tell me what to do about that," I say.

With frantic little movements, her eyes zigzag over every part of my face. I can almost hear the gears turning in her brain. There's a meltdown in the works, I'm sure, and at this point I'm ready to suffer it and get it behind me, because how could it be any worse than the afternoon I've just had?

"But if I *was* pregnant," I tell her, "I think I'd probably want to keep it, and that would be my business and nobody else's, wouldn't it?"

For what must be the longest stretch of dead air we've ever shared, she doesn't say anything and neither do I. Finally, she closes the notebook and folds her hands over the cover like it's a bible she's just given a reading from. "Oh, little lady," she says. And I know what's coming, because she thought her life couldn't stink any more than it already did, and because why should she have expected it to be any different? Why did she ever get married, have a kid, think there would be anything out there waiting for her other than one mess after another?

Her head is shaking no. No to me, no to my situation, no to the world.

I brace myself.

"I guess we should start thinking about names," she says.

FOUNTAIN OF YOUTH

Here's my morning routine (just to give you an idea of what my days are like now): I wake up at 6:15, as if I've still got a job. I go downstairs to the front stoop I share with five other units and hope somebody hasn't filched my newspaper. I take the paper inside and sit at the dining room table, and while I drink a glass of orange juice with Metamucil and eat a piece of toast with marmalade, I read the news. Christ, it's boring. Depends on your vantage point, I guess, but for me it's gutless. Meatless. *Vegan.* A dozen people blown up by an unknown attacker in a country I couldn't find on a globe if I had to. Some woman in Smalltown, USA, who drove her kids into a lake. Some guy in some other town who didn't like his neighbor's music and dusted off his old hunting rifle to deal with it. Politicians with hookers. Cops with too much power. That's the news: somebody's an asshole, and another asshole's got something to say about it. Which isn't really news, is it?

I go on the Internet to see what's happening back in Chicago, and it's like they gave typewriters to a bunch of cats. I turn on the television to check out the local affiliates, and it's all traffic reports and "human interest" stories. So I watch a few reruns. *The Big Valley,* which I still enjoy. *The Waltons,* which is corny, but better than a lot of the garbage they show now. *Kojak.* Good old Kojak, still with the zingers and still walking into the room with his dick swinging.

I turn the clock radio to the classical station, get in the tub, soak my joints. Put on my robe, go into the kitchen, pour a big glass of water and lay out my pills for the day. Atenolol, donepezil, hydralazine, quinapril—over the teeth, past the gums. I put on trousers or a pair of shorts, depending on my mood. A guayabera. Crocs decorated with little Mickey Mouse snap-ons the girl at the mall talked me into. SPF 30 sunscreen with zinc oxide I smear from my collarbones to the top of my head, which went the way of Kojak's long before I ever had a chance of going gray. Onto this slathered bust, I place one of three straw hats and a pair of Oakleys strong enough to block UVAs, UVBs, and UVCs, whatever they are. Watch, keys, money clip, loose change, and I'm ready for what my doctor likes to call my heart-healthy, low-weight-bearing ambulation. I'm the roaming prince of Villa Ponce de Leon. Do I love my life? Not so much. It's like the Players Club, only with none of the play.

*

Villa Ponce de Leon is a very proud place. It doesn't have bushes and trees; it has *landscaping*. It doesn't have sidewalks; it has a *promenade* of winding, wooden slats carefully painted with yellow caution stripes at every step up and step down. It has a Seniors Activity Center—shuffleboard courts, tile-laid tables for checkers and chess, classes in yoga and tai chi and scrapbook making. Its own battalion of big-bellied security guards who ride around on golf carts and wave hello. Signs telling you where you can and can't park, where you can and can't walk, where it's okay for your dog to do its business. Wooden dispensers with crap bags every twenty feet, and signs reminding dog walkers that the entire complex is a "Doodie-Free Zone." Its literature boasts of being the finest retirement community in all of Brevard County—huzzah!—and in the center of the superfluous roundabout at the entrance to said community stands the man himself: Ponce de Leon, painted to look like bronze, one hand on his hip and the other thrust out, offering up this bountiful wonderland.

"Good morning, Mr. Delacorte," one of the residents says as she passes me on the promenade. At the end of the leash in her hand is a Chinese crested, looks like he's got a toupee on top of his head.

I will never get used to being Eugene Delacorte—ridiculous name—but I've gotten used to faking it. "Good morning, sweetheart," I say, smiling my most devilish smile. She smiles back and might even blush if she had enough circulation to get the blood to her cheeks.

Down the way, one of the ancients, he must be close to ninety, is squinting at the notice board with his mouth hanging open. I can't tell if he's reading the board or drying his teeth. "Huh," he says just as I'm about to pass him. "Huh, huh, huh." Then he turns around and glares at me like I've startled him on purpose. "John Kennedy Jr.'s plane went down," he says.

"It sure did," I say. "About ten years ago." I pat his arm and keep walking.

The sky's gone from blue to a kind of ashy white. Blink your eyes and it'll be blue again. I follow the promenade around the lake they scooped out of the middle of the complex, past the playground for visiting grandkids, cut across the grass on a path of round pebble stones edged with a rope railing about as high as my ankle, and end up at the pool.

The pool is a fairly new addition to Villa Ponce de Leon. Finished just six months before I arrived, and still bearing the self-congratulatory banner across the entrance to the pavilion: *Our Beautiful Pool Is Now Open—Residents and Their Guests Only.* Maximum of three guests, that is, accompanied by a resident who's responsible for his or her guests obeying the rules. So says the president of the condo association, the one and only, ball-busting supervillain, Sophia Humphries.

She's a formidable opponent to yours truly, the roaming prince.

Under the umbrella of her presidency, Sophia is in charge of things like balcony etiquette (no barbecues, no storage, no nude sunbathing) and yard-sale etiquette (no yard sales). She's also the self-appointed Welcome Wagon; rings your bell right after you move in and presents you with—I kid you not—a basket of takeout menus, mosquito repellant, and a little stuffed-alligator key chain. I can only assume the sweet smile and the twenty-questions game are a regular part of her routine, because when I invited her in for a glass of iced tea, she sat herself down on my couch and was a jovial grand inquisitor. Where had I lived before moving here? Lincoln, Nebraska. What line of work had I been in? Drywall. Any children, grandchildren? Why not? Two of the former, five of the latter. A wife who passed away a few years ago. A sister who runs a daycare center in Omaha. Solid answers, and none of them true—if she was wise, she didn't let on. "I'd love to see pictures of your grandchildren," she said, and I told her I would, too, but there were a few boxes that had gone missing when the movers arrived and I was still waiting for them to turn up. "And what made you choose Cape Canaveral, Mr. Delacorte?"

It was chosen for me, just like the name Eugene Delacorte. But of course I didn't tell her this. There she was, half a cushion away, halfway through her iced tea, around my age, wearing her reading glasses on a chain around her neck, a blouse patterned with hibiscus blossoms, and a whole lot of makeup, including a red-coral shade of lipstick that would have looked just fine on a young fox. She was kind of a sexpot in her own right, and you had to give her credit for it. "Sunny days," I said with a shrug. "Balmy nights." I rubbed the side of my neck and then laid my arm across the back of the sofa so that my fingertips—just barely—brushed the collar of her blouse. "Maybe a little romance."

She glanced around as if suddenly needing to take inventory of my furniture. Then she looked me right in the eye, the smile gone from her lips but then back again in abbreviated form. "Well, aren't you full of yourself," she said.

"I am," I said. "I truly am. And I wish it weren't so."

The problem with becoming someone else is that you're still stuck with *you*. You can change your name, buy all new clothes, pretend you're from Nebraska when you're really from Illinois, pretend you used to work in drywall when, really, you were a bookkeeper for an extortion racket, pretend you're a happy-go-lucky retiree, no secrets, no regrets— and still, when you look in the mirror, you're going to see the guy you first saw, way back when.

D. B. Cooper, or whatever his name really was, could never be D. B. Cooper again once he jumped out of the plane with all that cash, but he still saw the guy desperate enough to make such a heist when he looked in the mirror. Ferdinand Waldo Demara, the great imposter who pretended to be thirty or forty different people in his lifetime, with thirty or forty different jobs and thirty or forty different personal histories, saw only one guy each morning when he shaved his mug: Ferdinand Waldo Demara. I'll bet even Mickey Rourke can still see himself if he squints hard enough.

So when I, Eugene Delcacorte, look in the mirror, I see Nick Parascos. And here's why it's no picnic, this brand-new life: I don't want to be either one of them. Eugene Delacorte is a cream puff, and Nick Parascos is a rat.

Sophia Humphries, I would guess, is not the happiest camper when she looks in the mirror. I say that not because of her features, but because of all the makeup, and because of her lust for power, and because of that forward lean in her voice. I know more about her than I do about anyone down here—she's a sharer—but she leaves out the tender parts and won't go near the juicy bits. She's divorced, like me. She played tennis until she had to have her knee replaced—a surgery that led to complications, two more surgeries, and a pending malpractice suit. She likes QVC, anagrams, Hummels. She listens to Tom Jones and Engelbert Humperdinck (so she's a private romantic, maybe, even while she's a ball-buster). I imagine she's been through a few wringers in her lifetime, had more than a few turns at the rodeo. And I suspect that, while she's glad to have survived it all, she's not exactly thrilled to be Sophia Humphries. She's got some Barbara Stanwyck in her, sure. She's even got a little Mae West, if I rose-color my Oakleys. But she's also got some dour in her dowry. Some Aunt Bee in her bonnet.

Nothing happened that first afternoon, other than that she finished her tea, complimented my Fiestaware, and went on with her day. Did I come on too strong? Not strong enough? Would she have liked it any better if I'd let her take the wheel? These might be questions for another man, but the rev in the engine doesn't go away, even if you're driving a jalopy.

The pool pavilion is a modest affair, given Ponce de Leon's lofty standards. Under the banner is an entrance that leads to the check-in counter, and on either side of the counter are the restrooms—ladies to the left, gents to the right, the only way in or out of the pool area. It strikes me as poor planning that you have to pass through the toilets to get to the pool, but there it is.

Sophia hires and fires the people who work the check-in counter. She hires and fires the lifeguards. She has her own test kit and goes behind the pool maintenance man, taking her own pH and alkalinity levels. She's breaking in a new kid for the desk today and, as I stroll in, she's also chewing out one of the lifeguards.

"We have to keep these children out of the hot tub," she's saying.

The guard is all muscle, shaggy haired and dimple faced. A smirker. He's got on a white tank top and this snug, little red bathing suit that might as well be Jockey shorts. He shrugs.

"It's too hot for them," Sophia says. "They're not allowed in."

She's right; it's in the regulations. But the guard shrugs again and says, "They jump in really fast," and he's right, too. I've seen them do it. There's a low wall between the pool and hot tub, and the brats make a game out of belly-sliding over that wall—plop!—right into old people's laps. I step around the two of them, wink at the scared-looking new kid sitting behind the counter, and cut through the men's room to the pool area. And what a crazy mix it is. A dozen retirees splayed out on lounge chairs, and half a dozen little hellions darting back and forth, up and down, asking for snacks. It's like flies on meat. I buy a Vitaminwater from the soda machine and carry it back inside.

Sophia's got her cinnamon-colored hair teased up into a bouffant, and aqua-blue earrings that match her nail polish.

She's still putting the screws to the lifeguard. "Can I just remind you," she says, "that it's your job to keep these children in line? I need one of you watching the counter, and two of you watching the pool, and if that's too much for you to handle, I'm sure they're hiring at McDonald's."

The guard is fingering the whistle around his neck. "We'll do our best, Ms. Humphries," he says, then heads out to the pool.

"I should hope so," she calls after him. "It's what I pay you for." When she turns away, her artificial knee pops and she lets out a small gasp. The lifeguards can be very mean sometimes. Behind her back, I've heard them give all kinds of descriptions for the noise her knee makes. They say it sounds like a squeezed aluminum can. Or the leg of a Barbie doll. Or—and I think this one is the cruelest—a wing being ripped off a cooked chicken. They watch her while she's doing her pH tests and they smirk at each other, waiting for the day that knee might give out and send her twirling into the deep end.

"And here's Mr. Delacorte," she says when she sees me. Like I'm one more thing she has to deal with.

"I'm just standing here," I say, smiling. "Is that against the law?"

"The rules say all residents have to be checked in, whatever reason they're here." She's talking to the new kid behind the counter now, who's nodding and blowing his bangs out of his eyes. "You've read the rules?"

"I will," he says.

"What does it take?" she asks—not the kid, or me. God, maybe. The ceiling.

"It takes a hope and a dream," I say. "A wing and a prayer. I heard about this stuff called Hint, supposed to be better than Vitaminwater. Healthier for you. Think we can get some Hint in the machine out there?"

"There are two file boxes," Sophia tells the kid. "One for In and one for Out. Someone comes in to use the pool—or get a soda—they sign their name on the sheet, you pull their ID card from the Out box, check the photo stapled to the back, and move it to the In box. It's the only way we can keep track of who's here."

"And it's *very* important to keep track," I tell the kid. "It's paramount. You don't want any covert operations happening right under your nose, do you?"

"Co-what?" the kid asks.

"Mr. Delacorte," Sophia says, "can I show you something?" She motions for me to follow her into the ladies' room.

I ape a *What's this all about?* expression for the kid's benefit and start after her with a goofy Red Skelton walk.

She hollers around the corner, "Anybody in here?"

No reply. A faucet is running. She shakes her head, shuts off the water. Checks for feet under the stalls. Takes my hand and leads me to one of the narrow, metal doors.

"Well, you little vixen," I say. "Got something naughty in mind?"

"Stop it," she says. Then she tells me these children are going to put her in her grave. The problem, she says, is that they all think they're living in a Space Invaders game and have lost touch with reality. (Adorable, right? I could kiss her.) Last week, some girl—and she thinks she knows who—stuffed a clementine down one of the toilets, so Sophia put up signs on the doors to both stalls spelling out the rules for proper food disposal. She's still holding my hand, and as if my eyes are attached to it, she tugs it up toward the stall door we're standing in front of. "Just look at that," she says. On the door are four little corners of ripped paper fixed with masking tape. "Would you have done something like that when you were a child? Would you ever dream of being so bold?"

"I was a rapscallion," I say. "I gave the nuns a run for their money."

"I don't doubt it," she says, letting go of my hand. "I'd just like to get hold of the girl who stopped up the toilet. I'd just like to shake that girl's shoulders."

The bathroom's got high windows cranked open, and through them I can see that the sky, which had already gone from cloudy to sunny, is now turning cloudy again. "Watch me, watch me, watch me!" we hear one of the hellions scream from the pool, and then a cannonball splash. I follow her back out to the check-in area.

The new kid's got his iPhone out and is about to put in his earbuds.

"No headphones," Sophia says. "I need you focused, sonny boy."

"My name's Todd," he says, tucking the iPhone back into his pocket.

"I know your name. I hired you." But then she smiles— maybe because it's his first day; probably because she's worried about running out of teenagers willing to work for $7.25

an hour. She reaches under the counter, pulls out a clipboard with a page fixed to it, and tells the kid it's the delinquency list. A rundown of all the tenants who are behind on their condo fees. It's a shame that some people think they can get away with not paying their share, and it's unfortunate that some people have fallen on hard times, but it makes sense that everyone on the list not be allowed past check-in, because the condo fees are mainly channeled back into what luxury?

Todd looks like he might get a nosebleed trying to follow all this, but then he says, "The pool?"

"He's a smart cookie," I say, reaching out to nudge Sophia's arm with my elbow.

She cuts me the kind of look you'd give a party crasher. The same person whose hand she was just holding in the ladies' room. "People will try to fool you," she tells Todd. "They'll ask you all kinds of questions about special circumstance this and check-in-the-mail that. But they're either paid up or they're not."

"Got it," Todd says.

I drink my Vitaminwater. I stroll around the little room, dragging my Crocs on the cement floor and watching the sky grow darker through the front window. My former employer used to tell me I was a significant part of his organization. Not that I was a genius with the numbers, but I was dependable. He knew if he asked me to take care of something, I'd do it. Cook the books till they're golden? I was the guy. Drive up to Evanston and talk some sense into a business owner? I was the guy. And now I'm *this* guy, as impressive as a goldfish. They tell you to save money for your retirement, but, really, we should all be saving up self-esteem, stockpiling it for days just like this. "Here's a question," I say.

Sophia sighs and puts the delinquency list back under the counter.

"I live in a world of beautiful women," I say. "I live in a world of spicy little numbers, they run around my place dressed in nothing but bikinis, and they can't get enough of me. If I bring them to the pool as my guests—assuming I'm all paid up, of course—do I have to stay here with them?"

Todd snorts out a laugh. Then he realizes Sophia's watching him, waiting for him to answer. "No?" he says.

"Yes," Sophia says, correcting him. "I can see we've got our work cut out for us."

"Another question," I say, because why not? I'm feeling my vitamins. "There's a little filly in Building C who's got her eye on me. A brunette, likes to wear a one-piece with zebra stripes." (This person doesn't exist.) "You think I could leave a little present here for her? A box of chocolates with a card, maybe? So when she comes to swim, she knows I'm thinking about her?"

"I guess," Todd says.

"Well, you guess wrong," Sophia says. "We're not the post office. We don't hold packages for people."

"It would mean a lot to her," I say. "And it might help my chances. I mean, you should see this woman." I jingle the loose change in my pocket. "Woof."

Todd snorts again.

Sophia taps her aqua-blue fingernails against the counter. "Are you *trying* to ruin this young man's first day?" she asks me.

"Absolutely not. I'm just livin' *la vida loca.*"

She turns back to her employee. "People flood through that door. You have to be ready for them. And some of them actually come to use the pool and not just loiter."

"Ouch," I say.

"And they aren't *all* as charming as Mr. Delacorte here."

Bless her for adding that. I'm done with my drink and just about to head out when the lifeguard comes in through the men's room.

"What is it now?" Sophia says.

"You hear thunder?"

She frowns at him, then peers through the front window of the pavilion. "No."

"Rules are, we close for thirty minutes if we hear thunder," the guard says.

I can see it in Sophia's eyes: If the pool's going to close, she wants it to be *her* idea, not his. Even if he's right. "No one heard anything in here," she says.

He shrugs. "Rules are, if the *guard* hears it."

"Well, maybe the guard needs to have his hearing checked."

"Thirty minutes for thunder, one hour for lightning," the guard says. "Storm's coming."

Sophia fakes a chuckle, which she doesn't do well—too much breath in it, too much staccato. "Do you have a connection to God we don't know about? Get back out there and do your job."

The guard's got a look on his face, I don't even know what

kind of look it is but somebody should smack it off. He turns and walks back through the men's room.

"The arrogance," Sophia says.

"That's right," I say. "That's what it is."

"Do you know I'm a volunteer? I don't get paid to do this. I do it because I care. This whole complex would go you know where in a handbasket if I wasn't going the extra mile."

"Punks, every one of them," I say. I glance at Todd. "Not you."

"The board didn't even ask me. They *begged* me. 'Please, Ms. Humphries,' they said. 'People look up to you. They respect you. Please provide us with the leadership we need.'"

I seriously doubt this is anywhere near an exact quote, more likely she grabbed the position before anyone else could, but I nod like I'm drinking in every word. "You're a godsend, Sophia."

"And you're a flirt," she says. "And a yes-man."

"And a loiterer," I remind her. "But would you have me any other way?"

There's part of me that doesn't want to be doing this in front of the kid, but there's also part of me that knows this is all I get: a daily stroll around the complex, a few wisecracks, some gutless flirtation. This is me with my dick swinging. Small shakes, right? And ol' Sophia walks a line you have to admire: a little nice, a little mean, cards held close to her chest and one hand on a lever that'll drop you through a trapdoor in a heartbeat. She's got nothing in common with my ex-wife and more than a little in common with some of the girls I used to date, back when I still had hair. And, believe it or not, I used to be able to make them swoon. But

Sophia's not having it—and why should she? I'm a joke in a straw hat.

A deep rumble rolls down from the sky. The three of us look toward the window.

"All the work I put in," she says. "And for what?"

The next rumble is louder and seems to echo back on itself.

I'm looking around for a garbage can so I can throw out my bottle when this bare foot crosses the corner of my eye. It belongs to a girl around ten years old. She's got wet hair and a T-shirt pulled on over her swimsuit. She's hugging a towel against her stomach and bolting from the ladies' room toward the exit.

Sophia glances at her, does a double take, and snaps, "Hey!" She steps around me and grabs the girl's arm.

The girl tries to tug herself free.

"I know what you did with that clementine," Sophia says. "And I'll just bet you ripped those signs down, too. Do you even realize how lucky you are to have a pool like this?"

The girl's eyes have grown wide in their sockets. She pulls her head back, and when she opens her mouth, her voice is buoyed by the next rumble of thunder. "Don't touch me, you old bat! You're not allowed to touch anyone! Get your claws off me!" She's like Linda Blair, this girl, her body snapping in one direction, then another, pulling Sophia with it because Sophia won't let go—or maybe *can't* let go, now that the girl's flailing. It's all about balance when you get past a certain age. It's all about not wanting to fall, which is probably why it's a good idea not to grab hold of someone who needs an exorcism. I take hold of Sophia's other arm, but my own

balance isn't what it used to be and I hear one of my Crocs
screech on the floor, so I let go. The kid behind the counter
looks entertained and says, "Awesome," and I don't know
what kind of universe it would have to be for a comment like
that to make sense.

Sophia's artificial knee pops once, twice. A third time.

"Let GO!" the girl screams, and when she pulls free, there's
one last pop, louder than the others, bouncing off the walls
like a rubber ball.

The girl darts out of the pavilion. Sophia wavers, leans
sideways, and takes hold of the counter. She's not just frown-
ing, now; she's wincing. Grimacing.

"You okay?" I ask.

There's a distant flash of lightning, followed by more thunder. She's still holding on to the counter and her lower lip
is pushed forward. She lifts her free hand as if to put us all
on pause. I'm about to tell the kid to move so she can sit
down when the lifeguard comes back in. He cuts a wide
berth around Sophia, reaches under the counter, and pulls
out a handwritten, cardboard sign that's got a string looped
through it and reads *Pool Closed Due to Weather*.

"I'm putting this sign out front," he says, waving it at her.

She doesn't respond, doesn't move.

"And we still get paid, even if the pool's closed." He heads
for the door, then stops and turns around. "And we don't
have to stay here."

He's all challenge, this kid, waiting for her to give him a
hard time. But not only is she not giving him a hard time,
she's got her eyes closed now, trying to work through what
I'm guessing is a substantial amount of knee pain.

"Check the rules if you want," the guard says.

I feel an old, familiar snarl in my upper lip. Life is fickle, you know? You can be somebody one minute and nobody the next, full of yourself in the morning and empty as a tapped well in the afternoon. I don't know who I am anymore, but sometimes, just for a second, I know who I want to be.

"Hey, cupcake," I say with more volume in my voice than I've had in a year. "Underpants. She heard you. You made your point and you got your little sign all ready to go, so do what you've got to do, okay, jelly bean? Hang it, lock it up, and get the hell out of here. You're fired."

He looks from me to Sophia, then back to me. "That's for her to decide," he says.

"Well, she decided and she asked *me* to tell you, okay? She doesn't feel like talking to you right now. So zappa-dappa and like that. You're gone."

He huffs. In an incredulous voice, he asks Sophia, "I'm gone?"

With her eyes still closed, she nods, backing me up on this.

As much as the tan can leave the kid's face, it does. And what a sweet sight it is. The rain starts pinging against the window as he's hanging the sign on the door, and when he walks past us, he keeps his gaze down and doesn't say another word.

I look at Todd and motion with my thumb for him to get out of the chair.

"Am I fired too?" he asks, standing.

"Nah, take a break, kid," I say. "But you be back here once this is over, understand?"

"Yes, sir," he says, and without another word he's out the door and gone.

I put my hand on Sophia's elbow. She opens her eyes, lets go of the counter, and I guide her over to the chair and help her into it. I squat down next to her and *my* knees pop because, let's face it, we're coming apart here as much as we're trying to hold it together. We stay like that as people file out of the restrooms, some of them with their towels wrapped around their shoulders, all of them grumbling about the rain. I hear the door at the other end of the men's room slam, and then the guard cuts through the entryway, a baseball cap pulled down low on his head and a backpack thrown over a shoulder. He doesn't look at us, but scratches his cheek with his middle finger, and I could break it for him, I really could, but happy trails, you dumb gorilla.

When it's just us, I ask her if she needs anything—some water, aspirin. I swear, I'd get her whatever she wanted if it would put the supervillain back in her face. I'd cook her a meal, take her to an Engelbert Humperdinck concert.

"I'm okay," she says. "Thank you."

But I don't want her to thank me. I want her to like me. Even if it's only for right now, for this one single minute. "That lifeguard?" I say. "He's a putz. He's a mook with a whistle around his neck."

She smiles—just a little, but she smiles. I'm still holding her elbow, and she lays one of her hands on top of mine. She says, "You're something, Mr. Delacorte."

I give her a wink. "Call me Nick."

GO FEVER

About a month after Challenger blew up, Wendell Troup told me his wife was trying to poison him.

Understand, we were all feeling a little rattled. Some of us had been in charge of checking the range-safety systems on the rocket boosters. Some of us had been combing over the liquid oxygen and hydrogen lines on the external fuel tank. Some of us—guys like me—had been double- and triple-checking the 31,000 thermal-protection tiles that covered the outside of the orbiter. The people who inspected the body flaps and elevons, the people who maintained the aft control thrusters, even the people who inflated the tires and washed the cabin windows had been involved in the incident. You didn't have to be the man who'd given the okay to launch on that cold Tuesday morning to feel responsible.

Wendell was my supervisor. His job was to oversee and sign off on every aspect of the Thermal Protection System, from delivery and unpacking to labeling and installation. I won't say he was any better or any worse at his job than I was at mine. He did what he was paid to do. Some days he took pride in it; other days he complained that he was superfluous to the whole process. We got to know each other on our lunch breaks, grabbed the occasional beer after work, teased each other about our accents (he was from Chattanooga; I was from Boston). We played racquetball now and then, watched a few football games together, got to know each other's wives.

Not that it had anything to do with his being from Chattanooga, but the more serious Wendell was, the more he overenunciated his words, so that he sounded like he was talking to foreigners. And he was the kind of guy who was always talking—to himself, if there was no one else to listen. The guys in our department called him The Yacker behind his back. They tuned him out unless it was work related. They'd say, "Oh, really?" or "How about that?" and move on. I listened because I felt sorry for him, and because, in his way, he could be amusing—a step up from the humdrum conversations the rest of the guys were churning out all day. Wendell could be telling me about how he'd unclogged a shower drain in his house with fishing line and a gasket coil, and I would give him my full attention.

"I'm telling you, Liquid Plumber is a joke, man. It's invented by plumbers who want you to feel like you've tried everything and need an actual plumber. Meanwhile, the means to fix the problem are sitting right there in your house. Look, you can use a gasket coil for anything you want. I've got one designated for clogs, nothing else. Do you think I'm not going to use a gasket coil just because it wasn't designed to go down a drain?"

I hadn't thought any such thing. I wasn't sure I knew what a gasket coil was. But sometimes I egged him on, just for my own amusement. "Well, now, Wendell, the EPA has issued a report about gasket coils and drain safety."

He'd fall for it every time. Get more wound up, more enunciated. "The EPA? Let me tell you something, friend: there isn't an Ex-Lax patty big enough to unclog the level of stupidity at the EPA."

And so on.

Wendell was enthusiastic about being at odds with the world. He was occasionally crude in his descriptions. And, in specific and maybe even deliberate ways, he was a slob. For example, he used Brylcreem to tame his hair but always left streaks of it in there—visible, unblended. He shaved every day and yet always had a single, long whisker or patch of whiskers sprouting out from his jaw, and he sometimes came to work with shaving cream stuck to his Adam's apple. He flossed his teeth after every meal and sometimes on a whim, right in the middle of an inspection, but he never cleaned his glasses, which looked felted with dust when they caught the sunlight. Even on the hottest days he kept his sweat-stained shirt collar buttoned and his tie snuggly knotted, but half the time, after visiting the men's room, he'd forget to zip his fly.

His wife, Loretta, was more refined. She looked just as put together when you ran into her at the grocery store or the mall as she did at one of their cocktail parties. Her face rested in a pleasant-enough expression, but when she smiled she had that quick, slightly irritated brightness of the not so happily married. That was my take on it, anyway. Her eyes were sad and pretty.

Loretta worked part-time as the school nurse at the elementary school and part-time as a volunteer at the local animal shelter. She delivered Meals on Wheels to the elderly two days a week and, as a hobby, made wallets and drink cozies out of vintage denim. In the realm of possibilities, I could imagine her one day becoming a born-again, or an Amway guru. But I couldn't imagine her trying to poison Wendell. When he first told me about it, I responded as diplomatically as I could while still trying to sound like a trusted confidant.

We were sitting on a bench not far from the Vehicle Assembly Building, facing the Crawlerway that stretched out through the marsh to LC-39, where Challenger had gone up. I was done eating and was watching an egret with an enormous wingspan circle overhead. Wendell was eyeing his sandwich. Our lunch break was over, we were going to be late getting back, but it didn't matter. There were no thermal-protection tiles to install or inspect. Columbia was supposed to be in orbit at that very moment, following Halley's Comet around, but the mission had been canceled. So had the other thirteen shuttle missions scheduled for that year, and the ten scheduled for the year after that. We weren't saying it out loud but we were all waiting—hoping—to be reassigned.

Wendell dropped what was left of his sandwich into the brown paper bag in his lap. "You don't know Loretta," he said. "She's got a devious side to her."

"Ha," I said. "Devious. Don't we all?"

"I mean, really devious. Crazy devious. Nobody sees it but me."

"Okay, let's say she wants to poison you. She doesn't, but let's say she does. Why in the world would she want to do that?"

"Your guess is as good as mine," Wendell said, worming an index finger into his ear. "The life insurance? The equity? Maybe she just can't stand me anymore." He rubbed his finger on his pant leg and then wadded the bag up, sandwich and all. "Doesn't matter. Point is, she's crazy and I'm on to her."

She's not crazy, I thought; you're crazy. But I wasn't supposed to have any opinion of Wendell's wife that didn't start and end with Wendell. My loyalties, at least on the surface, lay with him. I asked him what brought this on—not the poisoning, which I wasn't buying, but his suspicion of it.

"Get this," he said. "Sunday afternoon, I'm in the den minding my own business, watching *Wide World of Sports*. And here comes Loretta with this big bowl of vanilla ice cream in her hands. 'That's a lot of ice cream,' I say. And she says the whole thing's for me. Now, when's the last time I had dessert in the middle of the afternoon? Never. When I was six, maybe."

"So the murder weapon is ice cream," I said. "Death by ice cream."

"Would you listen? I tell her thanks, but I don't want any. And she says she already put it in the bowl. So I say, 'Then you eat it,' and she says she already had some. Now, when was the last time *she* had dessert in the middle of the day?"

"I don't know," I said. "I'm not really up on Loretta's eating habits."

"Probably not since *she* was six," he said. "But there she is, holding this ice cream out for me to take. So I took it, and I ate some of it. And she sat down right there on the couch and watched me eat it."

"And?"

"It tasted like metal."

I just looked at him.

"Metal's a dead giveaway," he said.

"Maybe you imagined it."

"Who eats ice cream and imagines metal? That doesn't make any sense."

"Maybe it was old," I said. "You know, freezer burn."

"Freezer burn tastes like cardboard, anybody knows that."

"Then maybe you have a loose filling."

"And maybe you're the wrong person to be telling this to. Look, I'm trying to share something important here, man."

I spotted the egret again—or a different egret, this one gliding along without even flapping, like he had a propeller attached to his beak—and I thought about what Wendell had said. I wasn't sure how many friends he had other than me, or, even if he had a hundred friends, how many of them would have sat listening to such nonsense without making fun of him. But he was right about one thing, at least: I was the wrong person to be telling this to.

'm a tremendous liar. I mean, I'm very good at it. That said, these things are true:

When I was seven, a commercial airline pilot visited our school, talked about his job, and then went around the room and asked us what we wanted to be when we grew up. Every boy in my class said he wanted to be a pilot, except me. I told him I wanted to be a lion tamer. I'd never thought about it before, didn't care about it one way or another, but that's what came out of my mouth. The pilot told me I was a brave little boy and wished me luck.

When I was eighteen, I wanted to move to Alaska and live in a cabin and raise huskies. I wanted to hitchhike across the United States, live in Belize, live on Koh Samui. I wanted to be the next Rodger Ward.

When I was twenty-five, I proposed to Renee, my future wife, by accident. I'd meant the question to be theoretical, Renee heard it as literal, and I went with it to save face.

When we were both thirty-six and had decided two kids were enough, no more for us, we inadvertently conceived another child. We love Teddy, and we wouldn't trade anything for his presence in our lives, but he wasn't part of the plan. Also, he was the reason I couldn't finally trade our station wagon in for something a little more sporty. I think about that every time he smarts off to me, which, now that he's eleven, is at least twice a day.

When Renee and I were both forty-four and approaching our nineteenth wedding anniversary, I got it into my head that she was having an affair. She'd made a new friend at work, some woman named Suzie, and she started having dinner with Suzie once a week—a "girls' night out," as she put it. But on one of those nights when they were supposed to be having dinner, Suzie called the house, asking for her. "I thought she was with you," I said into the phone, and Suzie said no, they'd talked about getting coffee or dinner sometime but they'd never managed to make it happen. Would I tell Renee she'd called? Yes, I said, but I never gave Renee the message. Instead, I steeped myself in suspicion. Felt cuckolded. Felt foolish. And then, flipping that on its head for no good reason, I began to feel empowered.

When I was forty-five, Loretta Troup and I locked eyes at a picnic. Specifically, the NASA Efficiency, Morale & Welfare Gathering at Kars Park. Nothing happened that day other than that I made certain we were standing next to each other during the horseshoe tournament—which Wendell was entered in, took very seriously, and won. But at their next cocktail party, I cornered her in the living room and said out of the blue, "There's something here, isn't there?"

"Where?" Loretta asked. She moved her glass back and forth in the space between us. "Here?"

"Yeah."

She rolled her eyes. "Ha. Maybe."

Two weeks later, at my suggestion, Renee and I hosted our own little cocktail party, and I invited the Troups. During an impromptu and unnecessary tour I gave Loretta of our one-story ranch house, while we were in the bedroom of my eldest daughter, who was off at college, I was working up my nerve to ask her if there was still something there when she leaned in and kissed me.

And so there I was at forty-six, in Florida, sitting on a bench next to Wendell, a year into sleeping with his wife, a month after he and I had taken part in sending seven people to their deaths out over the Atlantic, listening to him tell me that Loretta was trying to poison him and pretending I wasn't a heel, a cheat, and a traitor—which, when you think about it, is a far cry from living in Alaska, driving race cars, and taming lions.

W endell told me plenty of stories about Loretta—all of them revolving around his suspicions that she'd grown tired of their marriage, that she'd fallen out of love with him, and, now, that she was trying to feed him poison one meal at a time. Loretta had little to say about Wendell. That seemed appropriate enough—I certainly wasn't chatty with her on the subject of Renee—and it occurred to me after one of our early-evening rendezvous in the elementary school infirmary that I was always the one who brought Wendell up.

"Does he seem different to you lately?" I asked her. (I didn't mention the poisoning thing because I wasn't sure Wendell had told anyone else, and if she brought it back to him, I'd be pegged as the source.)

She was checking herself in the medicine cabinet mirror. "Different how?"

"I don't know. Like—*more* of what he normally is?"

"Wendell is Wendell," she said. "He'll always be Wendell."

I was standing next to her, waiting to use the mirror. She didn't like meeting in motels, preferred the sequestered privacy of the infirmary with its narrow bed—just a cot, really, with a foam mattress covered by a sheet she would change when we were finished—and once it was over she was always eager to leave. Postcoitus, she was anything but affectionate. "He's an odd guy," I said, retucking my shirt.

"You're one to talk. Can we get out of here?"

"Yeah, can I just—" I gestured toward the mirror.

She stepped aside.

As I combed my hair, I thought about how an affair can turn into a microcosm of whatever you're trying to escape. Surely I was not the first person to have that thought. Surely other men—and women—had realized the same thing, and what did they do once the realization hit? Find a third affair? Return, hangdogged, to square one? Loretta was holding her purse. I wanted to talk about Wendell; I was a little worried about him, in fact. But what I said was, "So I'm odd, huh? I don't think of myself as odd."

"Please. You're the fussiest person I've ever met."

"I'm not fussy. How am I fussy?"

"You're obsessed with your appearance, for one thing. How many times can you part your goddamn hair?"

I put my comb away. She reached for the door.

During dinner that night, there was an argument between Tania and Teddy about which show was better, *Murder, She Wrote* or *The A-Team*. Renee asked them if it wasn't possible that both shows could be considered okay by different people, and Teddy said that would be fine if some of those people were retarded.

"What about Dad?" Tania asked, looking at me.

There was nothing sarcastic in the question; Tania wasn't the smart-mouth; she was the sweet, even-keeled one. Tracy, who was away at college, was the mopey one. And then there was Teddy.

"Dad doesn't really like either one of those shows," I said.

"What's your all-time favorite, then?" Tania asked. "Like, if they were going to ban every show in history except one, what would it be?"

"I don't know. Something classic," I said. *"Sea Hunt."*

"Is Dad maybe a little brain-damaged?" Teddy asked.

Renee snapped at him, threatened to send him to his room. He stuffed a bite of meat loaf into his mouth.

"I also like *Riptide,*" I said, reaching for something a little more current.

This, for some reason, inspired Teddy to drop his head to one side and slap the backs of his hands together, letting the meatloaf fall from his mouth. Renee sent him to his room.

I thought about the sports car I didn't own. I thought about how terrible it was that I was thinking about that, and how decent it was of Renee to defend me, but how she wasn't meeting my eyes now. And how she really hadn't been defending me; she'd just been scolding Teddy. And how she'd maybe cheated on me, and how I was cheating on her with my boss's wife. And how my life had had a shape once, and then a different shape after that, and how now it had no discernible shape at all.

F lorida isn't built for cold. That's why, during the harder winters, pythons roll up dead in the Everglades and iguanas drop out of trees in Monroe County. It's why an orange tree laced with icicles makes for an exotic, even beautiful photograph in the newspaper, but it also makes for a dead orange tree. The temperature had dropped to eighteen degrees the night before the launch, and it was only ten degrees higher than that by morning. None of us were prepared for it.

Some of us didn't even own coats. The students at Merritt Island High School weren't given a choice, Tania later told me; they were all led out to the football field just before lunch and corralled into the north-facing bleachers on the home side so that they could watch the historic event. (TISP, it was called. The Teacher in Space Project—touted by Reagan, sought after by 11,000 applicants and filled by one: a brave, ambitious, and unlucky young woman from New Hampshire.) Somewhat closer to the launch site, Wendell and I were holding Styrofoam cups of coffee, wearing sunglasses, shivering in our windbreakers. The cold was all anyone could talk about. How the mission had already been delayed several times because of the weather. How there had never been a shuttle launched in temperatures this low. How fucking cold it was. There were icicles all over the launchpad, we heard. Icicles all the way up the tower and across the catwalk.

Then the countdown started.

I had surprised my family with our first VCR the previous Christmas, then had decided I didn't like the idea of renting movies from the one video store that had opened up on the island. All those rental tapes going in and out of strangers' machines, and then going into ours, seemed unwise to me. Renee and the kids thought I was being silly, but I told them the VCR was delicate. I showed them the new, blank tapes I'd bought, explained to them how to use the timer, told them we could tape any show we wanted without having to compromise the system. "Well!" Teddy said in a fake British accent, "we certainly wouldn't want to compromise the system!"

He'd set the timer before leaving for school that morning. He and Tania and Renee were all watching what had happened when I got home. They asked me to watch it with them, asked me what it had looked like, up close, but I told them I didn't want to see it, didn't want to talk about it.

That night after they'd all gone to bed, I sat on the couch clutching the remote, and I watched it over and over again.

Seventy-three seconds between liftoff and explosion. Viewed forward and back, forward and back, the breakup began to look like a flower blooming in a time-lapse nature film.

The solid rocket boosters began to look like a divining rod made of smoke.

The cloud that had just been a ship—a beautiful, streamlined, carefully put-together ship—began to look like a long-tendrilled jellyfish hanging in the sky.

And then it was done looking like anything.

Four months after it happened, three months after Wendell first told me about his Loretta suspicions, the Troups held their annual Memorial Day gathering. Their house was nicer than ours in that it was two stories and had a garage instead of a carport. But inside, it was ramshackle. Dusty. Cluttered with magazines and newspapers, a seam in the hall carpet repaired with duct tape, the dining room table taken over by Loretta's sewing machine and Wendell's jigsaw puzzles. Because of her work at the animal shelter, their home was the last refuge for unclaimed cats and dogs—the rattling, ghost-eyed ones too old for most people to get excited about.

That day, there were four cats roaming the floors and one ancient, shivering Chihuahua. "That's Urine Andropov," Wendell said, pointing to the dog as I was picking something—a hair, maybe—out of my drink. "He gives Hubba Bubba a run for her money."

Hubba Bubba, I knew from the previous party, was a tabby ballooned with tumors. Urine Andropov was a more recent arrival. I didn't care about the pets, nor did I care about Wendell's theories on how their personalities interacted. I always regretted coming to these parties. But Renee wouldn't go to them—she was allergic to cats—and it was hard for me to pass up an opportunity to see Loretta. Wendell stuck to the den, for the most part, where his framed jigsaw puzzles hung crooked on the walls. Loretta, playing hostess, roamed.

An hour or so after I arrived, I caught her alone in the kitchen, arranging deviled eggs on a tray.

"Hi," I said, patting her on the back.

"Not here."

"I'm just saying hello."

"Hello," she said. "Are you enjoying yourself?"

"Not especially," I said, but that sounded rude, so I forced a little laugh and added, "Sure, I'm having a great time. When can I see you again?"

She repositioned an egg on the tray, licked her fingers, repositioned another. "You and I aren't on a schedule. You know that, right? It's a whim thing."

I'd walked out of my own house that afternoon not particularly liking where I was. I'd driven to the Troups' house not particularly liking *who* I was. And now I was here, bored by Wendell, spurned by Loretta, and feeling like an idiot. *You know what?* I wanted to say. *Your husband isn't just eccentric anymore. He's crossed over. He chews my ear off about how you're trying to poison him. And maybe that means he trusts me more than he trusts you. There's something ironic about that, isn't there?*

"Earth to Kevin," she said, and held up the tray. "Deviled egg?"

"No, thanks," I said, thinking about how she'd licked her fingers and then touched the eggs. "Wendell loves those things, though. Why don't you bring him one?"

I watched the two of them from across the den. When she offered up the tray, he smiled and bent forward and kissed her on the cheek, then took one of the eggs and said thank you. He was going to eat it, I thought, and I felt a mild jolt of panic—as if I, too, believed the egg might be poisoned. But as soon as she turned away, he fed it to the Chihuahua.

The cats would have nothing to do with Loretta's cooking, Wendell told me. Not even Hubba Bubba, who, with all that cancer to feed, would eat almost anything. So Wendell had to rely on Urine Andropov to eat the suspect food. And Urine Andropov, after a few weeks of eating oatmeal, mashed potatoes, chicken pot pie, angel food cake, and everything else Loretta prepared for Wendell, along with the bowl of dry dog food that sat out 24/7, lay down under the coffee table and died.

Loretta was devastated when she found the dog. She cried while Wendell dug the hole in the backyard, and she cried as he tamped down the dirt. "He just got too old, I guess," she said, wiping her nose with a tissue. "He just decided it was time."

"Right," Wendell said.

He started sleeping downstairs, in the den, lying to her about how their mattress was hurting his back. He started making his own food and casually refusing to eat whatever Loretta fixed for him. But the springs on the couch were shot and kept him from getting a decent night's sleep, and he didn't know how to cook. Nothing could be trusted to the refrigerator, he told me, because nothing going into his body was going to leave his sight until he was chewing it. "From store to mouth," he said, pointing to his eyes. And so his diet became reduced to the likes of McDonald's hamburgers, Taco Bell tacos, and something called Yum-Yum Pies from the convenience store near his neighborhood.

I did what I'd always done with Wendell: I let him talk. I asked questions now and then, inquired as to whether he was maybe taking this suspicion of his to the extreme, but mostly I just let him talk. I was his trusted friend, after all.

Not long into this new way of living (fast food, poor sleep), he began to look run-down. He lost weight in his face and shoulders, even while his stomach was starting to push out over his belt. The back pain he'd lied about became real after several weeks on the couch, and his posture suffered for it. His skin started to look a little gray.

Loretta, he told me, had surprised him by noticing all this and seeming to care. But her concern only irked Wendell. She asked him, one morning while he was getting dressed for work, why he wasn't eating at home anymore.

He told her he didn't want to.

That was insane, she said. Nobody stopped eating in their own home.

Wendell said he did.

But why? And why the sudden problems with their mattress? She was fed up, she said; she really wanted to get to the bottom of things. She wanted them to talk about what was going on. (Was it hard for her, I wondered, to confront him while concealing so much herself? Or was it easy?)

There was a heavy rain that day, and Wendell and I were eating lunch inside, in one of the break rooms. There were four guys at the table in front of us, three at the table behind us. Another handful sitting off to the side, near the snack machines. From what I could tell, Wendell and I were the only people in the break room not talking about the Rogers Commission findings on the Challenger disaster.

"So I said, 'Okay, little miss, let's do that. Let's have a talk. Why is it I don't feel safe in my own home anymore? Why is it I get the feeling you'd be just as happy if I was dead? Happier, even?'"

"What did she say?" I asked.

"She said I ought to talk to a shrink."

There may have been a snicker from one of the neighboring tables, but I doubt it. They were discussing O-rings, at least one of which had cracked on the aft seal joint of one of the rocket boosters, according to the Commission Report. Hot gases had escaped and had turned into flame, and the flame had made contact with the external fuel tank.

I'd never been aware of the O-rings before. They might have been as wide around as the rocket boosters, or as small as the wedding bands Wendell and I were wearing. "Design flaw" was a phrase I heard more than once from the other tables. The O-rings had a design flaw. The manufacturer was claiming it had warned the NASA administrators that cold weather was a potential problem because the rings weren't designed to function in low temperatures. The NASA administrators were claiming that the warning hadn't reached them in time. But we all knew they'd been itching to get Challenger off the ground. The launch had already been delayed several times, and delays were costly. Delays looked bad. The conversations I overheard in the break room that day stretched all the way back to Apollo 1 and the deadly fire that had resulted from the rush to stay on schedule. "Go fever," it was called. There was a design flaw in the O-rings, according to the report, but there was also a design flaw in the administration's decision-making process. "Heads are going to roll over this one," someone said from a nearby table, and I thought, *Heads have already rolled.*

"Now, what good would a shrink do me, when I'm surrounded by poison?" Wendell asked.

Suddenly, the sound of his voice was like a finger jabbing into my brain. Or maybe I was just self-conscious about how ridiculous our conversation was, how nonsensical it must have sounded to our coworkers, if they were bothering to listen in.

"Well?" Wendell said.

"Are you seriously asking me if you could benefit from a psychiatrist?" I asked.

"Yes," he said. "As a prophylaxis against hemlock. Or polonium. Or dimethylmercury."

"Wendell, where do you come up with this stuff? Yes, I

think you could benefit from a psychiatrist. I really do. Jesus Christ."

My response caught him off guard. As I watched his face go slack, it occurred to me that he cared—he really cared—about what I thought of him.

It was still raining the next day, but he didn't eat in the break room. The day after that, the skies cleared, but he wasn't at our bench overlooking LC-39. I caught sight of him yards away, on another bench, peering into his lunch bag.

A week later, as he drove home from work, he lost control of his car and drove head-on into a magnolia tree. And survived.

A s with all events that touch more than one person, there were rumors floating around. We were full up on rumors lately. For example, there was the rumor that Challenger's cockpit had been found almost immediately, and not days later, as the official report said; the remains inside were unrecognizable, were pulverized, were like scrambled eggs; they were put into trash bags and flown by helicopter to the mainland, where they were tossed into garbage trucks so as not to catch the attention of the news crews lurking nearby.

The rumors about Wendell were directed toward me—I guess because no one at work felt like they knew him as well as I did and maybe I could verify what was floating around. Was it true he'd gotten so worked up, talking to himself, that he'd driven off the road? Was it true he'd been arguing with God, shaking his fist out the window? (I reminded them that there were no witnesses, other than Wendell.) The meanest rumor I heard was that he'd crashed his car deliberately, in an effort to end it all. I told the man who proposed this that Wendell wasn't suicidal. More than once, I told all of them what I hoped was true: Wendell had fallen asleep behind the wheel, end of story.

The police said his Plymouth had traveled along the shoulder for nearly a hundred feet before it hit the tree. The windshield had blown out, the hood had accordioned, and the front bumper had embedded itself three inches deep into the trunk. Wendell fared better than the car, which had to be scrapped. Both of his wrists were sprained, his left ankle was broken, and his right kneecap—which, despite the seatbelt and the airbag, had somehow managed to hit the dashboard—was shattered. He had a broken nose and two black eyes.

When I visited him at home two days later, he told me he was lucky to be alive. There was no mention of our recent spat or the lunches he'd been taking alone. He seemed to be in fairly good spirits, glad to see me, even. And he was letting Loretta feed him. She'd turned their bedroom into a convalescent area, had even rented him a rolling bedside hospital table so he could do his jigsaw puzzles. The table was pushed to the side while I was there. She was sitting in a chair next to him, holding a plate in one hand and a fork in the other. Wendell's hands, wrapped in bandages, were resting in his lap.

Finished with lunch, he asked her if there was any ice cream, and she went to get it for him. When she was gone from the room, I sat down on the edge of the chair and asked him how he was doing.

"I've never been better," he said, smiling.

I found that hard to accept. I felt I'd earned the right to question it, having been his confidant for what seemed like years of nutty rambling. But I said, "That's great. And you're— all taken care of here?"

"Oh, sure," he said. "Loretta's the best."

I ran my eyes across his raccooned cheeks, his bandaged arms, the rolling hospital table with its coffee rings, lunch crumbs, and errant puzzle pieces. "The guys miss you at work," I said.

"No they don't."

"They do. We all do. Everyone's been asking about you."

"Can I tell you something?" he asked. "Just between us?"

"Of course."

"I'm thinking about a career change."

"Come on, don't talk like that."

"Really, I think I'm ready to try something else, once I get back on my feet. Different pastures, you know?"

I felt a twinge of something—an unspooling in my chest. "Like what?"

He shrugged. "Lockheed, maybe. Hey, don't look so glum. It means a supervisor's position will be opening up. You deserve it as much as anybody. I'll put in a good word for you."

I nodded, but the feeling held. Outside the windows, the daylight was just starting to fade. How many supervisors were they going to need, I wondered, if the program was shut down? And even if they kept it alive and shuffled us all around, did I really want to stay?

I told him to call me if he needed anything. Then I stood, patted his shoulder, and walked out of the room.

Loretta was coming toward the stairs, a bowl of ice cream in one hand and a spoon in the other, as I reached the bottom.

"How are you holding up?"

"Fine," she said. "Thanks for asking."

"He's a miracle, isn't he? It could have been a lot worse."

"I guess so. But it's not like he's out of the woods yet." She said this with her gaze fixed on the ice cream, and for a moment—loony, head spinning—I wondered if Wendell had been right about her all along. But she added, "They might have to operate on his knee if it doesn't heal right."

"Oh, wow," I said. "That's serious."

"Yeah," she said. "Well. This is melting."

I glanced up the stairs, lowered my voice. "You have a lot going on right now, I know, but is there any chance, in the next week or so, you might want to—"

"No," she said.

"You didn't let me finish."

"I don't want you to finish. I have to get upstairs, okay? You have to go."

Driving home, I imagined what it would be like to drift off the side of the road and into a tree. I imagined the distraction that would be required to bring about such a moment of impact, and the chaos that would follow in its wake. Worth it? Not worth it? It didn't matter. There were too many variables involved in such an act, and I was too cautious—too fussy—for that kind of recklessness. Maybe that was my design flaw.

Dinner was waiting.

EARTH, MOSTLY

She had her granddaughter in the backseat, groceries in the trunk, and a watermelon next to her hip when she decided it might be nice to start eating junk food again. Just one bad choice a day, like before things had gotten out of hand. Why not? She'd be sixty-one soon and had been counting calories for almost a decade. Now that her situation had changed, now that all these new responsibilities had been thrust upon her when she was supposed to be basking in her senior years, who would begrudge her a Milky Way in the privacy of her own home? She slowed the Honda until she was sitting in the middle of the southbound lane, turn signal on, waiting for the oncoming traffic to pass.

"What are we doing?" Becca asked, head cocked to one side in the rearview mirror, her dark little eyes blinking.

"I forgot to buy myself a candy bar at the grocery store, so we're going to 7-Eleven."

"You don't eat candy bars," the girl reminded her. "You said you have too much self-respect to get fat again."

Lord, but there was almost nothing you could get away with in the presence of an eight-year-old. It was like having the Grand Inquisitor look over your shoulder every minute of the day. "Self-respect?" Gail said into the mirror. "That's a high-minded phrase to be tossing around when you might not even be sure what it means. But never mind, I don't feel like being judged, so we'll just go home."

She rolled forward with a sinking sense that something wasn't quite right. Then she slammed head-on into the side of a pickup truck coming the other way.

"Jesus on the cross!" she said, her voice cracking. "Becca, are you all right?"

"Yes."

"Are you sure, honey?"

"I'm in the backseat," Becca said. She'd declined Gail's invitation to "sit up front like a big person," having pointed out to her grandmother that children were safer in the back.

Gail got out and fast-stepped over to the other driver, a young man who was already standing in the road and staring at the spot where the Honda was crimped into the side of his truck. "Jesus on the cross, are you all right?" Gail asked him.

He spit what she feared was blood but turned out to be tobacco juice onto the asphalt next to one of his flip-flops. "Great," he said. "Just great."

As violent as the impact had been, the damage to both vehicles was minimal, could be hammered out by mechanics and paid for by insurance. But the watermelon had burst open on the floor beneath the glove compartment. They used the pay phone to call the police, and then the three of them sat on the stoop in front of the convenience store and waited. "You just had to have watermelon," Gail said to Becca. She smiled at the young man, but he didn't smile back. "I bought you granola bars, and veggie crunches, and peanut-butter rice cakes," Gail said, "but you had to have your stupid watermelon." She put her arm around Becca's shoulder, pulled the girl against her and kissed the top of her head.

T he driving class was held in the evening at the high school, in one of those portable buildings propped up on cinder blocks, and was scheduled for three and a half hours—an ungodly amount of time for something remedial and mandatory, Gail thought.

The instructor opened his briefcase, took out a legal pad, and introduced himself as Mr. Burgher—which he spelled aloud so they would know there was an H in there. "If you're in this room," he said, "you've done something wrong. If you can see me, if you can hear my voice, you've screwed up behind the wheel of a motor vehicle and the state of Florida has ordered you to take this class. It's your job to see it through to the end and learn at least one new thing. It's my job to make sure you're not bored to death."

Gail turned around in her desk and glanced at Becca, who was sitting at the back of the room doing her homework (or at least pretending to), then returned her eyes to the instructor.

"Do I like my job?" Mr. Burgher asked them with a slight grin bending his mouth. "Absolutely. Do I want to be here any more than you do? No, I'd rather be home watching the play-offs. Regardless, ladies and gentlemen, prepare to be dazzled."

He was goofy, but he had a friendly face and a full head of flat, graying hair that reminded Gail of Tom Brokaw. Driving defensively didn't mean driving aggressively, he told them; it meant driving with the ability to anticipate what the other guy might do. On the blackboard, he drew diagrams of where to hold their hands on the wheel, how to visually correspond the left side of the vehicle to the center line, how to gauge blind spots—all of which Gail already knew. He asked them what possible scenario could exist wherein the driver of a car that had been rear-ended was cited for the accident.

Someone coughed. Someone else suggested that if a person came to a full stop for no good reason, it was their own fault for getting hit.

"Negatory," Mr. Burgher said. "If you're traveling behind a car and you collide with it, you're going to take the blame. It's why we have the two-second rule." Then, with the help of another diagram drawn on the blackboard, he explained what the two-second rule was.

"Brother," a woman next to Gail said under her breath, but Gail had decided that Mr. Burgher was at least as sexy as he was goofy.

"Another interesting fact," Mr. Burgher said. "Some people think it's a good idea to throw themselves from a car when it's gone out of control. Well, that's fine except for a little thing we call physics. If your vehicle is flying into a ditch, say, and you jump out, which direction do you think your body's going to go?"

The question made no sense because who would throw himself out of a moving car, other than a stunt man? But Gail took a chance. "Same as the car?"

"Bingo," Mr. Burgher said, touching the end of his nose and pointing at her. "You land in the ditch and you think, *Good for me, I'm safe!* And then, ka-wump, your vehicle lands on top of you."

He wheeled a cart that held a TV and a VCR out of the corner and popped in a videocassette. "Let's take a look at a little movie called *Better Think Twice,*" he said, reaching for the light switch.

The movie was a mix of reenactments and true crash-site footage: actors sitting in cars and pretending to drive while exhausted, while smoking dope, while doing a crossword puzzle; then footage of similar cars smashed to smithereens on the side of the highway and actual people dismembered, half-crushed, the top of one man's skull sliced off like a Halloween pumpkin's. Gail peered behind her, but Becca was still engrossed in her homework.

"Fun and games," Mr. Burgher said, switching on the lights. "Fun, and, games. Or is it?"

During the break, Gail walked to the back of the room, pulled a plastic-wrapped candy necklace out of her purse, and laid it next to Becca's copybook. "Surprise," she said.

"I'm almost nine," Becca said, glancing at the necklace. "And those are bad for you."

"These, too," Gail said, producing a box of Junior Mints. "All for being my well-behaved little girl who didn't look at that awful movie."

"I saw most of it," Becca said, reaching for the mints.

How like a Thin-Makers meeting the whole setup was—right down to the coffee urn and the bland, cracker-like cookies on the folding table next to the door. Half the participants wandered outside to smoke. Gail poured herself a cup of coffee and carried it down the wooden steps.

Mr. Burgher was standing apart from the other smokers, staring out across the football field. His short-sleeved shirt seemed to glow in the dark.

Gail looked up at the stars and turned a little as she walked, as if trying to find a particular constellation. "Oh!" she said, feigning surprise at having come upon him.

"What brings you here?" Mr. Burgher asked.

"The craziest thing. I was going to make a left turn and changed my mind, and this joker—"

"No, I mean what brings you to me?" Mr. Burgher asked, taking her aback. "Care for a cigarette?"

"No, thank you," Gail said. "It's not my bag, as the teenagers would say."

Mr. Burgher exhaled a thin layer of smoke that fell like a curtain over his upper lip. "Aren't you a button?"

Gail found she didn't mind being called a button. "How'd you get to be such an expert on driving?"

"Common sense, most of it. I worked at the DMV for years, administered driving tests, even gave the eye exams. Guess you could say I've done it all. You married?"

He was nervy, but she admired his moxie.

She'd been married three times. Her first husband, the orthodontist, had been outwardly chipper and privately gloomy—so gloomy that he kept a dank little apartment she didn't even know about on the mainland, where he sealed himself up a year after their daughter was born and swallowed sixty Nembutals. *It's not anyone's fault,* his note read, *but my life has been no picnic.* So there was that.

Her second husband had been a tax attorney who announced his desire for a separation out of the blue one night and then moved all the way out to Wyoming, where he bought a thousand acres populated with buffalo and got himself named one of *Roam & Herd*'s Fifty Most Awe-Inspiring People.

As for her third husband, the water-park owner, she couldn't even say for sure which one of them left the other; they seemed to inch apart slowly, like continents, until he was living four towns over with a woman half his age. But, like the rancher, he paid his alimony.

"Not married," she said. "Most decidedly not. You?"

"Most decidedly," Mr. Burgher said. "Is that your daughter in there?"

"God, no. My daughter's run off to California to ruin her life. That's her kid."

"Well," he said, throwing what was left of his cigarette onto the sidewalk, "we should get on with it."

He was even sexier during the second half of the class. He explained ambulance and fire-truck etiquette, told them what to do when they were in the vicinity of a school bus or were confronted with a funeral motorcade, lectured them on the dangers of hydroplaning. He told them an ironic story about Johnny-the-time-saver who just had to speed and ended up spending most of his time in traffic court. Then he sat on the edge of the desk with his legs spread wide and gave an impassioned closing speech about how safety was a communal responsibility, how no one was above it, and how no one—but no one—was beneath it. How could anyone be *beneath* safety? Gail wondered if he'd written this out ahead of time or was just making it up as he went. Never mind; he was taking hold of the air in front of his chest as if holding a volleyball and he was talking directly to her, as if she, more than anyone else in the room, needed to hear it.

At the end, he handed out Certificates of Completion.

Becca had eaten all the Junior Mints and was wearing what was left of the candy necklace. There were little tattooed dots of color on the back of her neck. Gail licked a finger and rubbed at one of the dots. "Let's go," she said.

At the door, she turned to face Mr. Burgher. "Captivating."

"I aim to please," he said, closing his briefcase. "Did you learn anything?"

"I did. I never knew to put the sun visor so it's not aimed at my forehead."

"Common sense, like I said." He looked down. "What's your name, princess?"

"Becca," the girl said.

"I'm William," he said, smiling, "but I go by Billy."

"Billy Burgher? You should open a restaurant," Gail said— a silly joke she immediately wished she could retract, but he didn't even seem to have heard her.

"Becca's a pretty name," he said.

"It's Rebecca without the ruh," Becca said and looked up at Gail. "She told the police officer I was distracting her and made her have the accident, but I wasn't. I was just sitting there. She wanted junk food."

"Ha ha!" Gail blurted, reaching down to smooth the girl's bangs against her forehead. "If you made any sense, I'd have a heart attack."

Mr. Burgher smiled at Becca, then smiled at Gail. "I wonder if you might benefit from a private driving lesson."

S he'd torn off a corner of her Certificate of Completion, written her phone number on it, and palmed it to him while they were saying goodbye. And now, just watch: two weeks would pass, then three, and during all that time she would think about Billy Burgher, each and every day, and he wouldn't call. That was just the way some men were: interested when you were standing right in front of them and oblivious to whether you lived or died once you were out of their sight. And he was married, wasn't he? *Most definitely,* he'd said, but that was an odd way to say you were married. If she fluttered her mind's eye, she couldn't be entirely certain there'd been a ring on his finger.

It didn't matter, because he wasn't going to call. She told herself this over breakfast, muttered the words aloud while power walking through the mall. *It doesn't matter. He's not going to call.*

But two days after the class, while Becca was at school and Gail was at home bent over the bathtub with a bottle of Tilex and a scrub brush, she heard the phone ring from the bedroom and then this smoky voice rising out of the answering machine. She banged her knee against the side of the tub getting up. "Lord almighty," she said, limping toward the phone. "Hello?"

"Is this Gail?"

She sat down on the bed. "Yes, it is. Who's calling?"

He could have said his full name. He could have reminded her where it was they'd met. Instead—an encouraging sign, she thought later—he said only, "Billy."

"Oh, Billy! I'm so glad you called."

He chuckled. "Why's that?"

Tilex was running down her wrist toward her elbow. She angled her arm so that the scrub brush was over the floor and not the bedspread. "Your class made me realize how I really do need a hands-on refresher about road safety."

"Never hurts," he said.

"Seriously, I'm a menace behind the wheel."

"Just remember the old adage," he said. Then he cleared his throat and went quiet, as if he couldn't remember the old adage.

"To err is human?" she offered.

"All learning starts with unlearning," he said.

"Is that right? Well, there are a few things I've learned to do quite well that I wouldn't want to unlearn—know what I mean?" She waited for him to run with this; he didn't. "Anyway, you're the teacher."

He suggested three o'clock on Saturday, and she told him that would be perfect. She would arrange for a sitter and be free as a bird. Should they meet back at the high school, for old times' sake?

"I'll be in a white Mustang in the Denny's parking lot," he

said, and then clarified: not the local Denny's, but the one two towns over, in Titusville.

B ecca's grandmother was wearing her church dress and had gotten a new hairdo that was rounder and higher than Becca had ever seen it. The whole inside of the car smelled like hairspray. She'd asked Becca what she wanted to bring to Mrs. Kerrigan's, and when Becca had told her nothing, her grandmother had said, "Nonsense," and had taken a grocery bag from under the kitchen sink and filled it with Safari Suzie, Safari Steve, and all their safari equipment. She'd added a *My Little Pony* activity book and a matching glitter pen she'd bought at the drugstore.

The paper bag sat next to Becca on the backseat, its top rolled up and crinkled.

"You're going to be nice to Mrs. Kerrigan," her grandmother said, "because I'll pluck you bald if you're not. Mrs. Kerrigan is a sad, lonely woman, and she doesn't need to hear anything idiotic coming out of your mouth. You understand me, baby girl? No shenanigans."

After her mother had moved away, Becca had been switched from Freedom 7 Elementary School to Tropical Elementary, which was closer to her grandmother's house. Becca preferred being in school to being at home. At Tropical, nobody threatened to pluck her bald. Nobody warned her not to say idiotic things. Half her class thought she was from Paris, France (she was very good at fake French).

"Are you listening to me? I thought I told you to put that bag on the floor."

"You didn't."

"God, I'm looking forward to being around somebody new. That's not a reflection on you, honey; I'm talking about men. Somebody who appreciates a grown woman's company!"

"Your hair smells," Becca said.

From the front of the car, her grandmother shot her a look in the rearview mirror.

"It does. It's making me sick."

"Stop it," her grandmother said. "That's exactly what I'm talking about, that sarcasm you think is so cute. You're not going to ruin today for me. *Nothing* is going to ruin today. Do you know what you are?"

They were sitting at a red light. As soon as the light turned green, the car behind them honked and they both flinched. Her grandmother tried to honk back, but this wasn't her car, it was the car they'd given her while hers was in the shop being fixed, and she pushed the wrong spot on the steering wheel.

"Bastard," she muttered, moving the car forward. She found Becca again in the mirror. "You're a hardheaded girl who's actually nice, deep down, and the sooner you realize that, the sooner you're going to start enjoying life."

Becca traced a finger over the flower petals printed on the skirt of her jumper. She'd decided that if she didn't like it at Mrs. Kerrigan's house, if it was as boring as it had been the last time, she would pretend to be poisoned. She would moan and clutch her stomach, and she would scream if Mrs. Kerrigan tried to touch her. She would become delirious, start flailing, and break something precious. Then, while

Mrs. Kerrigan was weeping because whatever Becca had broken was irreplaceable, Becca would dump all the toys out of the bag, fill it with food from Mrs. Kerrigan's refrigerator, and leave. She would find a bus station and get on a bus that would take her to the airport, and at the airport she would follow some woman who was about to get on a plane to Paris, and as soon as the woman boarded the plane, Becca would start crying, *"Mamá! Mamá!"* and push her way through the other passengers. She would slip into one of the bathrooms on the plane, and by the time the stewardesses figured out she was a stowaway, they'd be airborne, nothing to be done about it. In Paris, she would buy two postcards of the Eiffel Tower and send one to her mother in California and the other to her grandmother in Florida, and both postcards would say the same thing: *You had me to lose.* She didn't know what this meant, exactly, but a lady in a TV movie had written it in a goodbye note to her fiancé, and the words had left him teary eyed and speechless.

On the front porch of the Kerrigan house, her grandmother rang the doorbell and then reached down and straightened Becca's collar. "Best behavior," she reminded her. "We're nice people who do nice things, and if you want to see daylight again before your ninth birthday—"

The front door swung open.

"Hello, Teresa!" her grandmother said.

The person on the other side of the screen door wasn't Mrs. Kerrigan but a withered-looking man with a small beak of a nose pushing out of his face and dark, curly hair scattered around his head. His bathrobe was untied, and between its folds was a pair of floppy camouflage shorts and a

T-shirt whirlpooled with colors—as if someone had melted down every crayon in the box and swirled a finger through the puddle.

"Friend or foe?" he asked, squinting through the screen.

"What in the—" Becca's grandmother said, then exhaled. "We're the Nicholsons. Can you please tell Mrs. Kerrigan we're here?"

"Friend or foe?" The bird man didn't sound mean or challenging; he sounded curious.

"For godsake, we're *friends.*"

He receded into the house.

"I don't have time for this," Becca's grandmother said, glancing at her watch.

"I'm not a Nicholson," Becca told her. "I'm a Watley." She'd been meaning to announce this for a while now.

"Oh, come down off your magic cloud. Brian Watley is hardly what I'd call a proper father. He didn't get around to marrying your mother until after you were born, and then he took off a year later—and good riddance. Anyway, would it be the end of the world if you took my name?"

"Was that Mrs. Kerrigan's husband?"

"I doubt it. She doesn't have one."

"Maybe she got married since the last time we were here."

"And maybe I'm the man on the moon." Her grandmother's voice dropped to something between a groan and a whisper. "I told you, she's sad and lonely. Who knows, maybe she got so lonely she's started taking in strays."

"I'm sorry!" a voice called from inside the house. "I'm coming!"

And then Mrs. Kerrigan appeared and pushed open the screen door.

"Well, hello there," Becca's grandmother said brightly. She tapped Becca's shoulder. "Say hello."

"Bonjour," Becca said.

"Please come in," Mrs. Kerrigan said. "I was out back and didn't realize you were here." They entered the house, which smelled to Becca just like her grandmother's hairspray—until she realized it was still her grandmother's hairspray she was smelling. Mrs. Kerrigan's own hair wasn't done up at all; it was gray and parted in the middle and hung down either side of her head like two horse tails. "Becca, have you gotten taller?"

"Je guess," Becca said.

"Can I get you something to drink?"

"Nothing for me, thanks," Becca's grandmother said. "I'm going to be late if I don't scoot. Did I tell you what I'm doing?"

She proceeded to tell Mrs. Kerrigan all about the car accident, which she said was Becca's fault, and about the driving-school man, and about how he'd been calling and asking to see her and wanted to give her a free driving lesson. By the time she was done talking, they were all sitting around the living room except for the bird man, who was at the dining room table hunched over a notebook, scratching at it with a pencil.

"Well, I hope you and Mr. Burgher have a pleasant afternoon," Mrs. Kerrigan said.

"I do, too," Becca's grandmother said. "In fact, more than

pleasant would be all right with me. But what do I know about people? They're all puzzles." She glanced toward the dining room. "For instance, who's that man?"

"That's my youngest, Frankie," Mrs. Kerrigan said. "You've seen his picture."

Becca watched her grandmother's head crane forward an inch or two as she gazed at the bird man. "I wouldn't have guessed that for a million dollars," she said. "I thought he lived in the Panhandle."

"He used to. He moved home about a month ago."

"Huh." Becca's grandmother returned her voice to its whisper-groan. "What happened to him?"

"Nothing," Mrs. Kerrigan said. "He just lives here now."

"Is he not well?"

Even Becca knew this was an awful thing to ask, especially when the bird man was sitting right there within earshot. She felt her face heat up as she clutched the paper bag.

Mrs. Kerrigan moved her chin in a little figure eight without saying anything. Then she said, "He's been under the weather, yes. Some problems with his immune system."

"Oh, sweetheart. I'm so sorry."

"It's not airborne."

"No, no, I know. I saw *Philadelphia*."

"I actually think he might be on the upswing," Mrs. Kerrigan said.

"Say no more." Becca's grandmother patted both her knees and stood. "I just want you to know it means the world to me, Teresa, you watching this little firecracker for an afternoon."

"We'll have fun," Mrs. Kerrigan said. "Won't we, Becca?"

"Moi stomage ez hurt avec poison," Becca said—but

without much enthusiasm. Pretending to be poisoned had lost some of its appeal now that she knew the bird man was sick with something.

He lifted his head and announced from the dining room, *"Nuzwah fear, mon guest. Antidotus miracallus voot be toi!"*

"I shouldn't be but a few hours," her grandmother said.

M rs. Kerrigan put a cassette tape into the stereo— something without words, all soupy horns. The bird man led Becca into the kitchen, where he offered her a stool at the counter beneath the pass-through and then stood mixing orange juice, mayonnaise, and coffee grounds into an empty Smucker's jar. After inspecting the results and adding a dash of milk, he handed the jar to Becca, who wished she'd never mentioned being poisoned. *"Voila!"* he said.

"Je feeling bet-wah," Becca said.

"No, no," the bird man said. *"Voo complexion ez teree-blah."*

Was he fooling with her? Or was he crazy in addition to being sick? She raised the jar and swallowed the smallest sip she could manage. Her shoulders rippled.

"Le miracle du science!" he exclaimed.

"I speak English," Becca confessed.

"Me, too. Want to see my design for a machine that can communicate with rats?"

"Can we eat real food?" Becca asked Mrs. Kerrigan.

The three of them sat at the dining room table and drank soda and ate Cheetos, pretzels, and Vienna Fingers while the bird man showed Becca his design. Biomagnetic receptors, he explained, would be noninvasively fixed to the heads of rats in order to record their neural oscillations. The oscillations would then be translated into a mathematic scaffold corresponding to our own alphabet, and that scaffold, measured against a formula he'd designed using multiples of seven, would produce a blueprint for a shared system of language. In the notebook, he'd drawn several pictures of rats wearing helmets wired to what looked like car batteries. Surrounding the pictures were numbers—so many of them that there was barely any white space left on the page.

"Why would you want to talk to rats?" Becca asked.

"Because they're experts on escape and survival. And because they're our ancestors."

"No they're not."

"They are. They were brought here by the inhabitants of Delfar, in the Libra Quadrant, and some of them stayed rats, but some of them turned into monkeys, who turned into us."

"I think it's a very nice drawing," said Mrs. Kerrigan, paging through a catalogue on the other side of the table. "Becca, would you like to draw something? Frankie has lots of paper."

"No, thank you," Becca said. She pushed a Vienna Finger into her mouth. "In Paris, we don't have to draw. Everyone draws for us."

"I see," said Mrs. Kerrigan. "And in Paris, do they chew with their mouths open?"

Becca brought her lips together.

"You're from France?" the bird man asked.

She swallowed. "Where are you from?"

"Earth, mostly."

"Why don't we play a game?" Mrs. Kerrigan suggested, closing the catalogue. She got up from the table and told them she'd be right back.

There was a saucer next to the bird man's elbow holding pills of different shapes and colors. Becca counted the pills—there were nine—and ate another Vienna Finger. The bird man sharpened his pencil with a tiny, silver sharpener. He selected two of the pills and washed them down with soda. Then, for what felt like a long time, he just sketched, darkening lines he'd already drawn.

"What do you mean, Earth *mostly*?"

"I spent some time on Delfar when I was twenty-seven. The Delfarians came and got me, and I lived with them for half a year as part of their species-exchange program. They're coming back soon and collecting a whole bunch of us to colonize one of their outer territories. It's different from any place on Earth. It's better, because they don't have any disease and they don't wage wars. The trees are blue and the sky is orange. Not *orange* orange; more like—"

"A Circus Peanut?" Becca offered.

"Exactly. You have big eyebrows."

No one had ever mentioned Becca's eyebrows before.

"And their moon is a kind of silver and purple paisley, a lot more interesting than ours, which is just gray. I have a fragment of *our* moon, by the way, if you want to see it. An astronaut gave it to me."

Mrs. Kerrigan came back into the dining room carrying a stack of long, flat boxes. The boxes were scuffed, their corners broken open. "These used to belong to Karen, Frankie's sister," she said, setting them on the table. "Becca, you're probably too old for Candy Land and Chutes and Ladders, but what about Monopoly?"

Monopoly, Becca knew from experience, took hours to play and ended in crying. The money wasn't real, the jail had no walls, and the pieces looked like charm-bracelet pendants. "What else is there?" she asked.

Mrs. Kerrigan slid the bottom box from the stack. "Mystery Date. Karen used to love this when she was your age." She searched for the directions, but they were nowhere to be found, so she opened the board and began to fiddle with the white, plastic door fixed to its center. "The gist, if I remember right, is you roll the dice to find out how many times to turn the knob, and whoever's behind the door is your date. Sometimes you get the hobo. But sometimes"—she turned the knob and opened and closed the door over and over until it revealed a picture of a young man dressed in a white blazer and a black bow tie, holding a corsage box—"you get the man of your dreams!"

"I don't like his tie," the bird man said.

Becca didn't mind the tie, but she didn't like the man's blond hair. Her mother had dyed her hair blond the day before she'd left for California. "He's ugly," she said.

Mrs. Kerrigan sighed and closed the door. "Then you try."

Becca turned the knob and opened the door to find another young man, this one wearing torn jeans, a leather vest, and a headband with a peace symbol on it.

"There you go," Mrs. Kerrigan said. "The hippie's your date. Or is that the hobo?"

"He's the one I like," the bird man said.

"You can have him," Becca said, and then came to a momentary full stop. Why would he want him?

"Frankie," Mrs. Kerrigan said, "would you like to take a turn?"

"Not if I've already got the hippie."

"Too bad the directions have gone missing," Mrs. Kerrigan said. "What about Jenga?"

Becca was on the verge of saying she wasn't really interested in unstacking wooden blocks when the bird man declared that Earth games were far inferior to those on Delfar.

"Why?" Becca asked.

"Because on Delfar they've learned how to neutralize subwindows of gravity. Their version of Jenga—even checkers—involves miniature ionic-propulsion engines. Every piece is like a miniature rocket."

"Frankie, please," Mrs. Kerrigan said.

Becca wiped her mouth with her hand. She wiped her hand on her jumper. "I wish we could play one of *those* games."

G ail saw no sign of the white Mustang as she pulled into the lot of the Denny's in Titusville. She parked away from the restaurant, left the engine running so she could listen to the radio, checked her hair in the rearview mirror. The digital clock on the dashboard blipped from 2:59 to 3:00. Another minute passed. Then another five. What an idiot she was to think he'd come—but why have her drive all the way to Titusville just to stand her up?

While it would have been hard for her to imagine the right song for her agitated state, it certainly wasn't "It's All Coming Back to Me Now," which only made her think of her ex-husbands, her ex-boyfriends who had preceded them, all the touching and cuddling that had occurred so long ago, it might as well have happened to another person. She turned the dial, found something more upbeat. Intense, familiar. A TV opener, she thought, then realized it was a new, jazzed-up version of the theme song from *Mission: Impossible*. As the music filled the inside of the car, the white Mustang appeared: gliding toward her across the parking lot, so suddenly and stealthily present, it might have climbed out of an underground passage.

Billy came to a stop next to her with his car facing the opposite direction. His window was down. She brought hers down and turned off the radio.

"Well, hello there," she said.

He pushed himself up in his seat a few inches and peered at her. "You look nice."

"Thank you," she said. "Thank you very much." Then, not wanting to sound starved for compliments, "Now I guess I'm supposed to tell you that you look nice, too. You do, by the way."

"Let's go somewhere that isn't here," he said.

"In your car?"

He shook his head and told her to follow him.

Because she wasn't feeling entirely foolhardy, Gail fished a pen and a deposit slip out of her purse while she drove and wrote down his license plate number. They were headed to another high school, she assumed, or maybe to a mall parking lot, some place where they could at least pretend for a little while longer that this was about a driving lesson. But what if he had someplace truly desolate in mind? Would she continue to follow him mile after mile, until she had no idea where she was and no one to hear her scream if things got dangerous? She would, she decided. And wouldn't she look pathetic, left for dead in the woods with a pair of jumper cables around her neck, after having followed a virtual stranger to the place of her own demise? As they waited to turn onto Route 9, she wrote beneath the license plate number, *I, Gail Nicholson, am spending time with Mr. William Burgher of the Brevard County DMV. If I fall into harm's way, he is the person the police should question.*

She folded the note and left it sticking out of the mouth of the ashtray for whoever might happen upon her car. But the note was a bit grandiose, wasn't it? She wasn't the sort of person who warranted a scandalous story or a headline-making crime. This wasn't *Diagnosis: Murder.* Truth be told, when you got him alone, Billy Burgher was probably as boring as a textbook. He was probably so charged up about driver safety that this was how he enjoyed spending his Saturday: teaching someone he thought was a road risk the finer nuances of hydroplaning, the two-second rule, all that hoopla. And right on time, she spotted a school up ahead, with a parking lot spread out beside it wide enough to land the space shuttle. How many years had she wasted trying to make a connection with someone who might find her just the slightest bit desirable? How many conversations had she struck up with retirees on boardwalks, in grocery store lines, at the Blockbuster? And yet here she was, dressed to the nines and feeling like a fool.

But they passed the school with its massive parking lot. They passed acre after acre of asphalt connected to super-stores and office parks and boarded-up businesses. They con-tinued north, and she grew so irritable that when he finally put on his turn signal at the entrance to a purple-bricked motel called The Juniper Inn, she assumed he'd overshot wherever they were headed and was just turning around.

AIR CONDIT ING, the marquee read. POOL. HBO. And on a hand-painted sign hanging from a post, *By the Week, By the Night, or By the Hour.* The Mustang came to a stop in front of the building. Its brakelights went dark.

Well, then.

n general, Becca wasn't what her grandmother would call a "people person." She liked a few of the children at her new school, but she didn't like any of her teachers, or the princi-pal, or the janitor (who was constantly whistling songs like the ones Mrs. Kerrigan played on her stereo). She didn't like Danny Desouka, the son of her grandmother's next-door neighbor (who'd told her she was pretty, but then had asked if she wanted to touch his "baby-maker"). She didn't like the man with the gold tooth at the post office, or the woman with the sunken chin at the Hallmark store, or the pale lady at the movies who always made a point of telling her there were no free refills on popcorn (which Becca had never once asked for). She didn't like either of the two priests at

Divine Mercy, or any of the people who sat through Mass repeating mush-mouthed sentences and wailing hymns. She hadn't liked her previous babysitter, and she didn't much care for Mrs. Kerrigan.

But she was starting to like the bird man. He had pretty blue eyes and he seemed smart, even if it was about things like talking to rats and playing Jenga on another planet. She could no longer imagine stealing Mrs. Kerrigan's food and sneaking off to Paris alone, because the food would have also belonged to the bird man and she would never steal from him.

When the phone rang and Mrs. Kerrigan went into the kitchen to get it, the bird man asked Becca if she wanted to lie down with him on the living room floor.

"I'm too old for naps," she told him.

"Not to take a nap. To look up."

They could look up from where they were sitting, but she didn't say this; she walked into the living room and spread flat out beside him on the carpet between the coffee table and the television.

"What do you see?" he asked.

"The ceiling. What do you see?"

"It depends on the time of day. Right now, I see a ship breaking through particle clouds. Sometimes I see seahorses pulling giant ice statues on sleds."

She understood then that he was talking about the swirls in the plaster—the same way you could look at a cloud and see a face or an animal. She let her hand flop sideways until her fingers brushed his. "If I go to Paris," she said, "do you want to come with me?"

"I've got stuff to do."

"Well, maybe we could go to that place you were talking about."

He made a little humming sound that may have been a yes but may have just been a hum.

"That planet," she said, in case he didn't understand. "We could go there together and get away from all these crappy people. We could leave and never have to see any of them again."

Done with her phone call, Mrs. Kerrigan leaned into the pass-through. "You know what?" she said. "I don't think we need to hear any more about other planets today, or about rats, or about how crappy everyone is. I told your grandmother we were going to have fun, Becca, and we're going to do it. Did you bring anything fun in your bag?"

"She brought Safari Suzie," the bird man said. "And Safari Steve." How he knew this, Becca had no idea. He'd looked in the bag, maybe. Or had X-ray vision.

"Well, then, let's have a safari," Mrs. Kerrigan said. "Chop-chop. No arguments."

They followed her out to the backyard, where she chose a spot near the cumquat tree, plopped down with her legs folded beneath her, and upended the bag. The bird man squatted on his knees and began picking through the miniature equipment, while Becca sat Indian-style and tried not to sneer. All she wanted was to be alone with the bird man. All she wanted was to be lying next to him, holding hands, the two of them talking about how they might run away together. But that wasn't going to happen with this horse-haired woman insisting they play with dolls.

Mrs. Kerrigan handed Safari Suzie to her. She tried to hand Safari Steve to the bird man, but he said he'd rather be the elephant with the double saddle strapped to its back. "I guess I'll be Steve," Mrs. Kerrigan said.

They pretended to ride the elephant around, Mrs. Kerrigan holding Steve at the reins and Becca rolling her eyes as she wagged the Suzie doll nearby. After they'd done this for a while, Mrs. Kerrigan suggested they dismount and set up camp. She unfastened the tent, which sprang into shape, and laid out the pots and pans, the little ice cooler, the shotgun no bigger than a pretzel stick. The bird man used the elephant's head to butt the tent away from the plastic fire, and he used the elephant's trunk to pound pretend stakes into the ground, even though the tent didn't need any stakes.

Becca made Suzie pace back and forth listlessly on the grass.

Noticing this, Mrs. Kerrigan walked Steve over to Suzie, raised the doll's unbendable arm so that his hand rested on Suzie's shoulder, and said in a voice much deeper than her own, "You look preoccupied, darling. What's troubling you?"

It was all too retarded. Becca opened her mouth to say so, but changed her mind at the last second. "My grandma's having sex with that driving school man."

"Uh-oh," the bird man said.

Mrs. Kerrigan's grip went slack, causing Steve to tilt to one side. "Do you even know what that means?" she asked Becca.

"There's a thing, and a hole, and the thing goes in the hole—"

"Never mind! I know you're going through a hard time right now, Becca. I think maybe you're angry at your parents for not staying together, and you're angry at your mother for traveling so much."

"She's not traveling. She moved to California."

"Okay, then you're angry at her for moving to California. But that doesn't mean it's okay to take it out on your grandmother."

"I can't stand that witch," Becca said. "She smells like hairspray and she farts."

"Your grandmother is a good friend of mine, and I happen to know she's doing the best she can."

"She doesn't even *like* you," Becca said. "She told me you're lonely. And sad."

Mrs. Kerrigan's chin quivered for a moment. "Well, I don't know anything about that," she said. "What I do know is that life can be very difficult sometimes, and it can seem like it's not going to change, but believe me, things change. And one day—"

"Oh, look," Becca said. She lifted her doll and held it horizontally a foot off the ground. "Suzie's dead."

Mrs. Kerrigan blinked. "No, she's not."

"She is." Becca opened her hand and let the doll drop. "She's dead."

Mrs. Kerrigan reached for Suzie, but Becca snatched the doll back up, held it by its legs, and whacked its head against the ground several times.

The bird man looked fascinated. Mrs. Kerrigan looked shocked—until her eyes narrowed with what was probably annoyance. A breeze stirred the air and delivered something tiny and winged into Becca's ear, where it buzzed with a furious noise. She wanted to reach up and brush it away but felt unable to move.

"I might have left the stove on," Mrs. Kerrigan said. She set Safari Steve down next to the tent, stood, and dusted her hands together. "I think I'll go check."

The insect finally backed its way out of Becca's ear as Mrs. Kerrigan walked into the house. Becca smiled at the bird man, thinking, if only he'd smile back. If only he'd tell her more about the planet with the blue trees and the Circus Peanut sky. She would listen to every word, if it meant the two of them could be friends.

And then, miraculously, he did smile. Not an over-the-top, I-love-you smile, but a jumpy-sad smile that made her want to hug him. "Should we have a funeral?" he asked.

"A what?"

"A manifestation of the human need to pay respects to the deceased."

"Okay," she said with a little shrug, unsure if he was being serious but wanting to go along. "And you can show me your moon rock, if you want. And then can we go to that planet you were telling me about? To"—she racked her brain for the words he'd used—"colonize the outer territories? For the species exchange?" Of course they weren't going to travel to another planet any more than they were going to talk to rats, but she ached for him to like her.

"I don't think so," he said calmly.

"Why not?"

"They don't take just anybody," he said, looking somehow both regretful and satisfied at the same time. "They're very particular."

"Because there's not enough room? Or food? I don't eat much."

"No, there's plenty of room and all the food you could want. The Delfarians are just—particular. So, should we pray? Or was Suzie an atheist?"

T he room Billy got for them was at the back of the inn, across from a small, kidney-shaped pool blanketed with pine needles. He took an overnight bag from his trunk. When he opened the door to the room, a smell not unlike boiled meat wafted across Gail's nose. She stepped inside, set her purse on a table, and for lack of anything else to do, started walking around the room, turning on lights.

He stepped behind her and turned them all off again, except for the standing pole lamp next to the door. Still holding the overnight bag, he sat down on the edge of the bed and patted a hand against the bedspread. She sat down less than a foot away from him. He had the beginnings of a bald spot, she noticed; his hair looked carefully arranged to hide it. But she hadn't appreciated before what nice ears he had or how prominent his Adam's apple was, rising and falling like a knuckle behind the skin of his throat.

"You strike me as an adventurous person," he said.

"So do you."

"Do you like to pretend?"

"I love it. More than anything else."

"Why don't you lie back and relax while I change into something more interesting?"

She was about as relaxed as she was going to get, given the circumstances, but she agreed. He carried the overnight bag into the bathroom and closed the door behind him.

Somewhere down the row of rooms, one of the outer doors slammed and she felt it in her ribs. Dear Christ, she thought, don't let him come out of there dressed like some kind of animal. Don't let him hop around the room with bunny ears on his head, wanting me to feed him carrots. I'd rather die. She slipped off her shoes and set them in front of the nightstand. She considered taking off her dress and hanging it on one of the coat hangers across from the bathroom, but she didn't want to be caught hastening back to the bed in just her bra and panties, which might have looked presumptuous.

When he stepped out of the bathroom several minutes later, he was dressed as—well, she wasn't sure what. His shorts and his shirt were the color of split pea soup. So were the socks that were pulled up to his knees. He was dressed as a pea, maybe. Except that peas didn't wear bright red, white, and blue scarves around their necks.

"How do I look?"

"Attractive," she said. "Are you some kind of vegetable?"

"I'm an Eagle Scout," he said. "This is my old uniform."

"What does that make me?"

"My hooker?"

That he'd asked this rather than assigned her the role suggested enough respect to tip her into going with it. "All right. We can pretend that."

"And I'm only sixteen," he said. "I don't have more than my allowance to spend."

"That's okay. Am I expensive?"

"No."

"What's my name?"

"I have no idea. Touch the front of my shorts."

He crossed the room and stood next to the bed, his hands hanging down at his sides. She reached over and slipped her fingers around his fly, searching for the tab of his zipper.

"Don't take it out," he said. "Just rub it."

She moved her palm back and forth over the pea-colored fabric.

"Tell me about you," he said.

"I'm retired. I used to work in bookkeeping at Montgomery Ward."

"No, tell me about *you.*"

"Oh! I'm a"—she couldn't bring herself to say *hooker*—"a lady of the evening."

"Have you always been one?"

For all she knew, he wanted her to have been a nun just previous to this. "I'm not sure."

"You have," he said.

"Yes, I have."

"For how long?"

"Forever and a day," she said. He grunted, and she kept rubbing.

"So all you do is turn tricks for money?"

"I suppose so. By definition."

"Say it."

Her eyes were beginning to sting. "All I do is turn tricks," she said.

"Like a hooker."

The logistics of this were confusing. Was she *like* a hooker, or was she a hooker? "Wouldn't you rather get undressed? Both of us, I mean."

"Trick-turner," he said. "You've never even had a respectable lay."

"Well, that's just not true, Billy. I know we're playing, here, but I don't want you really believing that. I've had lots of boyfriends. And three husbands."

He grunted again, then shuddered.

She felt a dampness on her palm. When she brought her hand away, there was a dark stain the size of a dime on the front of his shorts.

"Three times I've been to the altar," she said, turning away. "And they were nice men. I wouldn't have married them otherwise."

A s she pulled up in front of Mrs. Kerrigan's house, the person looking back at her in the rearview mirror could have been about to walk into a cotillion. Perfect hair, perfect makeup. Her lipstick wasn't even smudged—and why would it be? She and Billy hadn't kissed. He hadn't even touched her. She'd washed her hands three times at The Juniper Inn and had to shake them dry because there weren't any towels.

Mrs. Kerrigan was smiling as she opened the front door. "How was your afternoon?" she asked.

"Lovely," Gail said. "It really and truly was! I hope Becca wasn't too much trouble."

"She was an angel," Mrs. Kerrigan said. "Weren't you, Becca?"

Grocery bag in hand, Becca was already stepping around Mrs. Kerrigan and moving past Gail.

Mrs. Kerrigan's withered son jumped up from the sofa and

came to stand beside his mother in the doorway. "Don't forget about the star charts," he called after Becca. "And the Doppler trajectories!"

"What in the world?" Gail asked.

"I was showing her how to make reverse maps of the galaxy, and how the Doppler effect can predict wormholes."

"My, my." She looked down and saw that Becca was already off the porch and halfway across the lawn. "Hello? Rudeness? Get back here and say thank you to the Kerrigans!"

But the girl long-strided to the car, where she opened the passenger door and flung the grocery bag into the backseat with such force that it smacked against the opposite window. She climbed in after it.

"That is not my car, so please don't ruin it," Gail called out. She thanked the Kerrigans on Becca's behalf, then thanked them again as she stepped back from their doorway, and they both nodded and smiled at her like they would at an earnest but bothersome solicitor. Mrs. Kerrigan eased the door closed.

How, would someone please explain to Gail, had this become her life? What series of events had been so unavoidable that not one single thing could have been turned in her favor along the way? Two years wasted on a high school sweetheart who never bothered to tell her he had to marry Orthodox. A year wasted at college before her father started losing his mind and her mother insisted she move back home to help take care of him. Six months in Miami at the Barbizon School of Modeling, and not a shred of work to come of it. Three failed marriages, one suicide, thirty unwanted pounds, a daughter who'd told her to go to hell in their last conversation. Well, bring it on, brother; she could take it. But did all those rotten twists in the road have to lead her to a place where she spent eighty dollars at the hairdresser's just to lie in a motel room with no towels and masturbate an overgrown Boy Scout?

On the way home, as she aligned the left side of the car with the center line and counted two seconds' worth of distance between her and the car in front of her, she wondered what the chances were that she might have earned, at this point, one Holy Grail of a candy bar without having to suffer any backtalk. Becca, she saw in the rearview mirror, sat silently chewing in the backseat. "I wasn't late, so don't tell me I was," Gail said. "I see you've found the Fruit Roll-Ups I bought you."

No response.

"A person should thank people who are nice to them," Gail said. "I don't know what gets into your head sometimes, but if you don't start thanking people like the Kerrigans when they're nice to you, you're going to run out of—"

"They *aren't* nice!" Becca all but shouted through a mouthful of candy.

Gail saw that the girl's cheeks had gone red and her eyes were glistening. "What are you talking about?"

"The bird man pretended to like me and said he was going off to some other planet, then told me I couldn't go with him! I didn't even *want* to go with him, it was just stupid, made-up stuff, but he didn't have to be so mean about it! And that horse-head woman is crazy!"

Gail didn't need this on her plate, not after the day she'd had. "I'm sure you're exaggerating," she said.

Becca was practically hyperventilating in the rearview mirror. "They made me bury my Suzie doll!" she hollered. "It's still in their backyard! You're always telling me to say thank you, but why should I thank anybody? For *any*thing? Everyone's awful!"

Gail brought her foot down on the brake and yanked the steering wheel, throwing gravel as she brought the car to a stop along the shoulder. In one semifluid motion, she got out, folded the seat forward, reached for Becca, and dragged her from the car.

Becca's legs went limp. If not for Gail's hold on her arm, the girl would have sprawled out flat. Gail gripped both her shoulders and shook her hard enough to make a piece of Fruit Roll-Up fall out of her mouth. "What did you say?" she asked. "What did you say to me?"

With less volume and a slight tremble in her voice, Becca said again, "Everyone's awful."

Oh, I hate you, Gail wanted to tell her. All the work I've done, everything I've tried to make right, and this is how you act? I *hate* you.

But in the next moment, she didn't. There was a line of spittle running sideways across Becca's cheek, a look of horror on her face. Gail's breath caught in her throat and her eyes spilled over with tears. "My only babe. My sweet lover!" she gasped, pulling Becca against her. "You're absolutely right!"

YOU NEED NOT BE PRESENT TO WIN

"Come find me," she would sometimes tell her son over the phone, in advance of one of his weekly visits. "I might be anywhere." But Serenity Palms, by design, was not a sprawling place, and Ellie was ninety-two years old. Finding her was not a challenge. She would be in the community room, or in the activities room, or in the nondenominational chapel, or—more often than not—in her own room, sitting awake or asleep in the Arcadia recliner Martin had bought for her. The recliner swiveled and was throne-like, with its high back and wide arms, and if Ellie had preferred to keep her feet on the floor she might have looked like a wizened, B-movie empress when she turned away from the television or the window to greet him. Instead, she kept her feet up, used her cane to rotate the chair, and looked like a castaway rowing a life raft.

Her olfactory receptors had become so sensitive that Martin could no longer bring her flowers. The smell of flowers made her queasy, as did the smell of so many other things: candles, nail polish, aftershave, the stucco and terra-cotta exterior of the building, almost any kind of food. She liked both the smell and taste of Weetabix, and she tolerated Ensure—which was fortunate, the on-staff doctor had told Martin, because if she got much lighter, they would have to consider intravenous feeding, and Ellie wasn't amenable to needles. In fact, Ellie wasn't amenable to much of anything, and Martin, who'd recently turned seventy and felt every year of his age in nearly every movement he made, couldn't blame her.

When he arrived that Saturday, she was in the recliner and had it faced away from the door, toward the picture window and its view of A1A, the distant sliver of beach, and the ocean beyond. Her roommate—Martin had yet to learn this one's name—was sitting up in bed, working a pair of rounded scissors over the pages of a magazine. Over the past two years, Ellie had gone through four roommates, none of whom had passed away and all of whom had requested to be moved rather than suffer her complaints, her ramblings, and her observations about race that could only come across as insults.

As a rule, Martin tried not to startle his mother. Her hearing was as sharp as it had ever been, but she was easily alarmed and occasionally had to orient herself. Her eyes were closed, he saw as he drew near. Her cane was leaning against one of the recliner's padded arms. He set his windbreaker on the back of the plastic chair nearby, dragged the chair partway between her and the window, and eased himself down. When he cleared his throat, her eyes fluttered open and she stared forward in the general direction of both him and the window. "This again," she said.

"Hello, Mom."

She gasped. "Jesus, you scared me half to death!"

"I thought you knew I was here."

"How would I know that? You're like a cat."

Martin forced a smile. "You said, 'This again.' I thought you meant me."

"Not you. *This*," Ellie said, lifting a hand and motioning toward the window. She had been dreaming about Clermont, about the classrooms of children, about trying to teach the younger ones what an octave was. She could stand at the piano and strike the eight notes of an octave one at a time, low C to high, and get every child in the room to say *Yes* when she asked if they heard the difference. But when she struck the low and high C simultaneously, they heard only one note. "Listen carefully," she said. "It's this note." *Plunk.* "And this one." *Plunk.* "Low and high at the same time." And then struck the two notes together. "Hear them?" The seven- and eight-year-olds could distinguish between the two notes, but the six-year-olds couldn't. It was fascinating. Either their hearing hadn't yet developed beyond the monophonic, or their brains were capable of registering only one piece of stimulus at a time. If she were a scientist rather than a music teacher, she might conduct a study. But then she had opened her eyes and seen the palm scrub, and the beach, and the tiny man with the parachute going up and down over the water, and she had thought—apparently had said aloud—*This again.*

"Anyway, I'm here," Martin said.

"I was back in Clermont," Ellie said. "I was trying to drill some sense into those kids."

"But you're here now. Cocoa Beach. It's Saturday—you know that, right?"

"For godsake, I was having a *memory.*" She blinked at him, then narrowed her gaze. "Do you have a tardy slip?"

"Mom—"

"It's a simple question. Either you do or you don't. If you don't, I'm going to have to ask you to take a walk down to the principal's office."

This was what the on-staff doctor called "mental jurisdiction." Ninety-two-year-old Ellie was entitled to her own mental jurisdiction, just like seventy-year-old Martin was entitled to his. It was okay—even healthy, the doctor had said—to indulge her a little. And so Martin found his wallet, pulled out an ATM receipt, and presented it to her.

"Ha!" she said, ignoring the receipt and taking hold of her cane instead. She brought the rubber-tipped end of it down to the floor and gave a push, so that the recliner turned away from him. "You fall for that every time!"

Martin nodded and tucked the receipt back into his wallet. She was moving the recliner full circle—slowly, but she was getting there—and as he was putting his wallet away he had to stand a little and push the plastic chair back to make room for her elevated feet.

"That was a bad idea," she said, coming to a stop. "Now I smell something."

How a minute could feel like an hour in this place. How an hour could feel like a week. Martin had news for his mother, but the ideal moment for telling her wasn't going to present itself. The ideal moment didn't exist. He glanced at the roommate, who was watching the two of them as if they were on television, and then pivoted his head, listening to his neck crackle. "What do you smell?"

"I should never go all the way around. Partway around and back is okay, but all the way around stirs something up. Is it floor wax?"

"Is it floor wax?" the roommate suddenly piped up from across the room. "Is it floor wax?"

"Oh!" Ellie said. "I'm smelling a parrot! Have you met my parrot, Martin? Her name's Pauline, and she loves to imitate, loves to sharpen her beak on things."

"Squawk, squawk," the roommate said. "Go choke, you old bag."

Martin opened his mouth to say—something—but his mother and her roommate kept talking.

"She sheds, is part of the problem," Ellie said. "She *molts*. And, I swear, when she doesn't get enough attention, she picks up her poo with her feet and flings it across the room!"

"Gas bag!" the roommate said. "Gas bag from hell!"

Should he tell them to stop, call for assistance? Was there protocol for such a thing in an assisted-living home? A semi-emergency cord to pull alongside the regular emergency cords that were hanging next to each bed and in the bathroom?

"Do you hear the filth that comes out of the parrot's mouth?" Ellie asked him. "It's like a toilet flushing in reverse."

"Look who's talking," the roommate said. "Everyone—I mean, *everyone*—on this floor is sick of you."

"Ask her what she's up to over there, Martin," Ellie said calmly. "Go ahead, ask her what she's working on."

Martin didn't want to ask either one of them anything. He wanted to leave, but they'd come to a lull in their volley, and they were both looking at him. "What are you working on, Pauline?" he asked, then felt his forehead tighten, realizing her name might not be Pauline, that "Pauline" might only be Ellie's parroty nickname for her.

But the roommate seemed unfazed. Her scissors were still moving. On the nightstand beside her bed, Martin noticed, were cutout circles stacked according to size—some as small as quarters, some as big as coasters. "A collage."

"Ask her what kind of magazines those are," Ellie said.

"What kind—"

"They're pornos," Ellie said. "Ask her where she got them."

"Where did you—"

"She stole them," Ellie said.

"I did *not* steal them," the roommate told Martin. "And they're not pornos. They're *Playboy*s. The home fired Mr. Strickland, the head custodian, and they had to clean out his office before the new custodian got here. I walked by, and these magazines were stacked on top of the things waiting to be thrown out. No one else wanted them."

"She picks through trash," Ellie said.

"Liar," the roommate said.

"She *collects* them. Not the magazines. She collects the breasts and the lower-downs. She's got hundreds of them in a shoe box under her bed."

"So what if I do?" the roommate asked. "And how would you know, unless you went snooping?"

"Mom," Martin said, "can we go somewhere and talk? Somewhere private?"

"This is my room," Ellie said. "We can talk here."

"But it's not private."

"It's not private because of her. That's not my fault."

"I'm not blaming you for anything. But come on," he said, getting to his feet. "Let's get out of here for a little bit."

Her wheelchair was folded up and standing beside the dresser. Martin opened it and wheeled it over to the recliner. It was slow business getting himself around these days, but it was *very* slow business getting Ellie from one chair to the other. Her legs weren't much wider than his wrists, her wrists not much bigger around than his thumbs. Her skin was cool to the touch, and it bruised with the slightest contact, but she didn't seem to mind. She had dry mouth but it didn't affect her teeth, which had been swapped out for dentures two decades ago. She suffered from macular degeneration and mild glaucoma but managed, so long as her drops and her magnifying glass were nearby. She was unhappy with her bowels. Unhappy with the constant swelling in her feet. Unhappy with her hair, which was white and wispy and untamable, as soft and volatile as dandelion seeds. But she was still here and, for the most part, still operating under her own steam. Had she ever actually been sick? Martin had made a point of asking her that recently, and she had told him, emphatically, *yes:* she'd been as sick as a dog in 1943, on her honeymoon, and sick again right after Martin was born. She'd been on-and-off sick during all her years of teaching public school. And she hadn't exactly felt well since he'd moved her into Serenity Palms, if he wanted the truth. But she was holding on for a little while longer, thank you very much.

He held both her hands as he helped her into the wheelchair and noticed the absence of her wedding band.

"Did you lose your ring?" he asked. They'd already had it resized once to accommodate her weight loss.

"I traded it," she said.

"To who? For what?"

"To Mr. Hollingsworth. For Weetabix. The British Weetabix you can't get in the States. His niece sent a box over in a care package."

"Mom, for Pete's sake, you can't—"

"Take as long as you want," the roommate all but sang. "Take her to China, for all I care!"

"Enjoy your smut," Ellie said as Martin wheeled her past the foot of the roommate's bed.

"I will. I might even glue these to the wall over your bed."

"I think that's *wonderful*," Ellie said. "I really do." She reached over her shoulder and tapped one of Martin's hands. "Tutti-frutti, that one."

Poor Martin. When was he *not* in a rut? He had grown up to look just like a character in one of the comic books he used to read. Private Punky? Sargent Schlep? Ellie couldn't remember the name. Despite years of correcting him, he had the poorest posture she'd ever seen in a young man. "Tab neck," she used to call it in her students, and she would warn them that if they didn't straighten up, they were going to turn into bass clefs. Well, here was her own son: a bass clef. And getting a little soft in the stomach because of it, all that middle body pushing forward. It was sad, really, because with posture like that, how was he ever going to land a nice girl? Or a wife, for that matter? But that was wrong, she realized. Martin had a wife—had *had* a wife, and she'd died. That was a perfect example of a fact Ellie had to keep track of, because when you got something like that wrong—something big, like a death in the family—the doctors and the neighbors and even your children wrote you off as senile. Mr. Griffin, who used to live across the hall, got it into his head that he'd been hired by the mafia to shoot Lee Harvey Oswald but that Jack Ruby had gotten there first. So where did that leave Mr. Griffin, who'd never been reimbursed for his plane ticket to Dallas or for the gun he'd bought? One day, tired of waiting for answers, he climbed up onto a sofa in the dayroom and started demanding to know who was mafia around here? Who was going to get him his damn money? Well. *No one* took him seriously again after that, least of all Ellie. She pitied him, but she never again took him seriously. And so, certain facts had to be kept straight.

Claire was the name of Martin's wife. She'd had cancer, and she'd died the same week as Bob Hope.

And the comic-book character's name was Sad Sack.

They were passing the chapel room now, where she had one of the staff members wheel her several times a week just to sit in the peace and quiet and gaze up at the starburst on the wall that wasn't supposed to be Jesus or Buddha or anyone else a person could actually pray to. She thought about asking Martin if they could stop in, but it was against the rules to talk in the chapel, and hadn't Martin said he wanted to talk? That he had something to tell her? There were diamonds on the floor—big, ugly, turquoise diamonds against a mud-colored background. She hated the new carpet.

"I think you and your latest roommate are a good match," Martin said from behind her.

"She's an idiot," Ellie said. "And a typical Italian."

"I predict she's going to be the first one who ends up not asking to move," Martin said. "She seems stubborn enough to stand up to you."

"There is just no telling how perverted some people are until they show their true colors. Don't you think I'm right?"

An ancient but energized-looking resident in a bathrobe and tennis shoes strolled past them and nodded hello. They nodded back.

"Of course you're right," Martin said, and Ellie recognized the patronizing tone in his voice—the same tone she used to hear in her own voice when he was six years old and would come running into the house babbling about something she had no interest in. He was placating her, letting her prattle. They'd come full circle.

"What do you think about standardized tests?" she asked, reaching for a topic that would lend her authority and show how smart she still was.

"I was never very good at them."

"You certainly weren't. But I don't think they're fair to the teachers. They measure what's been *learned*, not what's been *taught*. See the difference?"

"Sure."

"If I teach you how to tie your shoes, that doesn't necessarily mean you've learned it forever. People forget things.

What if you wear loafers every day of your life except for the fifth of May? Do you think it's fair that they'd come after *me* for that?"

The question was most likely rhetorical; she would keep going if he grunted, which was good because he was trying to figure out where in this place you were supposed to have a conversation without people lingering around and listening in. Maybe that was part of the idea of assisted living: you were assisted, or accompanied, each and every moment of the day. His stomach was growling. He should have eaten lunch before coming here.

"I taught all those children how to read music, but it was just dots to them. And who can be expected to remember what you never had a passion for to begin with? One of those boys—his last name was Pratt, I'll never forget it because it rhymed with brat—told me I was a waste of his time. Can you imagine? A third grader sassing a teacher like that? Standardized tests would have weeded out the Pratts of the world, let me tell you, but the school board didn't want to use them for electives." She was vaguely aware of having gone back on the point she was trying to make. "Let's stop in here," she said, motioning toward the open doors of the dayroom.

Not that Martin's assessment mattered, but the dayroom was his least favorite part of Serenity Palms—the room he found most exanimate and depressing, the room he would avoid entirely if he were a resident here (and, indeed, some of the residents looked to be not much older than him). There were overstuffed chairs and couches laid out in a kind of grid. An entire wall of windows facing an over-fertilized lawn. And at one end of the room, a large console television around which a dozen people sat staring at Judge Judy. Thankfully, Ellie never wanted to linger in the dayroom. Today, for some reason, she wanted to show it to Martin as if he'd never seen it before.

"There they all are," she said, her eyes scanning the room, her voice lowering, but only by a few decibels. "Greeks and Jews and Irish and Italians. Mostly Greeks. And only one colored, which, if you ask me, is unusual."

Several residents looked their way.

"Mom," Martin whispered.

"What? I said 'colored.' And I'm pointing out there should be a few more of them, statistically. I'm all for the melting pot, so long as everyone behaves. The Greeks can actually be nice people."

Martin turned the chair around.

"Where are we going?"

He steered them out of the room.

"I'm not a shopping cart," she said.

"No, you're not," he said, as if he wished she were.

"Slow down, then." They were already moving at a snail's pace, but she disliked the surrender of control implicit in the wheelchair. She didn't need the chair for short distances— she had the cane and the walker for those—and being lowered into it always made her feel like she might never come out again. She could be as bossy as she wanted with the Serenity Palms staff when they wheeled her around, and they would either suffer it quietly or dish it right back to her in a jovial sort of way she didn't mind. But Martin was so sensitive. Always brooding. He'd never been in a full-blown argument in his life—not with her, anyway. Certainly not with any of the bosses he'd had, who'd been so stingy with their raises and promotions. And not with his wife, who, as far as Ellie could tell, got everything she ever wanted. And whose name was Claire. And who was dead, she reminded herself. There you go, that bit of information was secure and it was nothing to shake a stick at; she was a widow herself—since before Martin had ever gotten married—and she could barely remember what life with Howard had been like. The sound of his voice, yes. The stink of his cigarettes, certainly. But not how his presence had felt in a room, or in their bed. Sometimes it seemed as if her memory was as big as a hatbox. For everything she tried to fit into it, something had to be taken out. She had given up whole pieces of herself to make space for the clutter of other people, and who ever thought to acknowledge that? Who ever thought to thank her? "Where in the world is the fire?" she asked, gripping the arms of the wheelchair.

"We're barely even moving, Mom. Would you like to stop for a while and rest?"

"I'm not *doing* anything. Why would I need to rest?"

"Listen, about your ring. Who's this Mr. Hollingsworth? I don't know what kind of person would think it's okay to do that, but you can't just take someone's jewelry and give them a—snack."

"Weetabix," she said. "British Weetabix."

"But you gave him your wedding ring. It's valuable."

"Probably not, knowing your father."

"Sentimental value, then," Martin said. "It has that, doesn't it?"

"I suppose." She wanted to change the subject. More and more, she found that interacting with anyone made her want to change the subject. "Who cares? Is that what you wanted to talk to me about?"

She could still surprise him, now and then, by paying attention. He did want to talk to her about something; he just wanted to get her someplace private first because he knew that no matter how gently or diplomatically he phrased his news, she was going to react poorly.

"Are you hungry?" he asked. "Do you want to go to the cafeteria?" The cafeteria was sometimes empty between mealtimes.

"God, no."

"What about outside? It's not so hot today. It's nice, actually."

"Why are you so eager to get somewhere?"

"So we can talk," he said.

This didn't bode well, she decided. Martin wasn't usually crafty, or particular. Under normal circumstances, he was as clear and simple as a glass of water. He had something up his sleeve. "Come around here," she said. "Come around so I can see you."

She felt the chair stop moving. Then he was squatting down in front of her, his knees crackling. She was relieved to see that he didn't have a crazed, Richard Widmark glint in his eye. It was this godawful chair that was getting her so rattled. Unless you were Franklin Roosevelt, it was impossible to stand your ground in an argument when you were sitting on wheels.

She had to remind herself that they weren't arguing. But

he looked so somber, her Martin, such a little doughface. "There's my little man," she said, wanting nothing more than to see him smile.

He did smile a little. He even leaned forward and gently hugged her—something he usually did only at the end of his visits. Things were sliding back into Ellie's favor. Her throat, which had been fluttering just moments ago, was now regaining its grip. Her nostrils flared as she caught the scent of something disagreeable—the wallpaper, maybe, or the glue behind it. But all of this was going to be fine.

The atrium was a compromise, since Ellie refused to go outside. Located in the center of Serenity Palms, it had, until just a year ago, been a proper atrium: open-air, exposed to the elements, with a pond in the middle where koi and goldfish swam. But the fish couldn't keep up with the mosquitoes, and the summer storms scattered the mulch over the walkway—little sticks that might catch on slippered feet—so the atrium had been enclosed with a peaked skylight. The bugs were gone now and the walkway was clear, but the air was no different than in any other part of the building and hummed with the compressor of a hidden air conditioner. Also hidden were a set of speakers that dripped music—sometimes piano, today violin. The fish had been removed. The pond had been filled in with cement and was now a sitting area.

Martin put the brake on Ellie's wheelchair. He pulled out one of the patio chairs and sat down across from her.

"It's like the great outdoors without having to be there," he said.

"I liked it better when it was open."

"You never wanted to come in here before. The smells, and noise from the highway, remember?"

"Now it smells worse."

"But there's music. You like music."

She looked down at her lap and smoothed the fabric of her robe with both hands. "You don't need to tell me that," she said. "I know I like music. I used to *teach* music. I just don't think Vivaldi should get as much attention as he does. He's not serious enough, flits around too much. If Charlie Chaplin had had violins for eyebrows, they'd have played Vivaldi."

Fair enough, Martin thought.

"And you look spotty," she added, as if these topics were at all related. "When's the last time you saw a dermatologist? Some of those marks on your forehead could be cancerous."

"Do you like it here?" he asked.

Possibly a trick question. She glanced at the ficus trees, the bamboo, the Mexican fans.

"Not the atrium," he said. "The facility. The home."

"It's okay. There's a lot wrong with it."

"But you like it better than the other two homes, right? I mean, you seem at least a little happier here than you were at Garden View or East Haven."

"That's what you wanted to talk about?"

"I'm just asking," he said. "Just checking in."

"Do you want to take my temperature, too?"

"No."

"What is it? You're acting so strange today. Why did you even bother to come?"

It occurred to them both that she was getting ahead of herself. She usually saved this particular zinger for just when he was about to leave.

He sat forward and rested his elbows on his knees. The whites of his eyes looked pink all of a sudden. "I came because I love you, okay? And because I wanted to see you."

She didn't like the sound of that. "Go on."

"And there's something I need to tell you. The fact is—" He sucked in a shot of air through his nose. "I've gotten really tired of being alone all the time."

"Me, too!" she said with more spark than she'd intended. "I've been alone my whole life."

"No, you haven't. And neither have I. But I've been on my own since Claire died, and that was eleven years ago."

"Bob Hope's been gone for eleven years?"

"Who—would you just listen, please? For once?"

All she did was listen. All she did was get talked to. She pressed her lips together and widened her eyes at him.

"I had a great life with Claire. We were married for twenty-eight years, and we shared something that's always going to be special to me. I know the two of you never got along, but there was nothing I could do about that—"

"Stubborn," Ellie slipped in. "She was stubborn." Then pressed her lips back together.

"—and she always told me she wanted me to move on. So the fact is, I've met someone." He paused for a moment to let this sink in, but nothing changed in his mother's expression. "Her name is Beth. She's a landscaper—she's retired now, but she still grows orchids and takes them to shows. We've been doing that together for a while. We're serious, Mom."

He cleared his throat. "We actually got married six months ago."

One of the doors to the atrium—the front or the back, Ellie couldn't tell which—swung open and then hissed shut on its slow-moving hinges. No one appeared, though. "*That's* what you wanted to tell me?" There was an opportunity here, she just wasn't sure what it was. Martin had had a toy when he was little, a Volkswagen car that had flashing lights and a mechanism inside that made it back up whenever it ran into something, back up and redirect, over and over, until it was turned off. Her thoughts felt like that sometimes. They felt like that now. Back up, redirect. "Does this person have children?"

"Beth. She does. She has a son and a daughter. And her daughter has a daughter. Which makes me sort of a grandfather."

"Why didn't you ever have children? You and Claire, I mean."

"We didn't want any." Martin had always been indifferent about becoming a parent and had left the decision up to Claire, and when she'd waffled on the idea until she was too old to have kids, he'd been relieved.

"It would have been nice to have a grandchild," Ellie said. "A little Martin Jr. to toss around."

"That's beside the point."

"I guess I don't see what the point is, then. When do I get to meet this—" The name was gone from her head.

"Beth," Martin said.

"When do I get to meet her?"

"Well, that's just it. I don't think it's going to happen, Mom.

Like I said, I've been married for six months, and I haven't been able to bring myself to introduce the two of you—or even tell you about her. And I finally decided there was a reason for that. A good reason."

"What in the world are you talking about?" she asked. "Of course I'm going to meet her."

"I don't think so," Martin said. For all the mental preparation he'd undergone, his hands were shaking. He locked his fingers together to steady them.

"Why not?"

"We don't have to go into that."

"We most certainly do. She's your wife, for godsake. I'm your mother."

"And you were horrible to my first wife. You were horrible to Claire from day one, and right up to the end. Horrible."

"I was *not*. I was *not*. Don't you come here and rewrite history. Not while I'm still around to keep the record straight. I was *not*."

"You were," he said, eyes still pink but his voice calm.

"Oh, this just takes the cake!" Ellie said. "You're as stubborn as she was! I've never heard of such a thing in my life."

"Do you remember," Martin said, the moment so alive in his head that it might just have happened an hour ago—and, oh, how he'd longed to throw this back in her face for so many years, and how he'd sworn to himself that he never would because the past belonged in the past. Well, the ugly truth was that there was no real divide between the past and the present. The present couldn't be ignored, and the past never went away. They were like twins joined at the hip. "Do you remember when Claire was in the middle of chemo and radiation, the first time she was really sick, and you wanted to come stay with us and help out?"

"Of course."

"And I came to Garden View and got you and brought you back to the house, and you did nothing but complain? About how messy the place was, and how bad my cooking was, and how *preoccupied* I was?"

The house *was* a mess; she remembered that clearly. But she redirected her thoughts and said, "I was sad. It was a sad time—for all of us."

"It was. And you stood there in the hallway, asking what time we were going to eat dinner and saying you hoped it was better than what we had last night. I was helping Claire get dressed for her appointment, and you were complaining about the food."

"I was sad!" she said again. "It was a sad time! Your wife was dying!"

"She wasn't dying at that point. She was undergoing treatment. For all we knew, she was going to beat it and live another twenty years. But, yes, it was a really sad time."

He was going to cry, she thought. She *wished* he would cry. Comforting him would be easier than listening to him.

"I said, 'Mom, I'm not thinking about dinner right now.' And do you remember what you said back?"

"It was so long ago," she said. "I'm tired, Martin. I want to go to my room."

"You pointed at Claire, my wife, and you said to me, 'Of course you're not thinking about dinner, because all you care about is *that*.'"

She should have been keeping a ledger this whole time.

From day one of getting pregnant, the diapers, the spitting up, the scabbed knees, all the work she'd done to keep him alive and safe—only to have him zero in on one thing she'd said, one thing he *claimed* she'd said, which she had no memory of saying whatsoever. She should have kept a ledger.

He took his handkerchief from his back pocket and wiped it under his nose.

"Why even tell me, then?" she asked. "Why tell me you've married this person, if you don't want me to meet her?"

He wagged his head a little. "I don't know. I guess so I could tell you I was happy."

"Oh," she said. "And that's it?"

"That's it."

"Well, good for you!" she said, raising her voice, nearly shouting. "Martin is happy, hip hip hooray!"

Birds would have taken flight, if there'd been birds. Heads would have turned. But they were alone.

He wheeled her back to her room.

The Italian was sleeping. The magazines and the rounded scissors lay on her lap.

Martin brought the wheelchair up alongside the recliner, put its brake on, stood in front of Ellie and held out his hands. Ellie raised her own hands and held on to him as he lifted her and carefully moved her back into the recliner. He asked her if she needed anything.

"Some water," she said.

He took a cup from the shelf next to her nightstand, filled it at the sink, and brought it to her. She drank down half of it and set it in the cup holder built into the recliner's arm. For a moment he just stood next to her, and fearing he might want to resume their conversation, fearing the conversation itself, she looked out the window and pointed and said, "What *is* that?"

"What's what?"

"That tiny man with the parachute. Out over the water. He goes up and down, up and down, like he can't make up his mind. What's he doing?"

Martin followed to where she was pointing. "Parasailing," he said. Then he bent down and kissed her cheek.

He stopped at the front desk on his way out and asked the woman there if she knew a Mr. Hollingsworth. She did; she said he was a resident. "This might sound crazy," Martin said, "but is it possible he's traded some biscuits for my mother's wedding ring?"

She smiled. "Mr. Hollingsworth gives her the biscuits, and she gives him her ring even though he doesn't want it. So he brings it to us. It's happened several times." She reached over to a table beside her desk and found an envelope with his mother's name written on it. She held it out for him.

"That's okay," he said. "I'm on my way out. Would you mind giving it to her?"

"I'll make sure she gets it," the woman said.

He thanked her and walked through the automatic doors into the warm afternoon.

The sun beat down on the back of his neck and his forehead as he crossed the parking lot. For just a moment, he imagined he could smell the stucco and the terra-cotta radiating off the building. She was right about the dermatologist, of course; he would have to make an appointment soon. She was right to question why he'd told her about Beth. She was maybe even right to trade her wedding ring for a box of biscuits, if the ring was always going to be returned. But he was done, he decided. And if it confused her, wondering where he'd gone, even if it hurt her terribly—well, it could only hurt for so long.

ACKNOWLEDGMENTS

My love and endless gratitude to Fred Blair. Thank you for every moment of this ongoing journey.

Thank you to my editor, Noah Eaker, who is as brilliant as he is kind and who kept at me until I got it closer to right. Thank you to Susan Kamil and Lisa Bankoff for their patience, faith, and devotion.

Thank you to the people (all of them dear friends and fellow writers) who read early drafts of these stories and gave me sharp and insightful feedback: Michael Carroll, Sophia Efthimiatou, John Freeman, Laura Martineau, David McConnell, Keith McDermott, and Bob Smith.

Thank you also to the people who have rallied behind me in more ways than I can count: Nicole Aragi, Nina Arazoza, Maribeth Batcha, Denver Butson, Richard Canning, Lila Cecil, Donnie Conner, Darrell Crawford, Amanda Faraone, Rhonda Keyser, Joy Parisi, Kevin Pinzone, Steve Quester, Anna Schachner, Chris Shirley, Adina Talve-Goodman, Hannah Tinti, Dean Van de Motter, and Don Weise.

Thank you to Ann Patchett for her life-changing friendship and for seeing something in me that I didn't know was there.

Thank you to Edmund White—the hero who became the mentor and loving, guiding presence.

Thank you to my teachers: Sandra McInerney, JoAnn Gardner, Sheila Ortiz Taylor, Robert Early, and—gone but still resonating—Jerome Stern.

And thank you to Beverly Neel, Elizabeth Bles-Webber, Steven Webber, James and Debbie Bles, Patricia Ryan Green, my nieces and nephews, and Fred for teaching me what home is.

ABOUT THE AUTHOR

PATRICK RYAN is the author of the novel *Send Me,* as well as three novels for young adult readers. His stories have appeared in *The Best American Short Stories, Tin House, One Story, Crazyhorse, The Yale Review,* and elsewhere. He is the recipient of a National Endowment for the Arts Fellowship in Fiction. He lives in New York City.

patrickryanbooks.com

ABOUT THE TYPE

This book was set in Garamond, a typeface originally designed by the Parisian type cutter Claude Garamond (c. 1500–61). This version of Garamond was modeled on a 1592 specimen sheet from the Egenolff-Berner foundry, which was produced from types assumed to have been brought to Frankfurt by the punch cutter Jacques Sabon (c. 1520–80).

Claude Garamond's distinguished romans and italics first appeared in *Opera Ciceronis* in 1543–44. The Garamond types are clear, open, and elegant.

them wanted to know when they crossed paths at the water-cooler.

That was a real question, from a grown man who had a job and showed up five days a week and presumably tied his own shoes in the morning. Spotted a coworker wearing an eye patch and asked if the patch was leaching toxins.

The boys, of course, were fit to collapse when they saw the patch. Leo threw it away after listening to their spontaneous list of pirate names.

On the evening of the day Mitch and Howie tried to pull Julian apart, Leo came home from work to find Marie not in the dining room or in the kitchen, where she sometimes sat working on her lesson plans, but in their darkened bedroom, lying on top of the covers with one arm folded over her eyes.

She stirred a little when he came in. He asked if she was feeling okay.

"Just trying to escape from the world for a few minutes," she said. "I can't really sleep, though."

Leo seldom took naps, but suddenly the thought of curling up with Marie was what he wanted more than anything. He pulled off his shoes and lay down beside her, then turned toward her and folded his leg and his arm around her. He rested his head in the crook of her neck, and it felt perfect. Then Marie took the arm from her face and draped it over his shoulder, and that felt perfect too.

"Tell me something," she said.

He heard this as an invitation to tell her whatever was on his mind. "I'm slipping," he said, surprised at how small his voice sounded, how childlike. "I don't feel right anymore. I

feel like a—time bomb. Like there's another stroke just waiting to happen."

"What does the doctor say?"

"Nothing. Nothing that's useful, anyway. Basically, he says
I should cross my fingers. The thing is, I feel—" He almost
said *scared,* but even if that were true, he wasn't ready to
utter it aloud. He couldn't remember the last time he'd come
even close to speaking like this—had he ever in his adult life
told anyone he felt scared? "Fragile," he said. "I feel fragile."

"You're going to be fine," she said, patting the side of his
head.

Empty words, no more reassuring than Dr. Loudon's
babble. Still, Leo was glad to hear her say them. He tried to
hug tighter into their embrace but already felt her squirming
out of it, sliding herself up on the mattress to a sitting position.

"Tell me something," she said again, and he realized she
wasn't just making conversation; there was something specific she wanted to talk about. Not the boys, he thought, not
the boys.

"What are we going to do about Mitch and Howie?"

His head was now resting against her hip, hardly a comfortable position. He rolled over onto his back. "What did
they do now?"

She described for him the scene she'd come home to, the
scuffle in the backyard.

"Christ," he said. "They're kids. Isn't that what kids do?"

"They told me flat out they were trying to dismember
him," she said. "They shoved a *pig ear* in his mouth! I cleaned
him up as best I could, and told him there really wasn't any

need to mention this to his parents. I gave him an entire package of Oreos to keep him quiet. But honestly, Leo, this is getting out of hand."

"Did you talk to them?"

"They don't listen to me," she said. "They barely listen to you."

And so he got up, grumbling under his breath, and walked down the hall to the boys' bedroom. Outside their door, he stopped and listened for a moment. Then he grabbed the knob and pushed the door open.

Mitch was sitting on one side of the partner's desk the boys shared, leafing through a comic book. Howie was lying on one of the beds with his head hanging upside down, staring at his index finger. The finger had a piece of string tied around it and had turned purple.

"What are you two doing?" Leo asked.

"Reading," Mitch said.

"Killing my finger," Howie said.

Leo sat on the other bed. He waved them over, told Mitch to put down the comic book, told Howie to take the string off his finger. They stood side by side in front of him, looking down at the floor.

"Suppose you tell me what happened today."

"Suppose we don't," Mitch said, and in the next instant, without his even deciding to do it, Leo's hand crossed paths with the boy's face. The sting in Leo's palm was immediate, and the handprint—red and angry—was already rising on Mitch's cheek. It was the first time Leo had hit either of them on anything but their butts, and because he wanted this to be a one-shot deal, something they'd both remember, he smacked Howie too. Howie's head knocked into Mitch's shoulder.

"Tell me what happened," Leo said.

They started talking in tandem, at a rapid pace. They'd just wanted to scare the Ferris boy—he'd been calling them names—they hadn't been doing anything—really, they hadn't!—you know how joggers stretch before they jog?—that's what he'd said, that he'd wanted to jog, that he'd needed to stretch—so they were helping him—and they told him if it started to hurt to just say so, but instead he said he wanted to eat one of the pig ears, and—

"Stop," Leo said, holding up the hand he'd used to hit them. He was both impressed and a little saddened when he saw them flinch. His eye was spasming. He tried to squint, but that only made the drag on the opposite side of his mouth feel worse. Normally, he didn't touch the eye when he was in front of other people, but now he clenched his teeth and pressed the heel of his still-warm hand against the socket.

"Enough malarkey," he said carefully. "Just tell me why you have it in for this boy. Help me understand what's so irresistible about him." Meaning, he thought, *I know he's an easy target, but why can't you branch out a little? Pick on somebody else now and then?* But they weren't that ambitious, he knew, and they no longer seemed to care if they got into trouble.

"It's his hair," Howie finally said. "We don't like it."

Leo wanted to rub his eye again, but didn't.

"We don't like *this* hair, either," Mitch said. He reached up and tugged as best he could on his crew cut. Then he reached over and tugged on Howie's. Howie let out an exaggerated